MY TROUBLES BEGAN

MY

TRANSLATED FROM THE ITALIAN BY
BELÉN SEVAREID

A NOVEL BY **Paolo Volponi**

TROUBLES BEGAN

NEW YORK **Grossman Publishers** 1964

The characters and the events described in this novel are fictitious; the locales and the towns actually exist. The industrial complex has not been identified, because the author does not wish the reader to attribute the events of his narrative to a specific city or factory.

MY TROUBLES BEGAN

I

MY TROUBLES BEGAN a few months after my return from a German prison camp, and it seemed almost as if my country, after such a cruel separation, refused to welcome me. I was born March 12, 1919, in Avignon, France; but I am Italian of Italian parents— my father from Piedmont and my mother from the region around Venice, born in the country between the towns of Padova and Treviso; beautiful country, so she has always told me, but I do not know it. I am writing now at the age of thirty-six, and my troubles have become so unbearable that I can do nothing else but expose them. I write at home in Candia, the Canavese area in the province of Turin. My house is outside the town near the small lake in Candia, a bit toward the left between the town and the lake, not far from the hills. It's a farmhouse with a patch of vegetable garden, a red-brick porch, and an abandoned barn and stall inhabited by a few chickens, two roosters, and a family of half-tame rabbits. I don't look after the land or the animals because I work in a factory in the city, a factory bigger than the city it has conquered.

My troubles began at the end of 1945, a little before Christmas, the last days of December and the first days of snow. I waited for the snow and Christmas, hoping they would make me feel closer to home, hoping to find comfort in the birth of the Infant Jesus, hoping to feel once again part of the Christian family. I had had the Sacraments and begun the winter in peace. I had some money from the army, a fairly well stocked house and hope in the future. That was a time when I had a great deal of hope. I thought that perhaps the snow, beautiful and pure, covering the woods around the lake and lying all white around my house, would bring me peace and wipe all the ugly memories from my country.

I was coming home the night it first snowed, but I didn't want to take shelter from the snow or clear it away from the stoop in front of my house. I brushed some flakes from my coat, and once inside I opened the blinds, leaving the glass panes shut so that I could fall asleep in the twilight. I slept well and, as I had planned, awoke while it was still early but already daylight. The night had been filled with a great silence like the nights in the concentration camp and the nights when I was a boy in France, a silence that existed only for me and which ended the moment I felt through my sleep the murmur of my companions or of my parents or of the street. It was a white murmur. Even as a boy I slept with the blinds open, not so much because I was afraid but because I didn't want to be entirely alone. It was as if I tried to keep at the edge of my sleep a space where I could turn and stretch out my hand to feel something.

I never would have thought when I awoke that this was to be the morning of my troubles, the first morning of my sufferings. It hadn't been a heavy snowfall, but I was satisfied even though it didn't move me as much as I thought it would. The snow covered the woods and seemed to lie on the still water of the lake; it hardly touched my house or the little hill my house was on. I said good morning to my mother and put the chair with her folded clothes on it closer to her bed. I took a muffler from the chest of drawers and went downstairs to the kitchen to wash. My house is one of the few farmhouses with indoor plumbing. My father had it installed when he came back from France, and he did part of the work himself with his strong bricklayer's hands. The water, like all water after a snowfall, was not so cold as usual, and it tasted of roots. This taste fooled me at first for I thought it was the water, but as the taste slowly grew stronger in its sweet consistency I realized that it was the taste of my mouth. When I straightened up to dry myself I felt a pain in my chest like a seam that is difficult to iron out. I also felt a burning in my throat and in my stomach.

I didn't pay much attention to these symptoms, and I blamed them on the months I spent in the prison camp; I blamed them all on prison, mother of so much suffering. I didn't know then how much the pains would affect my future. I didn't know that because of these pains and the maliciousness of other men my life would become another prison, another agony.

I don't remember very well how I spent the days following the disappointment of that meager snowfall and the first pains. I stayed home most of the time, alone or with my mother, repainting the doors and the windows. My mother spoke little, and when she did it was only to advise me not to get married, something that I didn't want to do anyway because I was alone and uncertain and my life was still not settled. I read many newspapers. They were filled with stories of blood, revolutions, and political struggles. I have always voted for the Christian Democratic party out of respect for the Church that has never abandoned me, (not even in prison) and out of a desire to honor the cross of lights that shines at night over the church in Candia and has always kept me company, even now, at night when I can't sleep. I didn't trust the people like me or those worse off who gave themselves airs and belonged to the other parties. I believed that man should gain authority by quietly improving himself and by muting his failings in the face of the perversity of others through reason and virtue. Otherwise, nations become like Germany, which kept us prisoners and killed us by the millions, or like Russia which had the most ignorant soldiers of all and no roads.

My pains would come and go with varying time lapses between one attack and the next, just like changes in the weather which we have to bear and cannot control. Once in a while the pain worried me, and I noticed that I no longer enjoyed eating the food my mother prepared for me. It wasn't what it used to be, both in France and Italy, when her meals had been a feast to me. My mother ate with pleasure, and I would watch her and eat along with her, even though I was annoyed by her voracious appetite.

I had told her about my pains, and she had said that I should either pray and go to the doctor, or take naps after dinner and get a job. I had already gone to the doctor at the army hospital like all the other veterans. We stood in line single file, as you always do in the army, but without laughing or kidding and with a great sense of urgency. Standing with us were some ex-prisoners-of-war who were very sick and some others who looked depressed and scowled at everyone and everything. As a matter of principle I refused to let any of these men get ahead of me in line and besides, I had to get back to Candia before evening.

When my turn came, the army doctor thumped my back and my shoulders and poked my stomach. Then I told him about my pains. I named them one by one with precision, giving the hour and the date, on which each one had made its appearance. The doctor, a captain, looked at me with interest and amazement. He stepped back as if to get a better view, and before speaking he very slowly lowered the arm that had thumped me till it was hanging limply by his side. I watched the movement of that white military arm which seemed to be casting a spell, and I waited for him to speak. The words came fast, filled with the resentment and disdain that an army doctor always feels when dealing with a sick soldier. He told me that I was eating too much after having eaten too little in prison and because my stomach was not used to so much food it had trouble digesting. It expanded and contracted abnormally. According to the doctor, the soreness in my throat was due to excessive smoking. I didn't tell him that I didn't smoke and had never smoked in my life, not even when I went into the army, because I knew well enough that the purpose of this visit was not to discover the true state of my health; the visit was only a military duty that we both had to perform. I had recounted and denounced my troubles out loud because I was used to doing it in my mind. It was a daily or at least a frequent occurrence in my life. It was a process that enabled me to detach my troubles from my body and soul and that for a moment allowed me to see them clearly and from afar as if they were lined up on a ledge from which I could take them down or make them disappear at will.

I remember thinking while I was getting dressed that I was glad the army doctor had not discovered my troubles, and at the same time I was afraid that they might suddenly have disappeared. My troubles would have to be recognized and fought on another battlefield, once I had made sure of them, in all their numbers, frequency, and quality, so that I could conquer them completely and restore my body to perfect health.

I felt very well when I left the hospital, and in my hurry to leave Turin I ran all the way to the Porta Nuova Station to catch the train to Candia. I was forced to take the train, which was much slower and more uncomfortable than the bus, because the army didn't pay for any other means of transportation. The train left in the early evening. It was a train used by all the factory workers, and it stopped at every station along the way. It was as crowded as a military train, filled with workers returning home after leaving the factories in Turin.

Many of the workers had a contented look about them, with their caps, their newspapers, their lunch boxes, and their noisy talk. Others looked as if they were cold. Even in April surrounded by that crowd they looked cold, and the dirt on their clothes seemed to add to their discomfort. Small groups would get off at the different stations, laughing and shouting insults to each other. It seemed to me that the ones who looked happiest were the first to get off, leaving behind them their sadder and dirtier companions for the long trip ahead and the night.

Confused by the noisy and feverish atmosphere of the train, I hadn't even tried to find a seat, but when the lights went on in the car I saw some empty places and sat down. I sat next to a handsome-looking worker with a long, thin, well-shaped nose, a slim, perfectly proportioned nose that looked as if it were his most valuable precision instrument. He told me that he had been working for Fiat for seventeen years and that his job was to check the new motors. He said that his work was interesting and demanded all his attention. His father was still a farmer, who had land south of the river near Chivasso. Personally, he thought a farmer's life was a good life but difficult and unrewarding. A good life; still, there were those who didn't think so. A girl in Turin had refused to marry him because his family were farmers. The pleasant young man got off at Chivasso and disappeared into the station. Before the train pulled out I thought I saw him in the darkness rounding the corner of the station house on a bicycle, curved over the handle-bars but sure of himself, not with that stiff carriage and uncertain look that farmers have when they ride or that pained expression that makes you think they are wondering how it is possible for the wheels to keep their balance and move under the pressure of the pedals.

I then lit the cigarette he had offered me while we were talking. I had taken it so as not to offend him. I looked at the countryside and smoked. The smoke that drifted out the window caught between the lights of the train, and the blue night seemed alive. It was like an animal that lurks between the field and the hedges. I couldn't live in the city, I thought, not in the city where I feel alone and where I can see that people are mean and tricky, interested only in what they can get out of you. You have to be careful whom you talk to in the city. You never know when you are going to run into a thief, or a lunatic or a murderer or one of those women or into cheats and charlatans. The very air of the city tires me and makes me break into a sweat; my hands and feet perspire and so does my back.

The city is for girls who want to amuse themselves and who can work in shops behind counters and showcases better than in factories or in the fields; and then, as I was saying, the city is for thieves and other no-goods, it is for students and the condemned factory workers, it's for jails, hospitals and doctors, barracks and soldiers, bars and movie theaters, for thieves and their girls and unfortunate derelicts. It is hard work to find a street in the city and to know where to go. I love the country with its roads and lanes that tell you what you should do, the country that reveals itself at a glance, openly and honestly. I love the countryside more than I love my country, but I don't love it the way a farmer does because a farmer uses the land for profit and he digs and chops each day like those animals that gnaw on trees and ruin the timber. If the country were left alone to bloom wild, not only would it be more beautiful but it would produce more fruit to be picked in moderation. But I wouldn't like to own land, because you end up feeling that it belongs exclusively to you, and you want to take care of it and defend it and fence it off from the rest of the country, and you want to regulate the weather over your trees and field and perhaps even get rid of the crows and the other animals. These were my thoughts while the train ran toward the trees surrounding the lake in Candia and I sat and smoked the worker's cigarette, one of the first I had ever smoked in my life.

When I got off the train I went straight home. I walked slowly so that I could taste the countryside in the light of my talk and my thoughts on the train. I stopped for a second, held by the scent from a rosemary bush. It was such a good and subtle smell! It made me want to look up at the starry sky that glows on April nights, when the moon is still new but waxing with strange streaks of light (which of course everyone knows are only the looks the saints give each other across the heavens). I thanked Divine Providence, happy to be home after the city and the trip and above all the danger of having been sent to a military hospital. I stopped in the kitchen to eat the omelette my mother had kept warm for me between two plates and to drink a glass of wine. One half before eating; the other half when I had finished. As I went upstairs to the bedroom in the attic, I hoped my mother would still be awake and call me.

From the middle of April through May to the first days of June it always rains, not much but constantly. The rain dulls my senses and makes me silent. I stayed home, happy to be there where I could spend long hours on the porch or in my bedroom. I would lie down and think about the time when I would be healthy and strong again and ready at last for some kind of work. Before the war I had gone to a school for factory trainees run by Silesian priests, but I missed graduating by three months because of my father's death and an attack of pleuritis. Lying on my bed during those rainy days I thought of the things I could do, but I couldn't think of any job which really suited me or my new life. The rain poured down the windowpanes and lashed the lake and distracted me from my thoughts. The water of the lake rose visibly right in the center where it piled up and then would spread out, flooding the shore and slowly covering the muddy bank. I would touch my shoulders as I used to do when I was a boy during my illness and in my mouth I would savor a taste of myself, a memory of my youth.

Sometime during those days a letter arrived from my cousin in France. She had moved from Avignon to Paris and she wrote about herself and her family, about those who had disappeared or died during the war. She said that she wanted to visit Italy and meet us, the only relatives she remembered from her youth, and she asked if she could come and stay with us for the summer and part of September. I was happy about that letter, and often on warm nights I would sit in front of my house hoping my cousin from France would come walking down the road from Candia.

Other letters arrived. A letter from the Veterans Association reporting their progress on the matter of my claim for a pension. Another from the Placement Bureau kindly asking me to come to their office in the city to see if I was eligible for veterans training in factory work. I didn't like the idea that the Veterans Association knew my address. It made it seem as though the prison camp had traveled back with me from Germany and followed me into my home. Even the business of the pension bothered me because if they gave me a pension I would still be a prisoner with the stamp of an eternal sickness on my soul. The other letter from the new and unknown office couldn't really bother me even though it lumped me once again with the prisoners. It referred to the future —"Study for a position in industry." If I wanted to, I could almost interpret it as a sign of liberation and a step forward.

On the sixteenth of June, 1946, I went to the Municipal Placement Bureau. Just a few days earlier, the Republican party had won the elections, and even though I had voted for the monarchy, the Republic's triumph helped me by touching everything with the newness of its recent victory. Even the offices seemed to want to help by carrying on business as usual. At the employment bureau everything was filed here or there on a table or on a windowsill by a scurrying clerk who always seemed to know where to find the right piece of paper. He scattered his good mood all over the place like the ashes of his cigarette.

"Saluggia, Albino; Father, Ernesto from Candia; class of 1919; please go to the X Placement Bureau with this paper which I will sign and stamp." This he did hurriedly, using both hands so as not to waste time. "You are on the list of veterans assigned to be trained for skilled labor in the factory of X." He gave me the paper and then added, "The twenty-second of June, this month, six days from now, and good luck."

I nodded silently, accepting everything. I folded the slip of paper. When I came out into the square in Candia I stopped for a moment, and then I went to buy a pack of cigarettes.

The X Placement Bureau was bigger, dirtier, and more disorganized than that one room in Candia. I went there on the twenty-first of June, not the twenty-second, just to see what it was like. I was driven by the idea that if I went early I would be able to anticipate any trickery on their part and stop whatever preparations were being made to confuse me. Maybe I went early just to avoid a too definite appointment of someone or something waiting for me—someone or something that would then be lying in wait for me forever. This way, the initiative was nearly all mine and it was *my* will and *my* strength that would decide the first steps in my life. What hopes I had then for that new life! So many that I couldn't describe the extent of my expectations. I didn't know then just how cruel men could be to each other and how useless it was to try and develop through one's own strength and get ahead alone; how every refuge was denied one and how every man is every other man's enemy, ready to strike and hurt leaving the other torn and wounded like a Christ or a Saint Sebastian. Young men tied naked to a stake and tortured till their beautiful bodies are broken and all that is left is their mothers' sorrow.

I was so confident that day that perhaps I made the mistake about the date simply because I was in such a hurry to arrive. Things seem very different now. So much evil has been thrown in my way that it has stifled any hopes I ever had; so much so that the fear and submission of today have colored the memory of that bit of life I had when my mind was still tied to my youth. Today it is difficult for me to forgive, and although I write about my troubles and those who were the cause of my troubles I don't do it to accuse. Not even I felt singled out or accused by destiny during those first days of June in 1946 when I went for my appointment to the Placement Bureau and to the Personnel Department of the X factory.

At the Placement Bureau the clerk behind the large counter treated me with indifference. "Come back tomorrow. Tomorrow is the twenty-second."

Without accepting the piece of paper he held out to me, I asked for further information.

"There is little to explain about this paper. We have to register it and stamp it and you have to take it to the factory." As he spoke he registered and stamped the paper, looking first at me, then at the group of people standing in line behind me at the window. One of them noticed these looks and the endless stamping and complained. "There is room for all of you," answered my clerk. "All of you have the same rights;" and he gave me back my paper.

Why has the clerk behaved in a special way toward me, I thought. This thought frightened me, but I was quick to control myself, remembering that it was I who had taken the initiative.

Today I know I should have paid more attention to that thought, for it was like a sign marking the beginning of my troubles, unexpected as a fly you might find on the windowpane during the last snowy days of February, coming from God knows where to curse the winter.

A little later I stood in front of the enormous factory where I would have to appear in another five days. My curiosity was answered only by the most profound air of mystery. The huge low building hummed indifferently. It was still, like the lake in Candia when it alone in all the countryside reflects the light.

Not even in Germany had I seen such a large factory. Huge, sitting squarely on the street, without fences or gates so that people could go forth between the open and enclosed spaces. I thought a factory needed room for people to move about and that therefore it would need courtyards and open spaces, like a machine shop where workers in overalls go back and forth between the work bench, the machines, and the street. The doors of such shops are hung with keys and hammers and metal tubes for testing the different colored paints and the heat of the fire.

But the factory was immovable, solid, and silent, like a church or a courthouse, and from outside you knew that the interior was just like a church; you knew that in a high and empty space a thousand different kinds of jobs were getting done. After a second the work seemed all the same. The factory was the same in all parts, and it emitted the same humming noise from every side. It was more than just a hum. It was like a panting sound or a loud gasp. The factory was so big and clean, so mysterious that one couldn't even decide whether it was ugly or beautiful, and even after having worked there for so many years I still can't say whether the factory is ugly or beautiful. Because for so many years, even though I have thought about it sometimes, the question remains undecided, the same way that one can't decide about a church or a courthouse.

The factory was always in perfect order, even when they were enlarging or repairing the premises, always clean and always unknown. Maybe this means that the factory is beautiful; still I cannot really say that the factory is beautiful, looking at it both from within and without. I mean that it isn't beautiful to me, like a house or a tree. There were times during the course of many years when the factory did seem beautiful, but it was I who judged it so, inside myself, without really seeing it.

That day I went there hoping to get inside for a little while and to look around. I walked in, but a guard stopped me immediately. I showed him the paper that the Placement Bureau had given me and I told him that I was supposed to report for work in five days. The guard, who was well dressed and cordial, told me to come back at about eight in the morning to a certain door which he pointed out to me. I left without feeling rejected, because both the guard and his little speech had been perfect, as perfect as the order that prevailed in the factory.

I stood still on the street just a little way from the entrance, and I decided to wait for the workers to come out at noon. I wanted to see them close by and all together, and I wanted to speak to some of them if possible. Not far from the factory there was—and still is—a café on the corner of the street leading to the city. It is a wood-paneled café filled with a lot of different smells. The air inside tastes of coffee and mint and turpentine. And another pungent smell that I couldn't distinguish then but that today I recognize as the smell of the factory, the smell of grease, of metal and workers. The place is really more of a restaurant than a café, and in the back there is a bare room with tables and chairs. I sat down and ordered a vermouth. There were three workers sitting at the table next to mine, and now I know that they were workers waiting for the noon shift to begin. They didn't speak about work or about the factory. As matter of fact, they didn't speak at all; they only smoked and looked out into the street. They were dressed in street clothes, and one even had a hat on. Another worker arrived, bought some liquor, greeted the others, and left, saying, "I'm going to take a look at the papers." I remember wondering what papers he was talking about, and I arrived at the conclusion that they were work bulletins or instructions or even account ledgers. I also remember thinking that he must be a very able young man, in charge of some complicated work or other. The other three didn't strike me as having any particular ability. They seemed so much like me or like the others in Candia that I didn't have the slightest curiosity or desire to speak to them.

Other workers came into the café—young ones, older ones, some dressed in overalls. They all looked very pleased with themselves, although they were quite reserved, as if engrossed by a single thought. I decided that the reason for their thoughtful attitude was the sense of responsibility they all felt toward the delicate work they were doing in the factory. They all seemed very calm, and their hands were ordinary and steady, not thick and dirty like the hands of a mechanic, nor knotted and cracked like a farmer's hands. Only when the café was filled with people did I have the courage to speak to one of the workers. I didn't pick the one nearest me or one of the ones who had just arrived because I didn't want to seem too eager.

"Excuse me," I said. "Have you seen Manero?"

The worker answered no with the air of one who isn't easily surprised.

"Manero works in the factory," I went on, lying.

"I don't know anyone named Manero, at least not in my department. It's hard to keep track of everybody."

"Thank you," I answered. "I'll wait for Mr. Manero at the exit." The "mister" added to the fictitious conversation and put a stop to any attempt at tracing him. It also put me on a different level from the rest of the people in the café. Today I realize that it was the noonday rush and not the "mister" that ended our conversation.

I remember very clearly all the events of that overcast and blisteringly hot June. I even remember the minor events, less important than what happened later on, both in and out of the factory. I believe I remember those days so clearly because I still hadn't begun to work. I was still waiting for things to happen, and therefore every incident seemed very important. After a while, factory life dulls the memory. Things get buried at the back of our minds, and eventually the brain doesn't bother to examine too thoroughly our thoughts about work and the rest; our minds are free to wander and indulge in fantasies that have nothing to do with our immediate surroundings. While I worked I thought about the prison camp, my house, and my mother's health. I had never thought so much about them before. I thought about things that might happen to me instead of things that were really happening, even though reality was the basis for the daydream.

I remember exactly the pattern of the pavement in front of the factory. I remember each square and shiny stone I walked on while I waited for the workers to come out. I remember those stones better than the faces of so many of my companions, especially the faces of the men I worked with after my transfer to another department. Those stones, so thick and hard under my feet, made my legs ache; and the stifling June air that became even more stifling and oppressive in the vicinity of the factory, as if I were standing in front of an oven, made me want to escape. I didn't want to wait any longer; I just wanted to go home. The factory seemed like a meaningless building, but I still felt as if a part of my brain was forcing me to stay in that hostile, unnatural place.

Suddenly a mass of people started streaming out of the building. A large crowd poured into the street and still there didn't seem to be as many as three thousand people there. The factory employed three thousand workers. Many of the men rode off on their bicycles or on their motor scooters while others, very sure of themselves, sauntered off in directions that seemed to have been chosen at random. It was a mixed crowd of all ages, like the crowds one finds in a train or in the market. They moved quickly without seeming at all tired.

I thought that the only work each of them had to do was to pull a switch on some machine or something like that. More than anything, I was weary of them and a little dizzy from the vermouth I had drunk. I went back to the café; it was more crowded now, filled with people talking. I ordered a cup of coffee and sat down for a moment to watch the workers.

I gave most of my attention to a straw basket an old lady had put on the floor next to her chair.

As I left I thought how I would never learn to be like these workers, how I would never be able to imitate them. It was very hot. It was an unhealthy day; the sunlight lay shattered in little pieces on the metal factory. There was a different kind of light shining near the river. The heat bothered me. I felt dirty and as if I were trying to walk inside a glass bell. My pains awoke simultaneously and gripped my stomach. The pain in my chest, however, didn't begin at the same time as the others. Instead, I felt my shoulders tremble under the heat, tremble involuntarily, the same way your leg trembles when you leave it too long in one position.

I still have a job today in spite of all my troubles and the evil intentions of the doctors. It's a hard job but it's a living. Certain evenings, especially in winter, I leave the half-lighted factory by myself, after all the others have gone. I pretend that I am happy to leave, and I imagine that I can feel the warmth of other people's homes surrounding me, as if everyone were waiting for me in a thousand houses in the city and the surrounding villages. I am even lonelier at home because my mother grows more distant every day, and her long silences increase.

I know that one of the men who work with me has a crazy mother whom he has to lock up in the bedroom during the day so he can come to work. Another fellow I know gets drunk with his mother. He leaves his wife and goes with his mother to a tavern where they spend the evening drinking and hugging each other like a couple of drunks. Often they disappear for months, they rent a bedroom in some hotel, drink like crazy, and go to all the shows in town.

My fate is silence. My mother looks at me sometimes as if she didn't recognize me, and instead of helping and comforting me she cries and hides her face. I don't even think she prays for me any more, although she spends entire nights sitting on the edge of her bed mumbling to herself.

The only thing I have left is my fight for the triumph of justice, because at this point I don't think I will be able to conquer my troubles. I only want to unmask falsehoods, denounce the guilty, and sacrifice myself like a rebel to the cause of justice.

In the factory there have been times when I would find release in my work. Then I would whip my group into a frenzy of work, and I would stick to my job hour after hour just to show them that I was better than any of them. My ability gave me some comfort; it was one of the only things, if not the only one, that gave me a sense of progress. I knew I could do specialized work well, and I wasn't afraid of mechanical things any longer. But none of this did me any good.

To get on with the facts, I must tell about the day I was hired and the first weeks that I spent at my new job, up to the time the doctors made their fatal discovery.

16]

I arrived at the factory gates the morning of June 26, 1946. **One** of the guards took me to the Personnel Department. We walked quickly through part of the ground floor, but I didn't have time to look around or understand exactly where we were. The hum of the work going on around me grew stronger.

Inside the factory the noise was more distinct. It was the electric noise of many machines in action. The noise seemed to come from everywhere, even from the walls and floors of the factory. I couldn't see any work rooms during our walk, but just for a second through a half-opened doorway I saw a well lighted table, a glass table shining like the first light of morning. At one point I crossed an immense hall, a room roofed with enormous panes of glass bound in iron casings. Other hallways led from this room into still other rooms that seemed to dissolve the moment we left the light and walked toward the center of the building.

The guard led me down the cleanest of the hallways, the only one painted white. We went up three steps to where the light glowed higher, and on each side of me I saw many doorways spaced at regular intervals. The end of the hall led into a sort of waiting room. The guard left me with several other men who were also waiting. No one spoke, and the only noise was the sound of the factory which now seemed a little muted. Judging from the faces of those who were waiting, there were other things to listen to besides the sound of the factory. This was an enforced pause, and we waited in that bright white hallway with its linoleum floor.

During the five days that had passed since my first visit to the factory I had convinced myself that my call to work was a good thing, to my advantage. I wasn't afraid of being turned down because during those five days I had already felt myself present inside the factory. I had even dreamed about work, about having to perform a very exacting task constructing a complicated piece of machinery something like the mechanism of a clock. In the dream, just as I was about to finish, my machine would start clattering, while the machines of all the other workers busy doing the same type of work, lined up on either side of me, continued to function perfectly. I couldn't stop the clatter unless I removed one of the parts of the machine, thereby ruining the entire mechanism. But suddenly the foreman, who reminded me of the young worker from Chivasso, would arrive, and he would tell everybody that according to the latest instructions all the machines were supposed to rattle just like mine.

Many years before, when I left France with my mother and father I had experienced that same feeling of emptiness together with a confidence in the future. With the stubbornness and determination of a thirteen-year-old boy, I refused to accept the idea of leaving. I didn't want to go back to Italy, and my father tried to convince me with grown-up arguments which completely disgusted me. My father said that he was tired and even a little sick and that he didn't feel secure in a foreign country. He said that Italy had changed and that Fascism had brought prosperity to the country. Now there were many opportunities for the worker and still more for a young boy's future. All this only made my last days in Avignon more painful and drained me of every thought and image of youth. As our trip drew near I was overpowered by an overwhelming desire to return to Italy, to Candia which my father had described as a beautiful village.

In the hallway in front of the Skilled Labor Department I felt as I had felt at the station in Avignon moments before leaving: nothing remained of my past twelve years; I only looked forward to the train for Italy and to my arrival in Candia at the house near the lake. Instead, it was at that moment at the station—when I simultaneously lived my departure and my trip and bridged the distance between Avignon and Candia-Canivesa in one step—that many of my troubles began: my father's death, the two years' delay before I was enrolled in the industrial training school, the loneliness of my youth, and then war and prison.

If only for this reason I should have known that my exaggerated hopefulness and my self-assurance at the prospect of a new job would only bring me new troubles and sorrier times.

I blame those moments of forgetfulness while standing before the door of the Personnel Department.

Since the day I left Avignon my life has been a constant battle with evil, and evil has taken my innocent hopes and aspirations and forged them into weapons with which to strike me.

If the Skilled Labor Department had looked like an instrument of evil, I would have run away or fought with all my strength to conquer this evil. Instead I was so defenseless that I was completely fooled. I walked into that office unaware that such a step could revolutionize my life. I went in without hesitating, hoping that they would put me to work immediately.

"Sit down," said an old man with an enormous mane of white hair. He was dressed in black with a gray-green shirt and a black tie. He told me to sit down again even before I could look around to see whether there were other doors in that office that led to the workrooms.

It was a small white office with a green lamp and a yellow door. There were two or three desks, some larger than the others, and the old man moved among them as if he had to choose one of them and as if the rest of our conversation depended on his choice. However, he was sure of himself, and he had that kindly manner peculiar to old men. I sat down and showed him my paper. He slowly composed the mouth under his fat cheeks and mumbled: "Prisoner; prisoner in Germany. Good for you, soldier, faithful to your country." This statement surprised me, and for a moment I became suspicious. Were they about to refuse me what was already mine by right? But the old man continued: "So you want to work," and he got up to look for a pencil which he kept in a locked cabinet. "And what kind of work can you do? Were you doing specialized work in the army? What branch of the army were you in? Where were you captured?"

"I have had two years of industrial training, but I have never worked. I was in the infantry, the Sixty-second Regiment, and I was captured with all the others near Zagreb. I want to work in a factory. In Germany I worked in a radio factory."

The truth was that sometimes, together with the other prisoners, I would go to that abandoned radio factory in Germany to pick up odd bits of coal that had been left lying about in small heaps on the floor. The factory was completely bare, and one couldn't even tell what they had manufactured there. Once among the coals I found a small turntable and a pedal that still worked. I took it back to the compound, and I used it to work on an infinite number of senseless things. I remember that small turntable very well. Toward the end, one of the prisoners used it to smash another prisoner's skull.

[19

The old man's huge head kept nodding up and down; then it stopped, cocked to the left toward the window. (The old man is considered a fool by everyone in the factory, and they laugh at him because he has the rank of major and the age of a general.) He began to question me again: "How many are there in your family? Are you married? Any children? Do you own your own house?" I answered yes or no to all the questions, and I added that I spoke a little French.

"Ah, fine! Well I think they'll hire you; at least that's my opinion." He nodded to the yellow door and continued, "You'll have to go for your medical examination, and then some of my colleagues in this office will examine you to find out about your aptitudes. You've been a soldier for many years so you must know the value of discipline and obedience. These are also the two basic principles of the factory. You will receive a regular salary, according to the law, social security, bonuses, and paid vacations. You should never arrive late for work, and you should always do your duty."

This speech was fair enough, but it bothered me because it delayed the starting date of my work; it implied that I had to wait till others decided whether I could work or not. I was filled with a sense of doom. It seemed as if the old man wanted me to understand clearly that something important and unpleasant was going to happen, while at the same time he tried to hide the nature of the event under the flow of his polite words. I thought that it had been a long time since anything different had happened. My house was still and silent, waiting for an owner or some news that would bring light to its windows. Either I would get the job or a guarantee of a job, or something terrible would happen to me or to my mother.

The old man's huge head was still. It seemed as if I were watching him through a magnifying glass and each hair on his head stood out separate and distinct. Beginning with my father, people with large heads have always hurt me. This particular head made me uneasy, nearly frightened me in spite of the fact that the old man had spoken kindly to me. My forebodings made me so ill at ease that the old man sensed he had to help me.

"It only means a delay of two or three days. You can go for your checkup this evening or tomorrow."

"Tomorrow then." I left the office and the factory immediately, still holding on to my piece of paper, after having made still another appointment.

In those days I thought that the only thing I had to fear was myself. I refer to the pains and troubles I had noticed both within me and surrounding me and the forebodings that accompanied them. Only a new life, only work and daily progress could help me or my health. I had to save myself. I had to find a framework in which I could live and free myself from the sad harvest of my previous life and prison. I wanted to run home, go to bed, rest and analyze my troubles one by one, exorcise them and make them disappear by the following day.

Near the café I found a bus leaving for Turin that stopped at the beginning of the road to Candia. It was one of those buses that travel between Turin and the public gardens outside the city, leaving at regular intervals during the day. It wasn't one of the factory workers' buses that leave the dusty square in front of the station every morning and evening. The seats were very comfortable and the people were quiet; it was filled with women—young married women and girls.

I was lucky to have taken that bus because it gave me a chance to rest. I looked at the girls and their magazines; and outside the window the sunlit countryside seemed to be resting, like me. It seemed also as if a profound, thoughtful air were drifting over the landscape without touching the fields or the trees or the flowers, the same way that my thoughts, drifting out of my consciousness, left my hands still and undisturbed. There was only a small cloud far away where the countryside spilled over into invisible places and a few spotted pigeons, rising in flight from the grain fields. The girls on the bus were quiet, and their youthful presence comforted me. "When I go for my checkup tomorrow I must be as calm and serene as they are, looking forward to a new and happy life like theirs," I thought.

I got off at the crossroads, and I felt better because it had been such a pleasant trip. I thought that the walk from the crossroads to my house would do me good if I walked slowly and watched the lake appear little by little as I climbed the hill toward my house. At a certain spot I knew the lake would lie directly below me, the same way it lay under the wings of the swallows that circled the old castle on the edge of the lake. I would also see the village roofs, neat and red, apparently innocent but harboring so much human cruelty. That morning I had walked the same road in the opposite direction, but I tried not to remember that I had been sure my new life and work would begin that day.

I arrived around eleven thirty. My mother was in the garden, picking some onions. I said hello to her, adding that I would have to go back to the factory on the following day. I didn't want to remember the trick fate had played on me. I asked my mother to fix me a light supper, and I went to my room to face my heart and my sorrows. I lay down on the bed that has been my bed for so many years. I loosened my shoelaces and took off my jacket.

The space that this bed fills is mine. The one place of my own that I have, even though I have slept in many other beds, as a soldier during the war, in prison, and in many different sanatoriums. My bed has a definite place, a place that is mine and just for me, white, six inches from the wall. Here I find comfort or sorrow more acute and more constant, distinct and recognizable even though they often come from far away, from the days when I was a boy just returned to Italy, from the time when I first got my bed.

At first the bed with its big cotton spread refreshed me, but after a while the heat spreading slowly through the room hit me; it was an unbearable heat, not usual for this time of year. The lake mirrored the noonday sun against my window. I wouldn't be able to rest or relax in that heat, and my dark thoughts would return to find me more exhausted than ever; all my troubles would renew their attack and conquer me. I took my iron bedstead to the abandoned barn where it was cool and shady. My mother saw me carrying the bedstead across the courtyard, and she began to cry because she didn't understand what I was doing.

I lay down, relieved, waiting for dinner time. Not only was the barn much cooler, but it smelled of grass and earth just as did the lake. This smell soothed me and helped me to think. So did the spots and crevices in the wall and the red bricks held together by cement in an endless and orderly network of streets. Perhaps I fell asleep walking those streets. After the rest I had a moment of well-being, and then once again I began to battle with my troubles, or if you prefer, I began a discussion with my troubles.

I didn't know my troubles then as I do now, but I sensed them and feared them. Today my troubles are so distinct and all-embracing that they have become an integral part of everything I do. That day I felt them climbing over my body like a swarm of insects, each one choosing his favorite spot. "Troubles, troubles," I said. "You are the fruit of my difficult life. You accompany me like unfamiliar faces on a train. It may even be just, that my throat aches and my stomach burns till it fires my chest. Just, because it proves that I have been mistreated, that justice and I have been wronged. But this train ride of mine is finished, and you have to go so that I can begin a new life in peace.

"My throat aches because so many times as a soldier I have drunk and sweated ice water, because in prison I slept with only one blanket and wrapped a scarf around my throat, a scarf that was two parts dust and one part wool. My stomach hurts because I didn't eat, and when I ate it was only scraps fit for dogs. The circulation in my chest is bad because I lived so long with fear during those years when no one knew where to go or what was going to happen next, years when one wondered where on this earth and under what skies were those tall or short, thin or fat, half-crazed officers taking us. We spent the senseless months in uniform with our guns in our hands without firing a shot. More and more often we ran and hid in some foreign country, in villages that not even the enemy had discovered. Who would be able to find us? The men of the battalion were only poor soldiers; they didn't know how to speak properly and they were very ignorant. They only knew how to be tough and how to play practical jokes, many practical jokes on Saluggia, especially at night when we didn't know where to find a place to sleep. 'Saluggia,' they'd say, 'would you sleep with a girl? Saluggia, you son of a bitch, whatever made you leave France?' I ignored them and tried to remain aware of what was happening to me, to form an opinion of people and things and behave as much like a man as discipline would allow.

"I was nearly court-martialed twice. The second time they saved me from a sergeant who was beating me to death. They accused me of insubordination. While Vattino, the sergeant, was yelling at me and wrenching my arm, I looked him straight in the eye and prayed, 'Father, forgive them, for they know not what they're doing to themselves.' This is what had infuriated Vattino, and this is why he wanted to kill me. But I resisted. The more blows and ignorance I had to endure, the more distant I grew. I would leave the others and if it was possible I would try to find a place to sit down and think. I thought about France and about the streets in Avignon where I played when I was a boy. Or I thought about the training school and how much Father Caligari had liked me and how he would often let me visit him in his room. And how once he had given me some pears that came from his village in Monferrato. At other times I thought that everything would come to an end and I would be the only one left to return home, guided by justice. And everything would be over, everything was already over, but you, troubles, have to come at the very end, like certain orders that arrive after all the decisions have been made, like orders that arrive and fill you with terror.

"If the reasons for my sufferings have long ceased to exist, why, now that the tree trunk is dead, do you insist on building your nest inside me, like so many tiny ants? I am about to become a new person, so you must leave me. I sleep peacefully at night, and if for some reason I don't sleep, then I lie awake and listen to the sound of my mother's breathing or the rustle of the trees on the hill next to my house. And so you must leave me. You must go somewhere else and wait before you judge my new life. If I sin or others sin against me I should be chosen as a victim in the cause of justice and then you can return. Then it will be easier to attack me, and you will be more dangerous. Today I'm convinced that you're not dangerous—you're nothing but a memory and a shadow. I have eaten and rested, and I haven't abused myself. My throat is fine and so is my stomach, and I don't have fever. In moments of discomfort, when I despair of ever having a new life and find it impossible to see its design, then the shadow of past sorrows returns to cloud my mind and my spirit.

"I don't recognize the shadows of the sorrows that bit into my flesh in Croatia and in Germany. I was too busy fighting you. So

I can't remember you and you are destined to disappear. I'll know how to brush you off my body and tomorrow I will be well, ready for work. If you return, I won't be able to resist you because now I am home, and I would have to fight you for the second time but without any hope. When you first appeared, I knew that Croatia and prison had to end sometime. But what end can I possibly imagine now? I was younger then; I was a soldier destined to suffer. The conviction that I was involved in a just fight against the army and the cruelty of the other soldiers gave me strength. I was a stranger twice over; first, because I was in the army among strangers, then, because I was in a strange town. Somehow this was my comfort, and it justified my loneliness during the long hours I would sit on the steps of some strange house with my rifle on my knees. The towns were all alike, surrounded by thick woods where I would go and sit even though it was against the regulations. It was in one of these woods, two hours after curfew that the patrol led by Sergeant Vattino found me. I heard them looking for me, eight of them, armed to the teeth and worried. I had hidden myself deeper in the woods. I waited for an hour; then I started back through the path in the woods.

"I lost track of that beast, Vattino, somewhere in Germany. He was among the sick in the first prison camp. I was fairly well in that first prison camp, and I was holding on because I was happy over the collapse of the army. I was happy that the whole structure of the army including that hateful discipline had been shattered by the Germans in one minute. The camp was located at the edge of a river and a boat passed regularly four times a day. After a while I realized that there were two identical boats and that they carried barrels or wheat or crates. I would wait patiently for the boats to pass, and I would try to recognize the faces of the crew. If I watched them till they disappeared, I had enough time to count the barrels or the crates, and when they carried wheat I would just count the minutes during which they remained in my line of vision. Once in a while, about once a month or even less, I would imagine that a boat appeared painted like a battleship, going very fast. As it got nearer I'd discover that my mother was sitting next to the man that steered the ship.

"It was then, troubles, that you bit into me, and you bit even harder in the second camp when it rained for more than a week on my bed. The piece of cardboard I found to stuff the hole in the ceiling would soak through in a minute and disintegrate. That place under the crack in the ceiling, immovable, chained to the wall of the barracks and to the entire castle of beds, was a present from my companions. I didn't steal any food, and my companions certainly never gave me any. One evening, after a medical checkup, I found a small box of meat lying outside the door of the infirmary. As I picked it up from the mud, it didn't seem real, and I thought that it might be just another terrible joke. I divided the meat among all the sick prisoners without even tasting any of it.

"In those days, my troubles, you really bit into me even though I tried to resist you. Now your shadows have to disappear, they have to leave me in peace, or else this time I won't be able to resist you and you will destroy me. I can't struggle in my own house, in front of my mother, at the very moment when I should be well and begin to live like a civilized man."

I spoke to myself in the coolness of the barn while the sun passed over the lake in Candia. At a certain moment, a moment which I could predict and not one second before or afterward, the sun would suddenly leave the lake and disappear in back of the hills toward the mountains. Maybe my troubles would leave me in the same way, sliding down my arms; or maybe at least they would diminish like the sunlight and leave me in peace the following day.

Among the discolorations and patterns formed by the bricks in the wall, patterns that had been familiar to me for so many years during my childhood after my return from Avignon, I had no trouble finding the face of the Indian with the high brown turban, shining like a piece of beautiful silk. This immediately reminded me of the boot, and I looked for it higher up at the end of an old platform under the roof. The Indian had always been my fantasy: the inspiration for many fairy tales and the thrust that set my imagination spinning, creating new tales and stories and sometimes just different endings to the same fairy tale that began inside me the moment I spotted the picture of the Indian on the wall. The boot, high and round at the tip, always had a happy look about it and the air of a good friend who was always ready to cheer me up with actual happy memories of children's parties, beautiful

Easter days, and spring days, new clothes and presents of money. To have found these tracings on the wall after so many years, more vivid and fresh both on the wall and inside myself, must surely be a good omen. These were my thoughts, and I immediately put all my trust in the fantasies conjured by the Indian and the tender memories inspired by the boot. These fantasies and memories complemented each other, and I was so taken by them that I forgot my troubles during those last hours of sunlight before nightfall.

The memory of a particular event began to stand out clearly in my mind and take precedence over all the other memories that came rushing back to fill my head, my eyes, and my ears. It was the memory of my First Communion, and perhaps it was a sign from Heaven. Even then I was very worried. While they were in France, my parents didn't practice their religion. They hardly ever went to church and they hadn't thought about giving me any religious instruction, so that when I returned to Italy at the age of twelve, I still hadn't been confirmed. Once in Italy, my parents picked up the threads of their old friendships and habits. They started going to church again and they made sure that I received the Sacraments. After lunch, around two o'clock, I used to go alone to the parish priest, Don Achille Giglio Chion, for catechism lessons. He used to wake up from his hour's nap in the sacristy with his tunic unbuttoned and his watch dangling from a chain across his chest. I usually woke him up when I opened the little door behind the apse. I used to go alone because I was too old to be admitted to the regular catechism lessons.

"Albino," Don Giglio Chion would say, "there is only one God, just like this watch," and he would then wind it up and stuff it inside his tunic buttoning up all the little black buttons. "There is only one God, divided in three parts like this watch: the Father, the Son, and the Holy Ghost; the watch case, the mechanism, and the hands. One God, one tic-tock, and one law. There are many of us who look at this watch and who must believe in this one law, and listen to the tic-tock.

"How many Sacraments are there?" he would ask me immediately afterward as he got up and spat out the sacristy window. It was a horrible spittle, born in the throat and in the mouth together with the sacred word, spittle that would bounce like a coin on the pavement outside. Then he would close the window and smile at me, ready to begin the lesson. He was killed by the Germans one night as he was going to visit some partisans in the Val d'Aosta. He was killed by a single shot fired from far away.

In May, on the morning of my First Communion, I was upset and excited because I had to receive the Sacraments as a grown boy wearing long pants especially made for the occasion. I was ashamed to be so big in the middle of so many little children, and I was just as worried as I was in the barn this night before my medical examination at the factory. I thought something would go wrong and that some evil spirit would push me aside at the last minute just because I was so worried. I was the only one wearing long pants among all the other children with bare legs. Those pink legs lined up at the altar rail were the symbol of their purity. I was the last to receive the host and since the bishop wasn't there I couldn't be confirmed.

The memory of my First Communion calmed me and inspired me to go to communion the following day, in the morning, before my medical checkup. It was already night and I could barely hear the soft noise the lake made as the water washed toward the shore. The frogs and the crickets were louder than the lake, and once in a while I heard the sound of a car and voices coming from the road. The moon was out, and even without seeing it I felt the splendor of its three-quarters fullness through the songs the nightingales sang in the thick woods in the north. I saw the moon as I left the barn carrying my bed back to the house. Moonlight filled the kitchen and whitened the table still set with dishes for the supper my mother had prepared for me. I went upstairs, remade my bed, and came down to the kitchen to eat in peace filled with the serenity that had already become part of my spirit. My troubles seemed as distant as the noonday sun, and it seemed as if they would never appear again on my horizon. My new life would begin tomorrow, and I would find peace in my work. The night passed very quickly and quietly.

On the twenty-eighth of June, 1946, I left my house a little after dawn dressed in my best suit. Perhaps the suit wasn't entirely appropriate in that heat, but I left my shirt collar unbuttoned. I went to church but it was still closed when I arrived. I tried the sacristy, but even the little back door was closed. So I walked toward the center of town by the road that leads to the lake. The road was deserted. I saw an old man sitting in front of the last house in the village. It looked more like a farmhouse than a village house. The old man was curved over his cane, and he had a blanket over his shoulders.

When I returned, the church was open, and its great doors were standing ajar. There were four women inside already talking loudly among themselves. I asked the priest to hear my confession and he immediately knelt down at the altar, signaling me to do the same. The women lowered their voices, and I began my confession while staring all the time at the early morning sun dust that fell on the great golden chandeliers.

I didn't have many sins to confess, and I didn't even want to talk about my troubles because I feared they would come back. I hinted that I was afraid of the medical examination and that was the only time that the priest looked at me. I told him that every once in a while I despaired of ever having a better life and that sometimes I felt as if I hated my mother and her old age. The priest told me I should confide in my mother and make her a part of my life. He asked me if I was engaged and if I had made any plans for a Christian marriage. I was surprised for a minute, and I answered no. Then, because I didn't want to seem too brusque and also because I was a little embarrassed, I added, "I haven't thought about it yet."

He gave me absolution, but I wasn't entirely at peace. His last question remained suspended and unanswered within me. I heard mass and took communion with the women. I looked at them and I noticed that they were all old and ugly, dressed alike in dark or black cotton dresses, and only one of them had a round figure and breasts. I wondered how a man could live for so many years, so many nights and mornings with the same woman without eventually feeling disgusted by her.

I rid myself of these thoughts before taking Holy Communion, and when mass was over I was the first to leave. I walked to the railroad station in town. I bought a newspaper and a magazine so that I wouldn't have to think during the trip, and I sat in the last car so that I wouldn't be bothered by too many people. I sat with my back to the engine and began to read immediately. Every once in a while I'd look through the rear door of the car at the countryside split by the railroad while in the distance the shining rails looked like criminals in flight.

I arrived at the X factory and went immediately to the infirmary; a guard showed me the way. I was met by another guard and ushered into a waiting room with an enormous window with the windowpane painted white. How often I've gone into that waiting room since then! How often I've smelled the smell of medicine and trickery during these three years of suffering! That day I waited unsuspecting, and the others who were there waiting with me, either because they were ignorant or already under the thumb of that clique of doctors, didn't warn me. That morning a nurse with watery eyes called me and led me to a little table. Her torrent of questions terrified me, and the smell of medicine made my throat ache and my shoulders tremble.

There was a smaller waiting room in the back where you had to stand. That's where the real agony began. Whenever I've come into this waiting room I've always lost control, and I've hardly had the strength to rebel. All the other times I have always tried to get directly to the doctor and to enter the consulting room directly from the hall without having to go through that tomb. Sometimes I have succeeded but sometimes the nurses have pushed me out screaming as if I had dared profane some mysterious and sacred place. The doctors, on the other hand, hardly took any notice. Neither Dr. Tortora, nor Dr. Steffino, the specialist in nothing special, nor Dr. Bompiero, the number-one cheat, cared one way or the other about which door I used unless they were working on another unfortunate victim.

"Come in, come in," they'd say. "Let's see. Let's see how we're doing, Albino Saluggia."

The name Saluggia was their signal—their signal to wound me deeply with a smile.

"Saluggia, the silent one," or, "Ah, Saluggia, our colleague."

That morning, June 28th, 1946, there were two young men in the little room with the nurse, waiting to be examined by Dr. Tortora. One of them already worked in the factory; the other, like myself, was waiting for his pre-admission checkup, his bare chest covered by a blanket of black hair that spread over his back and shoulders as far down as his elbows. He had hair inside and outside his nose and in his ears. He had shaved but the black stubble of his beard was already showing. His hair was thick and shiny and he was a little fat with thick red lips. He laughed, full of self-confidence, and when he spoke his upper and lower lips never seemed to touch. He was a friend of mine, Francesco Pinna, a Sardinian sailor who had disappeared in Genoa in 1943. He had been a partisan in Liguria and in Cuneo. When the Germans captured him in Turin he managed to escape. I don't remember what he said to me that morning. He went in first, and he must have left shortly afterward by the other door because the factory worker was called in just a few minutes after he had left us. I stood for a moment with my eyes closed.

I heard someone come in behind me and I guessed that he, too, must be stripped to the waist. Maybe I thought so because as he came in he hesitated as if he were ill at ease. I heard the door open a little later, and then Dr. Tortora addressed me in his beautiful voice. "This way please. Here, in front of me, in the light, please; here, near the window. You are—yes, Saluggia, Albino." And he began the examination. He moved me back and forth between the light near the window and the examination table. I was shaking so much that I could hear my bones rattle. Dr. Tortora was serious and very kind. He prodded me all over with his clean, thick fingers. He paid special attention to my chest. He asked me to undress a little further.

"Why are you so worried?" he asked me. "Don't you feel well?"

"I didn't sleep last night," I answered.

"Prison was hard on you," continued the doctor. "Very hard. Your condition is not altogether perfect. Do you cough very often? Do you run a slight temperature? How is your appetite?"

This is the way Dr. Tortora's kind interrogation began. He who seemed the most solicitous of men would very shortly become one of my tormentors. Then he told me that he would approve my employment in the factory mainly because of the grave wrongs I had endured and because he wanted to give me a fresh start. He seemed to be sent by Providence to make up for all the injustices I had borne, he with his long white robe that covered everything except the collar and cuffs of his light-blue shirt and the knot of his flowered tie. He kept a rubber glove in the pocket of his robe. Great big handsome Dr. Tortora, beloved of all the nurses and the female patients.

"You'll probably be hired . . . I'm nearly certain; but . . . hemm . . ." And he moved solicitously between the bed and the window, convinced of the great work that he was doing. With his chest swelled up under his robe and his head bent slightly forward he reminded me of the pigeons that walk back and forth on the ledges of the Town Hall in Candia.

"Not that there is anything seriously wrong . . . anything specific that would stop you from working; but . . . but . . . you're a little run down. I mean your organism is weak. But you're still young and you'll get back in shape again. If they hire you . . . yes, yes I know, ex-prisoner, veteran, they'll hire you, they'll hire you. . . . If they hire you, maybe a well-regulated life would help you, and work . . . Who lives at home with you? Your mother? Oh well, your mother will know how to get you strong again. Eat a lot and sleep your full eight hours."

In the meantime he wrote out the first of his decrees against me. The first of those innumerable pieces of paper that have invaded my life and the entire Piedmont region for so many years, denying me peace and justice. I was far too trusting then to recognize the first warning signals, to realize that the pen the doctor held in his hand and pressed against that paper was the instrument of my misfortunes. Dr. Tortora reread what he had written and then called Nurse Ravetta. Nurse Ravetta is the kindest of all the nurses, and she has proved it from the start.

"Make out a file for Mr. Saluggia, Albino." He pronounced my last name without hesitation, without uncertainty, casually, as if it were already well fixed in his mind, as if I had already been chosen as the victim of his diabolical plot. "We'll take his picture later." He turned to me, holding out his hand, and he added cordially, "Till we meet again, Saluggia; till we meet again, because we'll certainly meet again. We'll work together till we get you completely well again."

I was deeply moved and thanked him. Instead I should have pulled my hand away and fled in horror because those kind words marked the beginning of my downfall. Today I say to you, till we meet again, Dr. Tortora; till we meet again on the day each of us has to account for his life. That day there won't be doctors and patients, executives and factory workers: everyone will be there with his chest bared so that all the others will be able to recognize and count the wounds. Then, Tortora, no longer doctor, you'll see that the holes in my lungs are your doing. The left lung belongs to you and the right one to Dr. Bompiero.

Nurse Ravetta came in as I was putting on my shirt in the dressing room. She said, "Your file is ready," and she showed it to me. It was yellow and new. They have added another two files since then in order to accommodate all the data, comments, descriptions, and observations they have reaped from my troubles. The first file is so worn that it is difficult to recognize: filthy, grimy, torn. My photograph becomes more faded each day, as if it too shared my bad luck.

"This means that you'll be hired. Don't worry," and she added that I had to go to the Skilled Labor Department right away. I found Francesco Pinna, the hairy Sardinian from the waiting room, standing outside the infirmary. I hardly recognized him. Dressed and without all that hair showing, he seemed much younger. He was also going to the Skilled Labor Department, and I followed him. I went down the same hallway I had used the day before; I went up the steps and sat down to wait. Pinna remained standing, leaning against the wall. I had to wait a long time before I was asked to go into Mr. Ducati's office. (Today, he is head of the Personnel Department and one of the ones helping to destroy me.) When I went in, Pinna was already talking in his round voice, round as his mouth. He was saying that he was an expert mechanic, electrician, and telegraph operator. Perhaps it was the Navy but I think it more likely it was his southerner's imagination which made him an expert in so many fields. As I stood before Ducati I saw that he already had all my papers in a neatly lettered portfolio in front of him. He even had my work permit that the company had gotten from the Placement Bureau. I was sure that the report from the old major with the huge head was there and the one from the doctor, and I thought that there probably were other reports from the police, the mayor, and the Bishop. I wondered if they had asked the Military Police for a report. All this was fair enough because my new life was really a matter of great importance.

After some routine preliminaries, Ducati asked me personally if I had done well in grammar school and training school and whether I remembered my mathematics and geometry. He also asked me very respectfully, without commenting on my answers, whether I had ever worked before and did I have a specific job in mind. Finally he asked me if I had ever seen a power saw. I answered all the questions truthfully and thanked him when he gave me a work card with the number 3743. It was Francesco Pinna who pointed out that the sum of the numbers on my card was 17, an unlucky number. He laughed and a thread of saliva shone between the lips that never touched. I was so optimistic that I didn't pay any attention to him and I told him that 3743 was a lucky number because it began and ended with a three and that by subtracting the four from the seven I also got three and that made me lucky all the way around. This made him laugh all the more, and as he laughed his left knee jerked in time to the laughter. His hands were small in proportion to his body: he rubbed them together and then rubbed his face.

We followed a guard who took us to the central offices. There was the same rancid smell everywhere, the smell of the machine oil, and from all around us came a clear, sharp noise different from the noise one heard when standing outside the factory. It was the noise of compressed air being forced through a hundred air hoses. From the other end of the room came the answering sound of the leveling steam presses. After a while you became aware of the continuous rattle of the clamps and drills and from somewhere the scream of metal. You had to wait before you heard the sound of men; they moved and talked to each other, but the movements and voices were noiseless. After a while you heard the footsteps and the voices of men at work.

From experience I can say that contrary to the sanatorium where the noise of a machine or a dripping faucet or a flushing toilet draws everyone's attention and overrides the screaming voices, the factory forces the ear to pick out the sound of men, their murmur, above the roar and clang of the machinery. A burst of laughter is the loudest noise in the room even at ten thirty in the morning when the activity of the factory is at its peak and nothing exists for the men and the women except work, and even if it only lasts a minute, everyone in all the faces in the room—those hundreds of work-drained faces—turns in its direction.

I write about the noise because at first it is the most striking aspect of the factory, and you do more listening than looking. Unwillingly you listen to that great shower of sound.

"What a noise," said Pinna. "It's like being in the engine room of a destroyer."

I looked at the guard walking ahead of us, fearing that he might be offended, but he hadn't paid any attention to Pinna. The noise was deafening, and the work rooms were awesome. They were large rooms, even then when the factory was only a third as big as it is today. Big, clean and orderly, filled with light. Each person in his assigned place, each person working separately with great self-assurance. They all looked very able and important. I was surprised that no one worked in groups, in groups where everyone works together, helping each other to pull or push something or hammering or lifting a heavy piece of machinery together. All the machines were made for one man working independently, and one man was enough to handle the machines easily.

It was nearly noon, but lights were on in most of the factory. Each man had his own lamp. There was no disorder; no tools piled in corners or broken-down machines. The ceiling was nearly covered with iron pipes of different sizes that extended from one department to the next. Each pipe was painted a different color so that you could trace its course across the ceiling till it was out of sight without feeling that you had a tangled and threatening mass of iron above your head. There was a photograph of Fausto Coppi, the champion cyclist, propped up on one of the machines. The men, for in the section we were just crossing there were only men, moved freely, but they didn't stray too far from their machines. One of the men had stopped working; he was cleaning his machine to get it ready for the noon break. Another man left his machine and walked toward a glass door at the back of the room. It was like a signal, and soon many of the others began to saunter away.

Our newly-hired group, four of us and a guard, was the only

group that moved as a unit in that part of the factory. The guard told us to stop; then he walked over to a man that was bending over the motor of one of the machines. He was peering down at the motor, one hand raised while the other gently turned a handle on the left side of the machine. The machine squeaked and oil, or some kind of milk, leaked into a pan on the floor. It seemed as if it were really suffering, like a wounded animal. The man was the foreman, Michele Grosset. The guard said: "Mr. Grosset, these are the new men. They can begin today if you like." And he left.

Grosset cleaned his hands. He looked steadily at all of us, then looked up at the clock. "Not now, certainly," he said; "and for today, the only ones who can begin to work are the ones who know how to run a power saw. This is Department A, the first department in the factory. Here we operate power saws. I am the foreman and my name is Michele Grosset. The man who works with power saws is a qualified worker who must work well. Today at two o'clock we'll see if you know how to work a saw. I'll have to teach the others. Now it's twelve o'clock and it's time to quit. Be back here at two, five minutes before. You can eat in the cafeteria if you want, or you can go home for lunch. You," he told one of the workers, "take them to the exit."

I followed Grosset who had stopped speaking. He took off his black smock and I noticed that in spite of all that heat and all that oil, he still wore a shirt and tie and gold cuff links. He put on his jacket which he kept hanging in a small metal locker and took out two newspapers from a drawer of a square gray desk. The papers were *La Stampa* and *Avanti*. He folded the second newspaper inside the first and put them both under his arm; then he walked off toward the cafeteria, winding his watch. I have watched Grosset go through the same motions on every working day for nearly a year, always the same. He had the same look on his face every time he ate in the cafeteria. This usually happened after a fight with his wife. He ate there often. His wife never cooked for him; she would stay in bed till late, then spend hours making herself beautiful, drinking milk, and eating fruit. It wasn't Grosset who fought with his wife; it was his wife who insulted him and threw him out of the house every time she had a new lover, or after a trip to Lake Viverone or St. Vincent or a week end in Turin.

Some of the lovers were men working in our section at the factory, but none of them lasted very long. Grosset was forced to arrive home late, after all the movie theaters had closed, sometimes even later. His wife would fix up a bed for him downstairs and take someone else to bed with her in their bedroom. Someone who is no friend of Grosset, someone who has probably slept in that bedroom, says that on these occasions Grosset doesn't even set foot on the second floor and is forced to wash himself at the water spout in the garden. He cannot even shave or change his shirt. The same man says that on one occasion Grosset didn't change his shirt for a whole week and that after a few days he would take off his shirt before he began to work and put on his smock over his undershirt.

Still following Grosset I arrived at the cafeteria. I began to eat surrounded by all my plates, sitting two tables behind my foreman. Looking at my food I suddenly felt a great sense of peace; but at the same time I felt hostile and envious of the seven or eight hundred others who were already a part of the factory and knew what to do. At the end of the meal Pinna came over to my table and happily accepted a glass of my wine. We followed Grosset out of the cafeteria and walked together toward the bowling fields at the back of the factory under the shade of many trees. There we waited for the first blast of the siren.

At ten minutes to two we were standing at Grosset's machine. I feared those first moments, and most of all I feared that the factory might resemble the army. The difference that existed between Grosset and Sergeant Vattino did little to calm me and I was overcome by the thought of the job I had to learn. Now that I was about to begin, I didn't stop to think about my new life. While I was waiting for Grosset I looked at the machine that he had been repairing. Perhaps that would be my machine: I hoped so, happy in the thought that it would also be a new beginning for the machine after its recent damage. A part of the machine that looked like its head was uncovered. Its air of surrender increased my confidence. Grosset arrived punctually; he replaced his newspapers, put on his smock, and looked at our little band of new men. In the meantime, the other workers were arriving in small groups, wandering in with an indolent and almost rebellious attitude, acting as if they were returning to their different sections to look

[37

for something they had forgotten. My attitude was very different from theirs as I faced Grosset and prepared myself to begin my work.

"This is an automatic planer-power saw," he said pointing to the broken machine. "It is built by our mechanics and it is called FP-3. Think of an ordinary plane that carpenters use on a table and then think of the chisel the same carpenter uses to cut and shape that table. This planer-power saw works the same way on metal and iron. It is run by industrial power instead of the carpenter's hand."

Grosset slowly and clearly explained every part of the FP-3, starting her up every once in a while, asking us to observe the others in his section in order to clear up any doubtful points, and to pay close attention to any explanations he might give any of the workers regarding the power saw or the particular piece they were working on. Every worker had to turn out thirty finished pieces an hour, that is, one finished piece every two minutes. He took the crude iron from the box of unfinished pieces that arrived once a day from the foundry. He worked it and then put it in the box with the finished pieces; all this in two minutes. It was a lot of work and the finished pieces looked like silver.

All the workers were serious men who worked quietly and well. Even when they stopped for a minute to regulate the auger or the compressed air hoses they were quiet and didn't waste time. They were all more or less my age, perhaps a few years older, with the exception of a very young man and two others who were about fifty years old. There were twenty-three men in Grosset's department; our group would make it twenty-seven. We were perhaps the largest of all the departments. All the men were dressed alike, and I thought that the sameness of the place, the machines, and the work would succeed in voiding any small differences.

By five o'clock Grosset had given us our first lecture, and we were ready to put theory into practice. First of all we learned how to stand in front of a power saw and we learned all the positions necessary to handle the work, regulate the motor, and follow the piece through to its completion. Grosset started the machine, stopped it, and then asked each of us to repeat what he had done. Everything went well. I felt fine even though my best suit was very heavy and it made me very hot; but Grosset never told me to take my jacket off. When the time came to try the power saw Francesco Pinna asked for first turn because he and the machine had the same initials: FP. I did well in the first exercise, even better than the other three. Grosset told us that after one week we could begin to work with the trainer and after the second week we could start in the production department.

A quarter of an hour before closing time the foreman sent us back to the Personnel Department. There they gave us our time-clock card and showed us where to keep it and how to use it. They showed us where to go for our working uniforms. I bought a two-piece uniform, very much like a regular suit.

I was very tired when I left the factory with the package under my arm. Once outside, I was struck by a different kind of heat, and many problems came rushing back into my head. I was afraid; I was terribly afraid that I had made a mistake and plunged back into the misery of army life. It seemed as if I were very far away from Candia and from my house, and I felt that I wouldn't be able to find my way back home. I was alone in the midst of all those people leaving the factory, shouting good-by in loud and confident voices, voices that were not meant for me and made me feel even more isolated from all the rest. I didn't take the factory bus because I was so uncertain about asking anyone where I could find the bus for Candia and Caluso. I decided to take the train again, the one that left at seven twelve and wasn't so crowded with factory workers.

When I arrived home it was already dark. I found my mother sitting in the kitchen; as soon as she saw me she began to cry. I comforted her and I told her I had a job, a good job with a salary of fifty-six dollars a month, free lunch, transportation, and all the rest.

She cooked me some vegetables from our garden, and even though it was late July we still had tomatoes, peas, and beans. Vegetables from our garden, that patch of ground at the back of the house, facing north, protected by two oak trees. I showed her the uniform I had bought, and while I ate she reinforced all the buttons with a stronger thread.

*

The night passed very quickly even though I awoke once or twice feeling frightened. I must not have been consciously afraid because as soon as I awoke the hand of fear would loosen its grip and I immediately managed to control myself. Fear was replaced by an icy sensation of waiting that gave me a clear vision of the things that were about to happen to me; my first day at the factory, working with so many other men, traveling, earning and spending my money. These things seemed certain and inevitable, as if they were predestined or as if I had to relive events that had already taken place. I felt the icy cold of these waking moments in my entire body, and it made me draw the bedclothes tighter and enjoy the warmth of the bed and fall asleep. And I fell asleep feeling secure about the events of the following day, events that would unfold upon awakening without further delay or confusion.

Everything happened as I had imagined it would, and I began work at the factory feeling as clear as a piece of crystal. I changed clothes in a second and, dressed in my uniform, I headed toward my department. In the presence of Grosset I felt as gentle and as willing as a child. The power saw he assigned to me was not the one he had been repairing when I met him. For the first fifteen days I didn't have a machine to myself, and I worked in shifts on different machines like the other new men. This fact kept me in a state of suspense because I felt something was missing from my new life. I felt as if I couldn't channel my energy, as if I didn't have a firm footing anywhere. I was nervous working under these conditions, but this only drove me to greater exertions. I was only tired at night when I got on the bus to go home. Then my weariness would wrap itself around me like the noise made by the other workers traveling with me. They all came from villages around Candia, from villages in the interior away from the main road and the train. It seemed as if being together on the trip home gave them new energy, gave them eyes and tongues. I had never seen such outbursts in the factory as the ones that took place the minute the workers set foot on the bus. Here, if they spoke about the factory, they did so in terms of people who had finally escaped it, never to return again. Even those who had worked in the factory for more than twenty years spoke of it that way. They spoke with animation, nearly violence, and they settled down to the trip charged with the excitement that precedes a drunken outing. Some evenings during that first month of July, if the weather showed signs of changing, they would speak about the farm, the wheat, and the vineyards. During these discussions they grew calm and profoundly serious. They would look out the windows toward the Alps and the valley of the Dora, commenting on the light and the air, and often they would finish their trip in silence. Later I learned that conversation was much more difficult in the factory. It always ended in a burst of laughter, or gossip, or resentful and disdainful words.

Even though I was still waiting, I felt the need of finding a sincere person in the factory. I felt the need of finding someone who could help me, but so far I hadn't been able to find anyone like that in my section. I didn't have any real friends, and conversation was always about unimportant things, ending always in jokes or curses. Pinna was the kindest, but he often didn't understand me. He hadn't even understood Grosset and he had laughed with all the others when Manlio, the oldest in our section, would go over to Grosset seated at his desk and make the sign of horns behind his back.

This business began the third day after we four new men started working in the department, and it made me distrustful of all my companions. Even the youngest laughed. He was only seventeen and the one nearest Grosset's desk. When he laughed he got all red and hid his face behind the machine table and the clamp. I felt the goodness and kindness in Grosset, and it hurt me to see him ridiculed that way. I felt the same way about the vulgarity and double meanings in the conversation with the girls in the cafeteria or in the halls. Pinna was a master at this sort of talk, and he was very popular.

But no one ever spoke about work. You spoke to the foreman about work or to someone who asked advice over some difficulty with his machine. For that same reason illnesses and cures are not often discussed in sanatoriums: except in those moments when the death or the arrival or departure of someone makes the air burst with talk about the common sickness. They speak together and separately, passionately as if a new fever had invaded the place. This is what made work harder for everybody. It wasn't fair to think of work as a sentence passed on all those who worked in the factory, as so many would have you think with all their complaining. In any case, the men who worked in the factory would have had to work somewhere, either inside or outside. When I questioned them, nearly all of them would answer, "We work for the boss." This phrase put an end to any discussion but I didn't agree with them and I noticed that this justification didn't even satisfy its most ardent supporters.

The day I started to work at my own power saw I hated my companions more than I hated the boss. I wished that their machines would stall and cut the metal badly. This hatred helped my work by inciting me to do better than the others. I removed the pig iron from the box as if it were an enemy I had to destroy, but by the time I had finished working the metal I had become as attached to it as if it were a part of myself. The noise of the power saw goaded me on, and the more I listened to its biting sound the more passionately I threw myself into my work. Its noise and its bite were the harsh proof of my ability to work; they gave my hands a strength they had never had even though I realized that it was the machine that guided my hands and not my hands the machine. Grosset would often come around to my post. One day he stopped and looked at me thoughtfully. Then he put his arm on my shoulder and said, "Take it easy, Saluggia." He understood my state of mind. "Don't think of work as your enemy, or you won't last long." And he added, "Don't make it your entire life, either."

Since his kindness was greater than our intimacy, and because I didn't want to feel too indebted to him, I answered like the others, "One works for the boss." "For more than one boss," Grosset answered. "But since work is part of your life, try not to ruin it." And he left me without even looking into the box to see how many finished pieces I had turned out.

I still didn't work on a fixed salary basis but I'm sure that in those days I more than filled the established quota. Once I noticed that the color of the metal I was working on, ever changing under the biting saw, turned cloudy a second before it was finished. It turned the color of the lake in Candia. This was a great revelation —so much so that for a long time afterward, though not always all day long, I looked forward to the moment when I saw the color of the lake. The split second I needed to finish the piece was like the last stretch of the road, between the lake and my house but different from the real one. A different and easier road where I would find a symbol or a sign of my new life, a revelation of my new destiny. In the meantime my machine worked well, except that the motor was a little noisier than usual. As the motors whirred on, I used to imagine that I was at the auto races. I imagined that I was in the lead with car number 17, the number that Pinna had given me, and I had kept on because my race was truly a challenge against an opposing destiny and the plotting of all the other contestants. At the height of the race my car would stall and only my ability would keep it moving. I would continue the race, holding my breath during the last laps and looking around at the other workers as if they were really going to surpass me with their power saws but then, with one last effort of will, I always managed to win. One more lap and my car would have gone up in flames. These thoughts didn't interfere with my work, and they saved me from the boredom of having to number the finished pieces one by one.

The hours passed by the thousands on the faces of the clocks in the different departments. I measured those hours by the time it took to complete each piece. The first day I started to work in the factory the clock in my department said 1227. Time is different in the factory, just like the men; it loses its own rhythm in order to follow the life cycle of the pieces we manufacture. The hours would pass, I would smoke a couple of cigarettes, Grosset would stop by once in a while and every so often Pinna and I would talk a little. Pinna always talked, even when he was alone.

The noise fascinated me. All parts of the factory throbbed in unison and, driven by this beat, I was compelled to adapt the rhythm of my work to that gigantic pulse. I couldn't stop myself; I was like a leaf of a great tree whose every branch shook in the wind. People ceased to exist, and I thought that even though we worked together, squeezed into the different departments, with the power saws and the vises and steam presses lined up three rows deep, even though we worked in long assembly lines, ate together in the cafeteria, traveled together on the buses, even though we did all these things—it was difficult to find a friend or someone who would help you. Unlike Pinna, I didn't mix with the others, nor could I join the men who at that time were demanding a wage increase of twenty lire an hour. If I had spoken to them about the poor farmers or the unemployed, they would have turned their backs on me. Pinna got along well with these men, I don't really know why; he hardly ever spoke and if he did, it was only to repeat what someone else had said. Pinna wormed his way into everything and I can't understand why they accepted him as a friend, with his great black head and that trickle of saliva always on his lips. They continued to admire him because he had been a courageous partisan and because he had escaped from the third floor of a hotel in Turin where the Germans were holding him prisoner until they could execute him. Pinna had actually suggested I join the Socialist party and the Federal Trade Unions, and laughingly he would add, "You'll see; you'll see . . ."

"I see very well now, dear Pinna," I answered, "and I'm not joining anything. I haven't anything to share with anyone." But Pinna had laughed and his leg had twitched a little more than usual. "You'll see how much the priest will help you . . ."

On the whole, in spite of my loneliness and the difference between me and the others, my first days at work weren't bad; as a matter of fact many things gave me pleasure and comforted me: the cafeteria, the locker rooms, the showers, the long halls and the neon lights inside and outside the factory. The tall silent engineers and the other top men who passed by in the corridors made me feel safe and at home in a well-run place. I thought with pleasure, but with a certain feeling of unworthiness, that I was part of a strong and beautiful industry and that part of that strength and beauty belonged to me and was there, ready to help me, the same way that the factory kept me warm and gave me light.

Little by little I began to love the factory more and more, in direct proportion to the decreasing interest I felt for the men who worked there. It seemed as if the workers hadn't anything to do with the factory, that they were its detractors or its enemies, that they were not aware of its unearthly beauty and therefore they made all sorts of unnecessary noise when they were working, talking and laughing, deliberately offending the factory. It seemed as if it amused them to abuse and dirty the factory and turn their backs on it every moment. The factory, on the other hand, seemed to become more beautiful, and I felt as if it spoke to me directly, as if I were the only one or one of the few who could or wanted to understand it.

Work was coming along very well. I mean my work and the others' work, even though they didn't seem to care. In certain moments of great vigor I felt the work bite into the iron foundation of the factory the same way a tractor plows into a field or an automobile bites the road. And it seemed as if I was the one who was plowing or driving, that the noise and the output of the factory depended on an accelerator linked to my work: when I increased my speed so did the factory, and when I slowed down I felt something slacken in the general tension and became aware of a door opening, or of a voice, or of an open window. This work, this child of the factory pleased me, so much so that on my way to the cafeteria at noon I would make a detour that took me past the Crating Department where the new machines, completed and miraculously shiny after so much handling in so many different assembly lines, waited in a row, with their faces full of teeth, to be packed in crates and shipped out to all the world.

Why didn't everyone love this work? Why did so many work and live in the factory without caring about this fruit of their work, ignoring the existence of this last door? Had I known the answer to this question, I would have known why some have always been against me. These breakers of every moral law hurt me in order to strike at the methodical law of the factory that gave them life, the same way that diseases turn on the body that feeds them.

After two months in the factory I realized that I had neither lost nor gained anything. I mean to say that I realized I was the same person I had been fifty days before, the same person I had been for so long, and that nothing inside or outside of me had changed. My life had remained the same, without showing any signs of approaching changes. I left my house every day, took the bus, worked, went to the cafeteria where I sat with thousands of other people, learned to do my job, and returned home; but in two months nothing had changed inside of me. I had to force myself to believe "I am a factory worker, I am part of a great industry and I belong in the factory." But even these thoughts didn't stir anything inside of me. I kept thinking about my locker in the dressing room, with its number written in my mind and its lock which had a different feel from any of the other metals I touched during the day. Its nickel plating gave a sense of relief to my hands and told me that work was over. I kept my work clothes and shoes in the locker together with some books that the Personnel Department had given me on the first day.

The locker room was full of the dampness of the showers, the smell of the toilets and the store rooms, the heat of the furnaces on one side, and the cold wind that came directly from the great piles of green and white steel. But in the locker room I recaptured the secret of human contact, that exciting and moving sensation I had experienced in the dormitory at school and in the barracks. It was a contact that happened in silence and never developed into lasting friendship. This is because I have always looked behind the mask of truth. How beautiful and innocent is a dormitory, with the beds made up all in order and the white pillows puffed up with love and kind feelings, and all the lockers neatly sitting at the foot of each bed! And how beautiful are the soldiers' bunks, those cots with iron bedsteads, and the knapsacks and bayonets propped up next to the foot lockers! The factory is beautiful in the same way, filled with glass and metal and great blue arches and all the machines in a row. The factory is beautiful when it is empty and you have the feeling that all the men who work in those clean spaces near the benches and the levers are sincere and courageous.

But the factory is filled with all kinds of people. A sense of confusion burdened by a smoky sadness, by a pale light in the corners where the oil shines on the water, made me feel as if all these men were repeating the same things. They all spoke the same way about their approaching vacations. Even the new men were given a two-week vacation, but we didn't get paid. If we wanted the money we could come to work. We could go to the Personnel Department, and they would assign us to the jobs that had to get done. Pinna arranged everything for us. He chose the night shift guarding the electrical control panel. I must confess that it was beautiful and fascinating to work at night, to walk into the shining and mysterious factory without disturbing the darkness, like a fragment of a falling star, to go from one empty department to another feeling as if I were walking in the sleep of all the men who had worked there that day, to touch their tools and move their chairs, always feeling as if I were walking in their dreams, in their houses, and in their minds, like a magician, living in silence, in an absurd silence within that noisy womb, to see the machines and conveyor belts silent and still. When I was in school I would go into church at night with the same sense of wonder, bringing bunches of flowers and leaves to prepare the tomb for Holy Thursday.

We walked into the room and closed the heavy door tightly behind us. We went over to the transformers, hung our jackets on chairs and ate the ice cream we brought with us. We spent many beautiful nights this way. The air came through the windows, stirred the curtains, and took us by the hand. Our friendship expanded in that atmosphere and so did our fancies. "We're in the electric chair," Pinna would say; I would stretch out my legs and lean my head against the back of my chair. That way I could see the moon shining low over the hills and pretend that it was the cause of the noise made by the high-voltage electricity.

"It's better than the power saws," Pinna would say.

"Only at night," I'd answer. "I wouldn't be stuck here during the day. I wouldn't do this sort of work, the same way that I would never work the power saws at night."

The two weeks flashed by and once more we returned to our department and the regular shift. I didn't mind going back to work in the morning surrounded by all the other men and the bustle of the factory. As a matter of fact, for a few days I felt as if I had again found a good friend.

In September we heard a rumor that there were going to be some changes made in our department. All the machines used for cutting or shaping or polishing the crude metal were to be combined in one department: power saws, multiple and high-power drills, the vise and metal polishers.

Toward the end of the month Grosset officially confirmed the news and told us that they were only planning to use sixteen power saws instead of the twenty-seven now in operation. The grumbles and suspicions began soon after his announcement. No one knew whether it was better to remain in the department or wait to be transferred. They were uneasy especially since no one knew where he would be sent. Opinions differed, but eventually several different groups emerged: the older men, the most able, the ones who lived in the city. Pinna and I didn't know what to think, although that didn't stop him from talking and flitting from group to group.

Grosset settled the matter on the morning of September thirtieth by choosing the men who were to remain with him. Pinna and I were in that group, together with the younger men and the ones who had just been hired. For this reason everyone thought that to remain in the department was some sort of sacrifice if not downright punishment. As a matter of fact, the older men were completely convinced that the best jobs had been reserved for them. In two or three days they had all left our section quite happily, taking their machines with them into one of the three departments to which they had been assigned. The skilled workers were also satisfied because they in turn believed that it was some sort of distinction to remain with Grosset, considering the challenge of the varied jobs we would be performing in the future and the responsibility of organizing a new department exclusively devoted to the complete processing of the crude metal.

The next day they sent us a new power saw. Grosset showed it to us and told us not to worry. "It's just like the old one, but it's easier to handle," and he explained the reasons why. He explained the improvements of the new aspirator. "You won't ruin your lungs any longer." I tasted the metal filing in my saliva. It was a taste I had grown to like the way a boy likes the taste of the bark on a stick or a blade of grass or a piece of iron or leather. That taste of metal had become a part of my life in the factory.

After a week all the departments had been reorganized, and by then our section extended to the stairs leading to the Assembling Department. The power saws, the drills, the vise and the polishers were at the back of the room, and they were run by both men and women. Women were even working the multiple drills, and as they worked their heads moved back and forth, back and forth. The machines had been arranged in a logical sequence in order to insure maximum efficiency. The crude metal arrived from the foundry and went directly to the drills, then on to the power saws and the polishers till it eventually reached the Assembling Department.

A question arose about wages. Would we still be paid by piecework and if so, how much? The wage scale of the other departments differed from ours, either higher or lower. Nothing happened for two weeks and even the bosses didn't know how to evaluate our work. Then the news came: there would be a common wage scale; no more piecework wages, the same salary for all. This way the average wages in all the departments increased whereas some of the individual salaries decreased. This was not acceptable. The different departments eyed each other suspiciously, and although we hadn't begun to work we were already plagued by dissensions. How could we let the women at the drills and the older men at the polishers determine our total output and in turn our wages? The same feelings ran through every department and since everyone was afraid to produce more than the required minimum everyone worked less. You had to work less even though you didn't want to because you knew that your diminished quota would be filled by someone else. The foremen tried to justify the bosses' decision, but even they were not entirely convinced.

"This way," they said, "there will be a fairer distribution of profits and less pressure on the individual worker."

"But this way," the workers answered, "the men who work more will earn less and every man will be keeping an eye on his companions to see that they work as much as he does without making any mistakes which would have to be paid by everyone in the department. We don't want to lose out because of the mistakes made by the women."

The women either kept quiet or spoke all at once, attacking the men. "This is exactly what the Directors want," one of our workers said. "They want to divide us and set us against each other."

In the meantime the four different factions reduced their output and appealed each on their own behalf to the Internal Commission. They all asked for piecework wages, which were to be based on the avarage wage in the department prior to the recent change. The administration refused. Then the departments asked for different wages for different groups.

I watched Grosset closely during these negotiations, and I noticed that even though he didn't speak very much he suffered a great deal. He didn't try to convince us one way or another and only held us responsible for our work. I would often catch him looking at me, and although he often came over to my work station we never spoke.

All this talk confused me, and I was almost happy when the administration put a stop to the negotiations. I looked at the women and saw that they worked as hard as the men and that their eyes looked even more tired. One day someone proposed a strike and the Internal Commission accepted. Since it was a Saturday morning, the strike was delayed till Monday. Pinna and two other workers asked me if I would join the strikers, and I said no. I really wasn't speaking to Pinna when I answered but to the other two who had been among the most violent agitators. One of them was from the Vise Department, and I had been struck by his arrogance on the very first day.

I spent my Sunday trying to justify in several ways my decision not to strike and fortunately the church, the boot, the Indian, and even the lake answered all my questions favorably. The lake obeyed my request and kept its blue streak of light till sunset, a streak that was clearer than a spoken yes stretched across the center from shore to shore. The lake wasn't marred by those patches of lighter water that the wind or some subterranean current spreads near the shores in the evening.

The strike was canceled on Monday. It rained that day, and many things calmed down, even in the different departments. It rained for many days and the weather affected the mood of the workers. The factory was as unalterable as the sky, all gray, without contrasts. The women were peaceful. They seemed refreshed like a grove of acacias, and they smiled as if stirred by a light October wind.

Pinna was worried because he had only one suit. He needed a new one for that dark autumn that was engulfing us so quickly.

It was no longer possible to establish any special contacts or friendships in our department with its hard businesslike atmosphere lit by a green light. Words were answered in one's thoughts, and they vanished from the mind like a puff of smoke. My work was going fairly well, and I managed to fill my quota.

II

THEY FIRED TWO FOREMEN, the one in charge of the vise and the one in charge of the drills. Grosset took over the drills, and the remaining foreman the vise. The women were pleased with the arrangement, and they seemed to like us better now that we shared the same boss. Pinna told me that he was dating one of the women. She was the darkest one he could find, and she had so many moles on her eyebrows and on her upper lip that she always looked as if she were scowling. Nothing new had happened to me. But I was looking forward to Christmas.

It was snowing when we left the factory Christmas Eve. It had begun to snow an hour before while we were getting ready to close up shop. The women had looked out the great plate-glass windows and breathed a prolonged oh, just like a bunch of schoolgirls.

Outside the factory the snow had already covered the street, and it fell in large flakes in the glow of the headlights and the open doors of the factory. Even I stamped my feet like a schoolboy. All of us, all of us were going home: everyone stopped at the café on the corner or one of the other bars near the station to drink a liqueur or a hot punch. And from every bar and café there streamed a blue haze, a ray of light that smelled of oranges and tangerines. The snow trapped in that ray of light whirled in every direction and flapped like a shawl in the wind.

I, too, went into a café for a drink and in the light of the doorway, a second before stepping inside, I noticed that my shoulders were covered with snow. I saw my dark overcoat, and I recognized myself in the midst of that festive atmosphere. I was aware of my body and my youth under the overcoat. I drank the tangerine punch in small sips staring at the glass beaded with tiny drops of moisture that reflected all the noise and all the fun. The alcohol burned my tongue and my throat, and I drank all the more eagerly; that burning sensation was yet another way to take part in the celebration. Everyone around me was drinking and warming himself with alcohol, and they breathed tilting their heads backwards.

We were all jammed together inside the café, and the smell of the drinks filled the stifling air. Even so, I enjoyed burning my tongue and my throat with the yellow liquor. The others were doing the same thing, earnestly, with all their hearts. As I drank my second punch the alcohol made me cough: it was an explosion that shook the entire group. I kept on drinking in longer sips but the cough always found me surrounded by men who seemed to be there for the purpose of thumping my back. The heat and the cough made me perspire, like a drinking glass just removed from a jet of steam.

I was happy, and the sweat poured over me like the confession of my happiness. I was thinking that at home in the darkness of that snowy night, overlooking the lake, in a darkness that was like hiding my face in the folds of one of her dark dresses to lose myself and feel only the beating of my pulse against the hard certainty of her leg, in that darkness, my mother was waiting for me. I took off my overcoat and left the café. I was still coughing but not as much as before, and my cough was swallowed by the falling snow.

The cough continued on the train, and I perspired. I looked out the window to see if it was still snowing. The snow wasn't coming down as hard as before, and it seemed to be falling far away from the train, in that last streak of light before the vast dark intimacy of the countryside. Even my cough was calming down. It shook me internally, but I could almost cough with my mouth closed. I kept on coughing so that it would keep on snowing. I fancied that if I stopped coughing the snow would stop. It was still snowing when I reaching the station in Candia, and I would cough with assurance every forty or fifty steps.

I looked forward to Christmas Eve, to those first minutes when my mother and I would leave the snowy night outside and walk into church to hear midnight mass. I arrived home. I coughed, and my voice re-echoed through the trees as if they, my brothers, had coughed with me; I walked to the door expecting to hear my mother's cheerful words of greeting. Instead my mother was in bed with a twisted ankle. All she did was complain, and she didn't seem to be interested in anything. I took off my shirt and washed;

I put on my undershirt and my pajama top, I opened the window and breathed the cold air. The snow went its own way like my hopes for a celebration. I stopped coughing and went to bed. My mother couldn't go out during the holidays, and I had to be content with going to one or two movies in the afternoon.

After the holidays and my thoughts during those days or, I should say, my attitude during those days, going back to work was neither easy nor difficult. It just seemed like something that didn't make any sense; myself surrounded by so many other men, acting, living, and almost thinking like so many other men.

Pinna would often come around to my work station, and his foolishness distracted me from my thoughts and my loneliness. When I thought about him, I understood the existence of a link between him, the factory, and all the others. As for myself, it was only a matter of going on. I amused myself, got angry, drove myself, and worked unwillingly, even though this unwillingness didn't seem to disturb either the power saw nor the finished pieces, nor Grosset who must have become aware of my attitude during the visits he paid me.

It was an ugly winter, dark and nervous, a winter of ugly watery snow and fog. The factory remained clean, with its shiny heavy doors and corners where neither winter nor night could ever penetrate. I was the only one in the factory aware of that hostile winter but more than hostile, barren and unreal. Perhaps there were others who were also aware. I was nearly convinced of their existence when I caught sight of someone with staring eyes and still hands. Then I would begin my winter song, the wind, the snow, the rain, the creaking cold. I discovered the notes in all the noises and sounds of the factory. This is how I spent my winter and managed to bear the passing days. The women brought me the snow in the small lost silver sounds of their drills. I could even distinguish the sound of the lake as it tumbled noisily about my head and cascaded down from the upper level of the Assembling Department.

In the evening, around quitting time, I often felt very hot. It was an exhausting heat like the heat from an overstoked furnace, like splintering glass and a rapid roaring in my ears. I thought that I could put out this burning stove at home; but I couldn't do it. It was cooler and I breathed better in the locker room. I would leave the door open while I dressed. But the heat wasn't fever and I wasn't sick.

As a matter of fact, I was planning a trip to France during the Easter holidays. I wanted to see the beautiful countryside around Avignon again and the great deserted river where we would picnic every first Monday after Easter. A little boat used to take us across, but on the opposite shore where the water was shallow the boat had to be pulled by a large horse, an enormous horse with a spotted tail. After lunch my father took off his jacket and his shirt and sat around in his thick, heavy underwear the color of the earth. The sleeves barely covered his shoulders and his great white arms hung out covered with shadows from his knotted muscles. The hair on his arms was very black and sparse, the fruit of some forgotten illness. The neck that disappeared inside his undershirt was pale and covered with black hairs, and it had two large furrows on either side. He had a mole with a tuft of hair a little above his collarbone and more hair showing all around the neckline of his undershirt. I knew that my father was sick although he laughed and kept on drinking.

I knew I wasn't sick, in spite of the heat I felt every evening in the factory. My illness was a desire to escape, to escape those interminable evenings of February and March, evenings that covered all the windows in the factory with enormous curtains of damp air. The lights of the factory seemed to bounce off an unseen wall while on the other side of that wall the lights and sounds of the city wandered off in the distance and the birds circled even higher. It was a wall that made me feel like a prisoner with an overwhelming desire to travel. To travel to a country, to a town that would be real, more real than the factory with all its machines, its noises, and its people. A person who wants to travel is not sick. I wasn't looking for adventure, nor was I hoping to return to some place I had visited before. I knew that the blanket of fire and air spread across the bloated windows wasn't real, and I wanted to run away, to escape its dangers and find a real life. Other times I thought that this somber winter that burned before the factory and within me at night, and the dank changeable spring with huge fans of clouds that covered the plain pierced by green, blue, and black gashes in the direction of the Val d'Aosta were merely the setting for my new life that would emerge like a perfect dawn, the backdrop for a sign or a call or a person. And I imagined this person returning from a trip or sometimes leaving, after having looked at my country, a country that even I no longer recognized.

One evening between May and June I looked at the lake and countryside from my garden, and they seemed new. I had finished dinner, and I was smoking a cigarette. A peaceful stream of smoke curled from my lips, circled my shoulders, and disappeared in the direction of another world. I looked at the lake and examined all its facets one by one, the shore, the evening shadows, the trees, and a ribbon of landscape behind it that vanished into the hills. Suddenly I heard my mother's voice, steady and sure, coming from the window above my head. It wound itself around my neck like a scarf, and it seemed as if it held me with one hand. It was as wide and profound as the night.

"What are you doing, Albino? Thinking?"

I was surprised, but the resentment I felt at being surprised was tempered by the tone of her voice. Since I couldn't see my mother's face, her voice sounded young and gentle, the way it had sounded so many years before. She had spoken with strength and clarity, like someone who prepares himself a moment before speaking and studies the attack and tone of voice he wants to use.

"No, I'm not thinking," I answered. And in fact the moment her voice reached me every uncertainty disappeared inside me, and I knew that I hadn't been thinking at all, that I had only been looking, noticing that the night covering the countryside, empty toward the left because of a lighter glow over the town, was just beginning at that moment.

"A beautiful night," my mother said.

"Yes," I answered.

"What are you remembering?"

"Nothing. I was only looking."

"What a wonderful scent those flowers in the garden have."

I became aware of it that instant: I found it immediately among all the sensations that the night moved before me.

"Yes," I answered. I spoke without turning so as not to break the spell but remain free in my expression, with that freedom one feels talking to oneself out loud or the freedom that comes in that instant of communion with oneself in which one feels that one can laugh at the most serious things, or grimace and gesticulate because the moment and the thought are united with other moments and thoughts of one's past life and together they combine to form a perfect whole. During that talk with my mother I was not only the one who answered—I, sitting in my chair. It was as if I were tenderly watching all my different selves. And those tiny fragile waves moved by the lake, even those were part of me, fresh and rippling like so many quiet days and so many things well done. My mother said a few more words and went to bed. I walked to the end of the garden, looked at the flowers, and walked back again.

The heat in the factory was unbearable. Even the noise seemed to expand. It was a great effort to work, but I kept on all afternoon driven by anger. It irritated me that the women at the drills sat with their legs spread apart and the buttons of their uniforms undone. I couldn't bear to look at them with their round bodies. The gestures they made while they adjusted a strap or a button or something more intimate were surprising in their vulgarity. There was one who bothered me more than the others, a middle-aged redhead who wore colored stockings and underwear. Grosset noticed my discomfort, and one day when it was hotter than usual he advised me to go to the infirmary to get a tonic or some pills. He himself took a pill every day dissolved in the glass of water that he kept ready on his desk.

The morning of June seventh I applied for an appointment in the infirmary. I was called at nine o'clock and sent to Dr. Tortora's consulting room. He received me with a charming smile, so charming that for a moment I thought that he remembered me and would treat me with the same solicitude he had shown on the first day. I told him my name, but he turned his head away, indicating that I didn't mean anything to him. He selected my file from the other files on his desk. He opened it with a single motion of his large hands as if he were cutting into an organ in my body. He examined me rapidly, concentrating on my chest and on my back. He barely listened to what I had to say about my fatigue. He didn't ask me anything; he only looked at my body and at my back with the concentration of an animal who is about to dig a hole. He told me to get dressed and called the nurse. He told her that I was to have X rays taken and that my file was to be kept handy. Finally he spoke to me and prescribed some pills and injections. He told me to come back in fifteen days. The following week they took my X rays, and after another week the doctor sent for me to give me the results. The grave must have been ready. He told me that I was seriously ill and in need of treatment and rest. I was silent and he spoke, trying to convince me. He referred to the specialist, Dr. Bompiero, and at one point he showed me the X rays, a piece of skeleton found God knows where. He suggested I stop working and stay home till after the holidays. In the meantime he and Dr. Bompiero would take further X rays and make further tests.

Why was he trying to convince me?

But the factory didn't seem as hot as before, and I was better. I would look at the glass of water that Grosset kept on his desk in the mornings and its presence reassured me, for it was a sign of friendship. The water absorbed the light in the department till it became the color of metal, as much a creature of the factory as the men. Its presence comforted me all morning, the way a rose standing in a glass in the kitchen or the smell of fresh vegetables can be comforting. I would stay in the factory till the holidays; I would go on like the others. I'd have a good rest during my vacation, and perhaps my cousin would arrive from France and we would go on picnics and swim together in the lake. I told the doctor that I wouldn't quit work. He pretended to believe that eventually I would obey him. He began to talk about other X rays and *tomography*, staring at me all the time as if I had undone one of the cords that held everything around him together. I decided that I would not let them take any more X rays and silently I left his office.

What do they silently speak about—those little birds that come in June to perch on the street and meditate, shaking their gray-black heads and tails? Those little birds with the long gray-black tails that I found on the road to my house couldn't live in cages. They couldn't even get X-rayed, but, turning their heads, they would speak to me. At home under the great red wheel of the sun everything was very quiet. The wheel was cut on one side, the side where the main road went steeply downhill in shade. The cars would throw themselves headlong upon that road. My mother was watering the garden, and the gush of water made the same subtle sound as a bicycle going downhill without brakes. It seemed as if the entire village were afloat. From the woods on the Serra to the hills behind Candia everything seemed to be gliding like a boat on the early evening shadows. Every evening till August I would return tired from another day at the factory.

When I arrived at the gate of my house, my mother would turn off the garden hose so that I could have more fresh water to wash myself in the kitchen. Then I would stretch out my hands, and she would hand me a towel.

The holidays arrived but I hadn't made any plans. I realized that it had been difficult to keep on going till the holidays that last night of work when I got on the train. I hadn't spoken to the others, and I barely managed a smile for Grosset. The only desire that remained was to travel, but to travel completely disembodied from any particular thought: to travel in some part of a nearly deserted country or city, a country colored a light shade of green or blue like a piece of metal, in some country or city like the ones I had seen from the prison trains during those moments when I nearly didn't care if they were taking me away.

I spent the first days of my vacation at home. Then because nothing new had turned up I decided to go with Pinna on a four-day trip to Genoa and the other large towns along the Riviera. Friday, Saturday, Sunday and Monday. Pinna had rented a motorcycle, and he came to pick me up early in the morning.

"We're going to the Riviera, too," he said, throwing himself down hard on the motorcycle which made a great deal of noise but didn't go very fast because it was geared low and stalled every now and then. "Even we, the workers of the machine-metal industry are going to the Riviera, even we," he screamed with his big round mouth and the familiar trickle of saliva that the air held glued in a white dot at the corners of his upper and lower lip. He wanted to go by way of Turin so that he could stay on the superhighway a little longer. To be in the midst of all those cars was like a badge of distinction, the exercising of his rights as a factory worker on vacation.

Once we had passed Turin around nine o'clock, he began to stop frequently to stretch his legs or fiddle with the motor or the tires. After a slight kick to the rear tire he would go into a café, one of the many new ones dotting the superhighway. He would alternate between espresso coffee and cappucinos, chocolates, caramels, peanuts and pastries: he spent money frantically and wasted half the things he bought like a child that has stolen too much money from his father's pocket.

Around noon, within sight of the sea, Pinna was perspiring like a fountain, and it filled me with disgust to hold on to his fat wet back. Because of all the things he had eaten and drunk, by the time we arrived in Genoa Pinna had a violent stomach-ache, a cold sweat, hot flashes, and a thick gummy taste in his mouth. His eyes were lowered, and he seemed to be melting away like a very bad dish of ice cream. He blamed the speed, the nervous tension of the long drive, the fumes from the exhaust on the motorcycle, everything but the food. He had an attack of diarrhea, but I managed to drag him just in time into a nearby café. The café was deserted, and it hadn't been cleaned yet. The air was thick with the rank smells of the night before. There, leaning across a bar stool with his shirt unbuttoned, Pinna drank a lemonade.

He eventually began to feel better; at least he controlled his spasms and began to talk, but still in the tone of voice of one who has been cruelly victimized. What a clown he is, I thought, and I was annoyed because I didn't want him near me. At the same time I knew that I couldn't abandon him because he was even weaker than I was. Even lonelier and more confused without any sense of pride and without my constant suspicion of people and the things of the world. After a while Pinna managed to leave the bar, squinting his eyes under the hot afternoon sun. It was two o'clock. We crossed the street where the silence was only disturbed by one or two passersby like us. We walked to the harbor and sat on the sea wall. We watched the ships and the smaller boats, black ones and white ones, lying still on the water. The white ships were deserted, and they looked like a summer painting. With all that heat and that color, with those thick hemp ropes hanging limp at their sides, it seemed as if they should only travel in summer, and then, only to Africa or to the islands near the equator.

[59

Pinna buzzed like a fly. He watched the ships and the sea through half-closed eyes. He raised his head slightly for a moment and said, "Sardinia," and then looking around at the things nearer to us he added, "How many tons, I wonder?"

He spoke very little and in a manner that wasn't natural to him. As long as I'd known him I'd never heard him speak this way, and I didn't understand whether the cause of his strange talk was his indigestion or his fatigue or a befuddlement caused by the sea. He spoke about the sailors, what it was like to be a sailor as he had been, what it meant to be free or mad, with a freedom that led to complete solitude. Then he fell asleep in the sun. I thought that the great Pinna was only a great big baby. When I compared him to myself, with a little malice and bitterness, I always pictured him asleep.

During the remaining three and a half days of our holiday Pinna regained his good humor and his total lack of organization both in thoughts and actions. Nothing ever went smoothly, even his most carefully calculated maneuvers, even when he said, "Would you allow me, Miss?" and tried to walk next to some girl in the midst of the strolling crowds. Only once, and then silently and at a run, did we manage to accompany two girls who were hurrying home after leaving the hotel where they worked.

I felt pretty well during that holiday even though it seemed a waste of time and my days were dedicated to looking after Pinna or at least given over to him and his decisions. During those days that didn't belong to me the sight of so many fragrant and luxurious gardens consoled me, and I enjoyed swimming in the sea, in the shallow water among the rocks where I could sit or lie down once in a while on the salty stones. A sweet lethargy would overpower me and dissipate itself without my having to sleep. I have often had the same sensation after a long intravenous injection in some sanatorium. My body filled with a comforting warmth, the smell of alcohol that makes me wrinkle my nose, a sleep that passes without consuming itself, like a trickle of urine flowing from the bladder during the night. In those moments I always managed to survey myself and my troubles with extreme kindness and compassion. I imagined that my bones were very light bamboo shoots with their roots still in the earth, still touched by the sun, still alive although not for long. I felt the same way about the other parts of my body, still alive and in some strange way even more alive because they ached and pained. They were smoothed and caressed by pain, a pain that was the measure of my time, like a well-defined cloud that lasts for days in some patch of sky.

On the Riviera it was difficult to find a place where I could gather these thoughts around me as I would often do in bed or on the verandah in the sanatorium. There were too many people and the ever-intruding Pinna, too many thoughts about going home and the factory and starting work again. I kept thinking that when I got home I would find that my cousin had arrived from France. That thought made me feel less guilty about having left my mother alone. But my more persistent thoughts were about my cousin. I imagined a beautiful dark girl in my house, washing herself silently, making only a very slight noise with the splashing water. A girl who would close the door and come down to the kitchen with her hair gathered at the nape of her neck and still a little damp at the temples. From thoughts about my cousin I would progress to thoughts about the factory, prompted by the memory of the girls that passed by without looking at anyone on their way to the ladies' room. I wanted to return very soon to the factory and start working again so that at last I would be able to find the proof of my strength.

Nothing happened as I imagined it. The factory was the same as before, beautiful and a little emptier. My mother was well, and my cousin had not arrived. No other news. October was better because it wasn't so hot, but in the afternoons I had the same attacks, my hands perspired, and I felt so exhausted that I had to lean against the power saw. I controlled the machine only toward the end of each piece I turned out and each time with difficulty.

In the meantime strange things were going on around me. Every time I went to work or to eat in the cafeteria it seemed as if some subtle change had taken place and that the factory and all those connected with it, from the cities, the town, and the surrounding countryside, were keeping something from me.

At home my mother lived the life of an old woman, dividing her time between the kitchen and the garden. I would go with her to mass on Sunday, walking slowly down the road, stopping every once in a while at some bend in the road or under a tree. Then I would go and listen to the football matches on the radio. I would read the newspapers and magazines and even a book or two. I would lose myself in my reading and find my feeling reflected in tragic tales of suffering. But this didn't bring me any strength, and it didn't help me to understand my situation any better.

The old newspapers that I collected in my room made me unhappy, as if the ruined paper faces creased by the folds had become monstrously ill and deformed in my company, just as their appearance was deformed—with only one eye, or one eye higher than the other and a broken mouth. The women in the corner of my room would vanish as they came near me. The priest told me that I should read better books. So I went to the library in the factory. It was a lovely room even if inside. Surrounded by those thousands of books I felt confused and as if I never would be able to leave that place free, as free as I had been when I had first walked in.

In the breaks between work shifts I would often go to the library or to the movies. I also signed up for a course in French and a series of lectures on the Unification of Italy.

Many young men used the library and attended these lectures, new and strange young men who asked many questions to clarify a point and shook their heads when they answered yes or no or just listened, the way that priests do. I noticed that some of the older workers went to the movies just to sleep. I was happy in the dark, and I enjoyed myself.

Once I ran into Dr. Tortora in the library. He was smiling as usual. He was leaving a lecture surrounded by a group of girls. He had the placid look of someone who hasn't any worries or disturbing thoughts, of one who is convinced he has the secret of perpetual serenity. He didn't see me, but when he got to the door he turned toward the corner of the room where I was standing. He stopped smiling, narrowed his eyes, and looked at me with malice. Then with an angry gesture he thrust his hands in his pockets and left the room. Had he seen me and recognized me? Did he mind my coming to the library to regain a little of my strength?

After a month I went to the infirmary because I had a nosebleed. A nurse told me to sit down and gave me some cotton and a little basin with water and a pink medicine. She left me standing alone in front of the sink in the bathroom. No doctor showed up, and the nurse didn't even come back. When the bleeding stopped I rested a while and left without seeing anybody. I almost felt as if I were escaping. Why hadn't Tortora taken that opportunity to see me again? I was almost disappointed that he hadn't done so.

But during the first days of December I soon learned the answer. Grosset told me that I had to go to the infirmary the next day for a fluoroscope examination. My companions told me that it was a mere formality and that everyone had to go through the same thing. But I was the only one who had been selected because that was the chance that Dr. Tortora had been waiting for. He wanted to act with authority, in other words when he chose. In order to strike with greater certainty he had deliberately turned down the more ambiguous opportunities to visit me, like the time of the bloody nose.

The morning of the examination I glanced at the Indian and the boot. If they resist, so will I and tonight I will be here at home like these walls. This lake will surely be here waiting for me. I prayed, but these thoughts and the small flicker of hope they gave me distracted me from my prayer.

On the way to work everything was normal. The factory seemed peaceful. The treachery was well hidden inside the souls of the conspirators. The glass panes of the factory didn't mirror this treachery the way they reflected the damp December street, the rain from the previous day, and the slight wind that ran with us across the street to the infirmary. We entered in groups of two and three after having punched our cards. As I was going in Pinna was coming out. I don't remember who was with me: they all seemed to be young and laughing, with their chins tucked inside their uniforms to protect themselves from the cold. They didn't seem to be paying any attention to me. Perhaps they didn't want to witness the terrible injustices in store for me nor assume any of the blame. A witness automatically assumes part of the blame.

Because of the constant stream of people coming and going I knew where I had to go for the fluoroscope examination. To a room on the second floor, at the end of the hall, on the side of the building that didn't have any windows. We had to take off our

shirts and undershirts and wait for the nurse to tell us to go in.
There were two nurses: one who held our personal files and called
us by name and also helped the other one run the machine and
place the man in the right position for the examination. There
weren't any doctors present, at least there weren't any there when
it was my turn to go behind the machine. They preferred not to
face me now that they had already made up their minds about me.
The first nurse wrote down my name and the date and selected
my file from among the others.

If only I had burned it then or if only I had been courageous
enough to read it and expose their trickery by taking it immediately to the old Major in the Personnel Department or to the
president of the company or to the police! Instead I waited my turn
and walked quietly to the machine. The second nurse had a de-
cisive look about her, as if she didn't have anything to do with the
people around her but only with the machine and the lights. She
did what she had to do and dismissed me shortly. She turned away
immediately and called out a number to the other nurse who had
been signaling to me to get dressed and leave. I left while the
stream of people continued to pour in for the examination, steadily
and innocently. I must have been thinking about something else
because I don't remember thinking about the consequences of
the examination.

I learned the results twenty days later, the morning of the twenty-
second of December when I was called by Dr. Bompiero. The
verdict was tuberculosis of both lungs, acute tuberculosis, infec-
tious and contagious.

"Why haven't you said anything? Why have you suffered like
this? How long have you been feeling ill? In this factory, at home,
surely we would have done everything possible for you." These
were Dr. Bompiero's words, and as he talked he clasped his hands
together and hid his hypocrisy behind a green lamp on his desk.
The light was on, even though it was only ten o'clock in the morning. The green light that spread over his robe left his face in
shadows and focused on his hands, which he moved to emphasize
the gravity of his words. His green hands became the tuberculosis
that burrowed in my lungs; in the large veins there lived a malig-
nant, acid blood dangerous to mine.

64]

"For how long?" repeated Dr. Bompiero, and in that moment time became one. From beginning to end all my time ended in that deception. "Forever, forever," I should have screamed at him, putting out the light and uncovering the plot. "I have always suffered, but it was not intended that I should suffer. Today it is you, the doctors in the infirmary, who are my executioners. You who on the eve of Christmas stop me from being reborn and actually want to kill me. Kill me with grief and despair." I didn't want to sit down, and I refused to be examined. I felt my heart beating rapidly because of the great effort it was making to keep me on my feet. I felt the blood pour down my neck and shoulders as if someone had cut a great gash at the base of my skull. My hands swelled up, and I could hardly bend my fingers. At this point Bompiero made a mistake in his wretched performance because he stopped for a moment and lit a cigarette. I saw him pull out a lovely packet and an even lovelier cigarette, all round and golden. He put it in his mouth and lit a match. The flame was brighter than the green light; a small thread of black smoke rose from the flame. This gave me a feeling of reality and woke me from my bad dream. I came to the immediate decision that I would run away. As Bompiero got up and came toward me pointing to the examination table, I turned and my voice shattered the air like thunder. "No," I said, "no, no." I screamed, louder and louder, as I ran from the room.

I ran back to my department and threw myself headlong into my work. The machine reacted as if it understood my despair. I kept to myself in the cafeteria, and I sat down at the table occupied by the assembly crew and the women in order to have time to decide what I should do. I was thinking so hard that I ate feverishly, but I was unaware of what I ate. I decided that I wasn't going to go along with Tortora and Bompiero. They couldn't take my work away from me; they couldn't lie to the point of violating my wishes. If I resist, I thought, I'll manage to save myself. To resist them I had to avoid them and avoid the consequences of their machinations. The deception was clear, the sick X ray was not mine. Either that, or it had been faked. Since the factory wasn't hiring new people, Tortora wanted to throw me out so that he could give my job to someone else. Or perhaps he had to show that he and the other doctors were capable of discovering the seriously ill and curing them; and all this just to make a bigger impression on the nurses and on the factory. And to establish the importance of the infirmary.

During the rest of the afternoon, after lunch, I did nothing else but try to put my thoughts in order and arrive at some decision. In the meantime I didn't talk to anyone for fear that the news would spread. I didn't even tell Pinna because I knew that I would be furthering Tortora's and Bompiero's plans; everyone, including my companions, would believe the doctors and reconfirm the reality of my illness. Perhaps Grosset was the only one who would keep my secret and help me; but I couldn't even trust him because he was foreman and tied to the decisions of the factory.

Once again all my thoughts had to remain within me, trapped between my mind and my heart, and I had to try and control them so as not to explode with them.

I left the factory prepared to carry out the first of my plans. I wanted to show that Tortora was lying by producing a diagnosis from a good doctor who was willing to uphold the truth in the face of Tortora's lies. I went to see Dr. Giordano, whom I had met in Candia when he came to organize the Catholic Action Center. I had discovered at the time that Dr. Giordano was the best doctor in X and the surrounding area. He had been chief of the medical staff at the hospital and a doctor to the poor. Dr. Giordano was retired and only saw people by appointment. His study, where I was led by his dog, was enormous; it seemed empty even though the doctor was present. He was standing in a corner next to a small, black table. There were other black tables in the room covered with jars containing various human organs. The sight of those vases brought back all my troubles, clamoring to be heard one by one and all at once, there, in that place where the skulls and tiny fetuses were like members of my family. Three of the walls in the study were heavily draped. There was no light or noise from the outside. On the folds of the draperies and on the carpets there swarmed the ghosts of many illnesses.

Dr. Giordano stood motionless next to the table. He bent down for a minute to write my name on a piece of paper. His handwriting was so large that even in the semidarkness of the room I managed to distinguish each letter as he wrote it down. He listened to what I had to say looking steadily at me during my entire speech. When I mentioned the name of Dr. Tortora, he gave a start.

"What," he said, "you work in the . . . factory?" I answered yes. "Well, why have you come to me? You have everything you need at the factory, all that medical science can invent. You have access to all the public health services and every type of assistance. Between the factory and the health insurance every last one of you has at least four doctors at his disposal. You can no longer choose your own doctor nor your own illness. Therefore you shouldn't try to do it. At least not with me. I don't want to get mixed up with socialized medicine, not I. I'm sorry, but I have to refuse your request . . ."

"But I am ill," I told him, "and Tortora is the one who is ruining me." This accusation took him by surprise, and in that pause I regained the strength to continue my story and tell him about the fake X rays and the verdict of tuberculosis. The doctor was silent and after a while he said: "I cannot, nor do I want to get mixed up in this. Go to a lung specialist, to Dr. De Saint Martin; if he decides to examine you, it will be the same as if I had done it."

I thought about Dr. Giordano during the entire trip home and I realized that he hadn't wanted to become an accomplice of the doctors who were plotting my destruction. I renewed my decision not to let them examine me again.

Only one thought revealed itself to me as I watched the white lake in the night: the magnitude of my troubles.

At a certain point in the conversation Dr. Giordano had said, "But such a serious diagnosis indicates that you must suffer a great deal and that you have been suffering for a long time. Such acute pain should certainly not be a surprise to you now."

Was it true then that my old troubles had returned? Had they ever left me? The doctors said I was ill because they knew how much I suffered and how from day to day there were times when it was almost impossible to resist and go on. And they, instead of helping me conquer my troubles, only strengthened them in order to ruin me completely. I could conquer them if I kept them within

[67

myself—I could even ignore them. But if others exposed them and set them against me I would never be able to control and master them.

Dr. Giordano's innocent comment had been enough to line them all up against me once more. Going up the hill toward my house I felt as I had felt when I returned from the prison camp. The pain and the disillusion prevented me from seeing the front of my house or recognizing the road and the familiar places. I didn't want my mother to see me suffering and beaten. So I stopped for a moment at the door and barely managed to comfort myself by renewing my decision to ignore my troubles and the doctors at the factory.

I spent Christmas in peace. It was the third Christmas after my return from prison, and we had a little snow. Once again the snow hadn't been able to hide anything or give me any comfort. I went regularly to the factory on the days between holidays but nothing happened. No one sent for me. The factory seemed totally involved with the holidays, and it was wrapped up in a special mood that even extended to the working days. There was less heat and less noise, and the metal pieces seemed fewer and lighter.

After Christmas everyone was full of talk about dances and plans to go dancing here or there on New Year's Eve. It was the beginning of 1948, the year of the second elections. I didn't know that I would be thrown out of the factory and my house and that I would be doing my voting in the sanatorium.

I spent Christmas and the remainder of the holidays with my mother but I wasn't at peace, even with her. One evening my mother gave me my father's wedding ring to wear. One Sunday I went to a football game in Turin where I got very cold. To get warm again I went into a movie theater that was so crowded I had difficulty getting in. I had stood during the football match and I was tired. So I leaned against whatever I could find—even against other people. A short time after I had been in the theater I felt a violent heat that left me even more exhausted. My breath was as thick as a sweet drink, but it barely reached my throat.

I was so tired that leaning for a moment against the wall or someone near me gave me short intervals of rest that were like snatches of sleep. It seemed as if my body was reduced to so little that I could sleep for a moment and rest against the shoulders of some stranger. As I leaned against someone I felt that I dearly loved them and their strength. I had to admit that I was alone and sick, but I only admitted it silently, to that unknown companion who seemed to be protecting me even from Dr. Tortora's attack. But even in that moment I didn't give in to him, the one who didn't want to help me. But my weakness depressed me and made me wonder if perhaps my troubles would win. This thought stayed with me till I returned to work after Epiphany, when the factory had lost its festive air.

The following Monday they called me from the infirmary: I had to appear that same morning. I told Grosset immediately that I wouldn't go. When he phoned back to tell them my decision he was asked to go and speak to the doctors in person. He went as soon as they blew the noon whistle, and I saw him return to the cafeteria three quarters of an hour later. He looked around him before he sat down, but I managed to hide among a group of drillers. When work began, Grosset didn't say anything to me. Around four o'clock he came over to where I was working and lit a cigarette the way he usually did. He looked intently at me and said, "Don't you want to talk to me?" I didn't answer, and as he turned to leave he added, "I think the doctor did his duty by telling me everything."

Then for the rest of the afternoon he didn't say another word. The doctors were fighting me according to the plan that I had discovered; since I hadn't told anyone about my illness because I didn't want anyone to think that I was really sick, it was up to them to spread the news.

I didn't go to work the next day. I stayed in bed nearly all day talking to the boot and the Indian. The December dampness blurred their images, so much that the boot became a dog and the Indian just an undefined spot on the wall. I told my mother that I didn't feel well.

Even though I had definitely traced a plan of action, my thoughts, like the damp patches on the wall, distended and lost their shape. They became confused in a maze of loose ends and connecting events. I lost myself in this uneasiness till at last my decisions seemed petty and unreal in my own eyes and so irrevocable as to be almost unchristian. I would touch my chest and my arms and it seemed as if the flesh was melting in my sweat. It seemed as if I could touch the heat and the sores under the skin on both sides of my chest. If I leaned on my body, I felt the same perverse pleasure I had felt in school together with the desire to be really sick, in bed, without homework, or any kind of work, cared for by my mother, in complete harmony with her, like a good son, happy to be protected. What made me react against this tendency was the fact that others had made the decision for me, in a deadly way, in a manner fiercely opposed to all the hopes that urged me on. I was afraid of giving in because of the conflicting feelings within me, or had my troubles become so numerous that I could no longer contain them all inside me? When my mother brought my supper she stroked my forehead with her hand to feel the fever and wipe away the drops of sweat.

If they would only let me stay home for the cure. This possibility increased my uneasiness because it conflicted with the decisions I had taken. I had the desire to fight back, to go to Tortora and show him up for what he was, unmask him. I wanted to run to him and Bompiero and tell them in front of Grosset and with his help that I was fully aware of all their plotting. I wished that Tortora would suddenly appear in my house, at the foot of my bed so that I could tell him everything right away. "Ah, if he would only come." I muttered these words with my head buried in the pillow to preserve my voice and the intensity of my desire. "If he would only come immediately, immediately, here."

I decided to return to the factory the next day to see what had happened during my absence and to find out if the doctors had looked for me, or were looking for me. I was so anxious to know the answer that I was awake until very late, but then I managed to sleep until the time came for me to take the bus.

As soon as Grosset saw me come in, he came toward me and even though the others could hear, he asked me how I felt; then he stopped me for a moment and told me that he was very worried and that he had to talk to me. "If you don't go to the doctors they may tell the Personnel Department for the sake of the other men." His words turned me to stone. I thought about my contagion, and I felt I was finished. Once more I was alone, excluded from the group just the way I was in the days of Sergeant Vattino and prison. This is it, I thought.

The end was so perfect, so hopeless, and so inevitable at that moment of my time that it seemed to be the completion of a pattern drawn on my skin. The most adverse of destinies could not have been so cruel and so precise; only man, only man could do this.

Rebellion sent me directly to the infirmary. Bompiero was not in. I was received by Tortora, who told me that Bompiero had informed him of everything. While I was denying everything he made them bring me a small glass of brandy to calm me down and help me catch my breath. I refused this last trick of theirs, and I accepted only some water which I made them take from the wash basin that was in the room. But Tortora didn't admit his trickery and continued to talk to me.

At last he said that he couldn't accept my refusal, for my own good more than for the others. In any case, he could only help me if I would take care of myself and cooperate with him and Dr. Bompiero, beginning that afternoon. A few months in the clinic, a thorough cure, a good long period of convalescence and then, well and strong again, back to the factory, where he and the infirmary would always be ready to help me. This was the opinion of the handsome Tortora, whose big eyes saw everything as beautiful and good.

"At four this afternoon," he said as I left, "and there isn't any need for you to go back to work."

I left, and I didn't go back to my department. I walked around the grounds and after having passed all the buildings of the factory, I found myself nearly in the countryside. In the distance they were preparing a building site. I stood in the January cold, in a very cold January without snow, uncovered, alone, threatened by death. Two steam shovels were digging at the ground, making a lot of noise; they would turn and head toward each other. They would stop, turn again, make an arc in the sky with their shovels, then bury them in the ground; another turn and they would begin to move in opposite directions. The noise that spread through the countryside kept me from thinking about my illness and Bompiero and brought more familiar thoughts to my mind. The machines were operating, and it seemed that besides their work it was also their duty to make enough noise to fill the country, the sky, and help me and my thoughts.

I heard one of the steam shovels turn its motor to maximum speed, and I saw that it was shaking violently. It complained, standing in the middle of its plot of ground, but it couldn't move. It could no longer move on that brittle, frozen soil, and the treads only bit the air. I saw the man who ran it thrust his head out of the cab. His gloved hands were bigger than his face. He gunned the motor once more, he shook the yellow steam shovel from side to side, but the machine gave one last shudder and stopped. After a moment the motor began to throb faintly as if the whole machine had given up. In the meantime the other steam shovel kept on working.

I felt completely free, free and disembodied like the noise and the morning. As the motor of the first steam shovel throbbed faintly, the other machine arrested its shovel in mid-air and turned around. It had understood immediately; and it went toward its companion. Its yellow body drew near the other. When they were side by side they stopped their motors. Then the first machine began to vibrate at regular intervals as if it were singing; the other followed suit at a slower pace. The combined noise of the motors grew in volume, the machines drew closer and closer as if they were hugging each other. I realized that one was helping the other and that together they were pushing in the same direction. One machine would push the other with its shovel from the back and support it with its body from the side. At last they were free, they turned their backs on each other and began to work again.

All this had a prophetic meaning on that morning when the leaden January sky seemed to clear a little because of the warm breath of the two machines; I hoped that somebody would really be able to help me, and since it involved my work, I thought that Grosset might be the one.

I waited for him in the cafeteria, and I asked him if we could have lunch together. "I need your help," I said softly, so that those nearby wouldn't hear me. Fortunately, they were all from other departments. As I spoke to him, trying to explain my situation, he ate slowly, removing the sauce from the top of his spaghetti. He picked at his plate carefully as if my words had fallen into it.

"I understand everything," he said. "You may be right, as far as your past and your life are concerned, but this time you're dealing with a real truth outside of yourself that you cannot ignore."

"What truth, Mr. Grosset?" I thought, and I said, "The truth of the deception that has even managed to possess your conscience? The truth of having to admit that my troubles have won?"

In a speech confused by my own visions I told him that I had to get rid of the bonds that were suffocating me and that I would not let myself be bound again till they buried me.

"No one is persecuting you," said Grosset.

"Yes, everyone. Tortora is the first to do so and all the others; I see how they look at me, what they think of me, how they listen to my talk."

Grosset led me out of the cafeteria toward the trees near the bowling courts and the benches. As I walked I suffered because I couldn't shake his conviction, and it seemed as if everything around me was siding against me. Not even the trees, or the halls, or the doors, or the stairs or the fire escape could help me; the entire world reflected a truth that was not mine.

I tried another futile speech, but it made me cry; I threatened all the doctors and the factory, and I told Grosset that he, too, was on the point of becoming an accomplice.

"You should calm yourself, because you are ill," he said harshly.

"Then you're a cuckold," I screamed at last, and I threw myself down on the bench, weeping.

He followed me to the bench and began to walk up and down the path under the trees. I watched his feet which didn't seem to have heard what I had said to him.

I had offended Grosset in order to bring him closer to me, to keep him with me, the only one left to me, unhappy and betrayed. He should never have left me. This is what I wanted to tell him: that he was like me and therefore he couldn't leave me.

He stopped pacing and said, "You suffer a great deal, Saluggia. I am sorry. See what you can do. Running away won't help you." And he left, he, the only one. The best man in the department didn't understand my fate because the doctors and the Skilled Labor Department had defined it in a different way.

There wasn't anyone else in the factory who could help me, who could back me up so that they wouldn't consider me incurably ill. Grosset had run away, and I was very sorry I had offended him, sorry and at the same time prepared to offend him again, more profoundly, to make him understand how much we were alike.

There wasn't a soul in the park, and only a few lights shone in the factory, in that immense fish bowl that reflected the dying January. I felt farther away from everything than the time I was in prison, alone, as if everyone had gone away and left me in that glass boat. I was sorry I had offended Grosset, but I felt compelled to offend him again, to lash out at him in the department in front of everyone. Perhaps a scandal could save me. The Communists would save me; on the other hand perhaps they would try to get rid of me immediately; but that would make the others take my side, perhaps even the doctors would take my side.

I got up to go to my department and say out loud everything I could think of against Grosset.

I left the fields and paths and took a short cut back. On the second floor I had to go through part of the Assembling Department and then turn left and go down the short hall that led to my section. When I was halfway down the hall Grosset came out of a doorway accompanied by a guard. He pointed at me. I didn't have time to say anything. The guard came up to me and told me I had to go with him to the infirmary.

I had been betrayed and handed over to the guards. I barely heard Grosset say that he could not have me back in the department and that it was his duty to force me to take care of myself.

I certainly was well taken care of, and only divine Providence and my Christian acceptance of suffering have helped me to this day and guide my hand as I write.

That time in the infirmary everyone stared at me. The nurses left their rooms to get a look at me, and the orderlies moved slowly around me, the way a farmer circles an animal that kicks. The doctors were nowhere to be seen. The shortest nurse appeared on the staircase and told me, nearly shouting: "Saluggia, come upstairs. Come up!"

When I walked in the door on the next floor Tortora and Bompiero were already together. Together they smiled at me, talked to me, and walked toward me. Then Tortora pulled open one of the green curtains covering the window in front of me and I saw a plane tree. My eyes and my heart rested on it and I waited. Toward the end, some birds flew from its branches, just at the moment when they decided to send me to a sanatorium. They telephoned immediately, and Tortora got angry when it seemed there might be some difficulty in finding a place for me.

I watched the birds, and I thought it was incredible that they should live so near human evil, so near to that infirmary and those instruments; it seemed incredible that they weren't frightened by those words and didn't fly far away from that iron factory.

III

ON THE TWENTY-FIFTH of January, 1948, the day commemorating the fall of Saint Paul on the road to Damascus, I entered the ——— sanatorium on the opposide side of the lake from my village.

"This way, your mother can come to visit you often," Tortora had said. "Not at home, but near, very near . . ."

I couldn't see the lake from the sanatorium, and I couldn't even see my house which was higher up. Sometimes at night I heard the sound of the water and of the main highway, the same sounds I had listened to at home. Then I would think of the Indian and his turban and the boot. It would have been enough for me to find that wall, the wall in the barn with all its roads that my eyes and my thoughts had traveled. The thought that it was so near and still not visible was a source of even greater torment because I realized that it wasn't the distance that separated us but something else. Another illness, the worst of all my illnesses.

In the sanatorium I was given a small room in the isolation ward; that means the contagious section. As soon as I arrived by bus like any other healthy person, carrying my suitcase, they handed me my admission papers and I was nearly lifted off my feet by an orderly. He must have been warned and instructed by Dr. Tortora because he acted as if I were deathly ill and in no condition to stand on my own two feet. He led me to a bathroom where, because of my insistence, he limited himself to bathing only my hands and face. He undressed me carefully and dressed me with clothes from the sanatorium. When I saw myself in that uniform, I cried. That bathroom seemed as far away from my mother and my house as the moon, and the water dripping into the tub dripped and vanished uselessly, like my sorrow.

As soon as I had put on their pajamas, my body no longer belonged to me; it became the body of a sick person, thin and twisted, shoddily covered by the seams and the rough material, and it already seemed to hide a different structure under the folds of the pajamas. Even the smell of my body was no longer my smell. Only the slippers belonged to me. My mother had packed them for me and managed to pass them to me under the bathroom door. In the hall I had the look of someone who had been in a sanatorium for many years. Tortora had fixed everything. Now my troubles had free rein, and they had already taken me over. Only my will could resist, but I was busy thinking, "How have the doctors managed to recruit the orderly in their sad cause?" He already knew everything, and as he meticulously washed and undressed me, he said, "Ah, prison . . . you at least came back. My brother didn't." The doctors knew that the love for his brother could turn to hate for all men who had managed to survive. That was the reason I had been placed in his care.

There was a statue of the Madonna at the end of the hall, just before turning into the isolation ward. In the glare of all those bright lights her eyes looked at me full of pity. They said, "Poor Albino." My room was furnished with a small, white iron bed and night table. There was another table against the far wall, two white iron chairs next to the bed, and a washstand next to the French doors that led to the balcony. There was a basin on a three-legged stand next to my bed. "In case you wish to spit," said the orderly.

"You must stay in bed for a while, as still as possible," said a doctor who had just come into the room. He spoke like a Neapolitan. "I don't see how you could survive another hemorrhage."

He already knew everything. Tortora had told them that I had hemorrhaged one evening at home and again on my way to the cafeteria at the factory. It had been Pinna's fault. He had made me run all the way, pushed me downstairs, and slapped me on the back.

My mother had told me that children often had nosebleeds and the blood would go down into the throat and occasionally their gums would bleed too.

I had to lie motionless in that small bed, bathed in my sweat. An orderly would come once in a while, nearly always the same one, custodian and guardian. He would open and close the windows and give me a drink of water. The only thing I could do was think.

Tortora and his wickedness still hadn't set foot there, not in my thoughts. Yet I realized that nearly all my thoughts centered around his cruelty. It was terrible to lie there thinking about battling my troubles and conquering them, trying to find a way to get well, to leave the sanatorium and go back to work.

It was terrible to lie there and think about my cousin from France who perhaps would be coming for the carnival season while I was still on this side of the lake. It was terrible to lie there and think about the lake that looks so different in February, narrow and silent till the night the ducks arrive. They fly over my house coming from the north, straight like stars, and as they penetrate the water they barely disturb the color of the surface. It was terrible to lie there and think about the factory and once again Tortora, Vattino, the orderly, Father Caligari, the Indian, Pinna, the cafeteria, my power saw so far away from my hands. I looked at my arms and my hands. I slowly moved my arms. They seemed hairier, and my fingernails were thicker.

Sometimes I tried to picture the life of the sanatorium from the noises I heard all around me. Terrible sounds ran along the water pipes under the sink and it seemed as if all the patients were standing and suffering into their washbowls. I heard pathetic voices, rattles and gurgles, an entire network of obscene communications that were without a doubt the noises made by the patients. Once in a while I'd hear someone walk by in the hall and sometimes I'd hear the voices of the cleaning women. The sound of many voices came through the window, even the voices of women and normal chatter and every so often a burst of laughter.

Once I thought spring had arrived. I found a pebble on my window sill, but I really didn't understand what was happening because it was soon after lunch and I was half asleep. The sun was shining into the room and the sun always brings something to the window or makes some sort of noise of its own. I was dozing as I often did after lunch because I ate with a vengeance. Eating did me a lot of good and helped me fight Dr. Tortora. In order to whet my appetite I would imagine that Tortora was standing near my tray like a voracious pigeon threatening to eat my lunch and jump into my plate to dirty my food with his feet and his wings. I had to beat him to the punch so I would eat faster and faster mixing all my food together. After lunch I would eat the fruit I had hidden under my pillow and drink the water and the orange juice I kept well protected by covering the glass with a plate. I ate a great deal and the food was not bad. I especially liked the strong taste of the American cheese that I managed to savor even though I ate so fast.

The doctors were happy about my appetite, and the doctor with the Neapolitan accent would laugh every time he gave me an intravenous injection or my medicine. "Our dear Saluggia is blooming again," he'd say and as he left the room he would invariably add, "In a month we'll be back at the factory and we'll be able to lift a two-ton machine with one hand. Then we'll go to the infirmary and make fun of Dr. Tortora and we'll split his desk in two with one blow." And closing the door behind him, he would make a noise of a desk cracking in two.

The only one who seemed upset about my determination to eat everything was the orderly, and every time he came to take away the tray he'd say: "So you ate everything again today, huh . . ." He was the one who one day toward the middle of May escorted Dr. Tortora into my room. Tortora looked at me, lifted the bedcovers, felt my arms and my chest and said: "Was I right? In autumn, in autumn." He left in a hurry without saying another word, no doubt he was upset by the progress I was making. The relief I felt when he left the room and the joy at his disappointment in my progress didn't last very long. I heard his words buzzing all around me, "In autumn, in autumn."

So, he wouldn't let me return to the factory till autumn; I wouldn't be completely cured till autumn. I still had to stay in the sanatorium for a long time. I didn't mind entirely because once I had escaped the traps set for me by Dr. Tortora I could devote myself to building up my strength and pursuing my reading and the new contacts I had made in the sanatorium. I thought these things were good for me.

The elections were over, but the discussions continued. They hadn't let me go down to the garden till the eighteenth of April. I voted from my bed and I voted for the Christian Democratic party on both ballots, and I prayed that my vote would double and redouble itself like Samson's strength. After the overwhelming

[79

victory of the Christian Democratic party I made a few friends. One of them was the chaplain who had quarreled with my mother because they wouldn't let her see me. The Neapolitan doctor was another friend. The others in my group were all patients who often couldn't come to the garden and even when they came couldn't speak very much. They came, attracted by the beautiful weather, the splendor of the hedges, by the insects and the sun, the sun they followed by turning their chairs, the tables, and their backs to its warmth. They were attracted by the words of the most talkative and healthiest among them. The ones who could take walks, gather stones, eat candy, and smoke. These were the things that showed you were off the critical list, and consequently the ones who could do all these things did them wholeheartedly.

My group was the most serious and subdued of all the groups, and we didn't talk so much about sports and women. In the other groups the talk was about very young and beautiful women, of Slavic women who had been freed from the prison camps and had remained in Italy, of a movie star ruined by her passions. This was the favorite subject, even of those who were very ill: they always ended up talking about women. Some of the men would jump the hedges and go into the women's section; others threw notes. The chaplain was very worried. He was especially concerned about the men and women who were allowed to go into town to send postcards and shop. They always returned very late, in couples, and the priest suspected that something was going on. He told me that they had had to put the contagious ward in that unattractive part of the building in order to separate the men's dormitory from the women's.

"It must be illness that causes such evil thoughts," the chaplain would say.

In our group we would take turns reading a book, then telling the story to the others. Sometimes someone would read out loud and the others would listen. I was considered the best reader, and they would come from the other groups to listen to me, especially the older men. We would end up discussing politics and I would tell them what I had seen in Russia. I had never been to Russia but it didn't seem wrong to tell them what I knew about the Russians I had seen or tell them what I imagined Russia was like. I would begin with Poland and go on toward winter and ignorance. I would tell them about the black countryside without roads, about the forests and about the mud villages without schools and hospitals. I would tell them that there were no churches; about how they tortured us soldiers and how they were always hungry.

There was an old man who tried to prove that I was lying, but he didn't succeed even though he said that he had been in Russia for thirteen years.

"Moscow, Moscow," they told him. "You haven't seen how the people suffer in the other towns and in the country."

After these sessions it was difficult for me to sleep at night, and I would lie awake imagining my life in Russia—the trips through the snow, discovering new villages, some of them burned to the ground and others occupied by Communists who had been sent to capture me. Once, just to contradict me, the old man mentioned the kindness of the women. This had stayed in my mind and every once in a while in the stories I made up I would invent a young girl, a good, religious girl who helped me escape from the guards who were hunting me down. She would take me to her house and feed me and hide me in her bed. She would sit on the edge of the bed, shielding me with her long braids and her voluminous nightgown while she answered the guard's questions.

Once I had seen a girl like that among the women patients. She was crossing the hall going toward the operating room. One night when I couldn't sleep and I was lying there thinking of a story about Russia, someone knocked on the wall facing my bed. I thought about the Communist guards and the girl who would save me. Then I heard a voice coming from the corner of my room nearest the window. It was late at night and you could hear very well.

"Are you men?" said a woman's voice.

"No," I answered.

"What do you mean no?" said the voice.

"I am alone," I said, getting up, covering myself, and walking toward the corner where the voice came from.

"What a shame," said the woman. "There are two of us." Then she added, "Are you in a bedroom?"

"Yes."

"Then there's a bed?"

"Yes."

"Big enough for three?"

"No, for one."

"I was kidding," said the woman, "because there's a beautiful girl with me. Her name is Vera, but it isn't true."

"What isn't true?"

"Her name."

"Why?"

"What if you were an orderly?"

"No, my name is Albino."

"My name is Falsa and this is Vera," and I could hear them laughing.

"But aren't you in bed?"

"No. This is the bathroom. We came to talk to you."

"Do you know me?"

"Certainly, you are the handsomest one, the one who walks the dog in the garden."

"What do you want?"

"To talk, dear. Don't worry. We won't touch you."

"But aren't you cold?"

"What? Are you afraid of pleurisy?"

"How old are you?"

"I'm eighteen and my friend is sixteen; but it isn't true."

"I'm twenty-nine."

"Twenty-eight and a half or twenty-nine?"

"Twenty-nine."

"Come and see us and bring some cigarettes."

"How can I?"

"Open the window and walk along the ledge. Once you are on the terrace, climb through the first window on your left. You'll have to do some climbing, but we'll help you."

"But it can't be done."

"Are you afraid to come alone? Then get a friend."

"But I'm alone. There aren't any friends."

"How long have you been here?"

"Four months."

"Then you don't know anyone. Haven't you ever come to the women's section?"

"No."

"Find a friend and come; there's a girl here for you."

"I can't find a friend."

"Speak to someone who has been here for a while and tell him that Marina is waiting. You'll see how he comes."

"But what are we going to do over there?"

"Just . . . do . . . yes, just do . . . you know . . ."

"What?"

"Are you really twenty-nine?"

"Yes."

"Where did you get sick?"

"In prison, but I'm well now."

"Oh sure, I bet you're well if you take such good care of yourself. But were you a soldier?"

"Yes."

"Oh what a love, beautiful green tree! Come tomorrow night. Get yourself ready and find a young friend but not from the contagious ward if possible. Come tomorrow night. When we get here, we'll knock; you come without speaking. Come alone if you like. We're the ones who sit under the cherry tree in the garden."

I listened a while longer and it seemed as if the wall were very light . . . very light, that the window open to the night was part of the fields, free, that I could walk out, walk through the wall and speak through the pipes under the sink, that the sanatorium was unreal, neither sickness nor patients existed, that everything was a sweet dream and that the night was the eve of a great happiness. Once back in bed I didn't think about Russia anymore. I was filled with a great feeling of friendship, even toward the old Communist. I warmed myself in this discovery, and I felt my blood flowing clean and free throughout my body. I tingled with pride on my back and on my chest. I pressed my hands to my side and that embrace protected me and eased all my anguish; it separated me from all my old troubles. Toward the end of my reverie, as I was about to fall asleep, I was afraid for a moment that someone had overheard my conversation with the women; but as sleep slowly penetrated my consciousness, I understood that this fear was not due so much to the suspicion of having done something wrong, but due to the thought that someone else might have heard my conversation and that he would cross all the balconies and take my place or continue my conversation with the women who sat under the cherry tree in the garden. In my half sleep I imagined this cherry tree to be very beautiful and heavy with fruit. It became a symbol of the reality of our conversation, a real symbol that would bring me luck.

As soon as I awoke the next day I remembered the entire conversation and my happiness increased when I thought that during the free hours in the garden I could remain alone on the dining room terrace to watch the cherry tree and the women who sat underneath. I didn't imagine that they were beautiful, but I was nearly certain that the youngest one was the one I had seen going into the operating room. This girl's beauty disturbed my thoughts; it took on enormous proportions to the disadvantage of the story and blocked my daydreams with a strange fear. The fear of her beauty developed into fear of seeing her, fear of being seen on the terrace and ridiculed, fear of having everything end in a monstrous joke. I was plagued by these thoughts all morning long and since it was Sunday, the women's nearness at mass heightened my uneasiness. Almost unintentionally I noticed that the girl in the nightgown wasn't present. I ignored all the others and I buried myself fervently in my papers. When the recreation period came around I didn't have the courage to go down to the terrace. I stayed in my room and sent for the chaplain. Sadly and crying I told him that I was willing to see my mother that day. I hadn't wanted to see her since I entered the sanatorium because I didn't want to expose her to the danger of contagion or make her suffer any more. She cried a great deal even though we met in the visitors' room with many others present. She told me that she was well and that the factory sent money so that she had enough to live on without worries. Pinna had come to visit her.

I was very tired when my mother left, and I abandoned the idea of going down to the garden to see the women. It was the last week of the football season, and I stayed to listen to the final scores and commentary. When I got back to bed I was sad, convinced that I had offended the two girls and that they wouldn't appear that evening. I decided that if they showed up I would be rude to them and scold them for waking me up.

I fell asleep without hearing anything. In the middle of the night I awoke with a start. I was desolate that I had missed the appointment. My ears were straining to catch every sound, and I was aware of the beating of my heart and the sound of coughing coming from the stairs. The wall was white and solid, inanimate. No light came from the window but the spaces between the blinds were white and flat like cut out pieces of morning light stirring in the direction of the lake.

At home the Indian and the boot would already be visible, standing out from the rest of the wall. Here in the sanatorium I was alone, and I couldn't rely on anyone's help. Even the chaplain when he had that argument with my mother revealed that he didn't understand. He had nearly always sided against me. The doctor who looked after me was good, but he was only a southern Italian. A hundred words today and a hundred more tomorrow, yet everything remained the same. In a month's time . . . "In autumn," Tortora had said, and in autumn it would be.

On Tuesday night, an hour after lights out, around eleven o'clock I heard someone knocking on the wall. It was a soft, gentle noise, nearly a scratching sound and it took me a while to realize that the women were there.

"Here is Marina, raring to go. There are three of us. Come."

"I am alone."

"Come, one of them is leaving right away."

"I'd rather talk."

"I'd rather smoke."

"Is Vera there?"

"Yes, she's here, but come. It's easy."

"How are you both?"

"Oh fine, and you?"

"Why didn't you come the other night?"

"I don't know, but what do you want? Just talk?"

"Why?"

"So that's why they gave you the room nearest us. You're pretty dumb, friend."

[85

"I can't come over because I don't know the way."

"Nobody knew it."

"And afterwards?"

"Now listen, do you like Vera?"

"Does she have dark hair?"

"Do me a favor, call somebody else, someone who knows how to get over here. Get out of the way and go back and suck your pills."

I heard them whispering together, and I imagined that Vera hadn't liked the way Marina had spoken.

"Open the window. I'm coming over to visit you," Marina said a moment later.

I went back to bed because I didn't want to endure such a serious imposition. I put out the light, but I didn't close my eyes. The noise of the bedsprings traveled from the veins in my arms to my chest and throat, together with the pulsations that went from my heart to my bed and to the walls. It seemed as if I could hear the plaster dust falling around me, and I felt its taste in my mouth. The whispers continued from the other side of the wall, followed by the loud sound of a flushing toilet. It was done on purpose to cover up another very distinct sound.

This noise continued for a while. Then as it came onto the open terrace the noise changed. A gasping sound, like an animal breathing in the night came from the window where the shutters were still closed. The noise assailed me, and I imagined there really was an animal ready to jump on me.

I heard a step drag along the ledge and then a hand at the window. I heard a loud knock and a voice.

"Open up, you idiot. Do you want me to fall? Open up. Put on the light on the night table."

I couldn't stand it any longer, and I put on the light. "Open up, you big idiot. Open and don't push the shutters."

I got out of bed and did everything the woman told me to do. I turned back to the bed, and I had to squeeze the covers hard so as not to scream as I watched the woman's figure at the window. She climbed over the window sill, her robe was open, and she put one foot on the floor of my room. I still hadn't seen her face for she had kept her head lowered as she came through the window.

I saw it when she stopped to rest for a minute inside the room. She was a very tall woman, dressed in the fashion of the sanatorium. Her nightclothes reached her feet. She was very pale. She had black hair streaked with white, very black hair and black lips. She had a mole on her cheek, and her hand was bandaged. She held a cigarette. She frightened me. My fear was no match for her courage, and I was powerless. She didn't move. She didn't advance any further into the room. She turned her head toward the window and looked out for a second then with one hand she closed the shutters.

"Don't you have a friend?" she said, looking toward the door.

"No."

"Why are you so frightened? We have to help one another in this place."

"Yes."

"Then call a friend if you don't want to."

"There isn't anyone."

"Let me come into your bed. I'm cold."

I started to get up and she said: "Not that way, idiot. Why are you in isolation?" she continued.

"I don't know. I'm better."

"Are you the one who cried all the time in the dormitory and had to be put back in isolation?"

"No, I've always been here."

"Oh you're that one! Now I understand everything. Poor idiot."

"Speak softly."

"Give me some cigarettes."

"I don't have any."

"What have you got?"

"Nothing, nothing. Speak softly."

"Have you ever seen this?" and she put her hand over her robe, at the end of the row of buttons. "What do you live for? Do you want to get well? Eat this and it will give you faith in life. If you see it, you'll die, soldier!"

"Go away."

She went toward the door. She opened it very slowly and looked down the hall.

"It's ugly," she said. She turned toward me, "What do you have?"

"I have some candy and some cheese."

"No eating. You shouldn't eat. What do you want to cure, idiot? What do you have to drink? Nothing to drink either? You're a real Piedmontese . . . and you're not ugly. Do you like Vera? I'll bring her here if you don't want to come. All you have to do is call another fellow, or ten others and throw in some cigarettes. What are you waiting for? To get out? Get organized, idiot. I'm leaving. Give me the candy for Vera and help me out the window."

I helped her and standing close to her I smelled the strong sanatorium smell of newly changed sheets, the smell of water in the pitchers on the night tables and the smell of the corridors before they open the windows. She muttered to herself and climbed over the window sill. I heard her move forward, climb onto the terrace and on the other side of the wall I heard the voices of the others. Or was it her voice? After a while she said: "Good night, idiot. Get a friend, somebody else. The two of us will come to see you."

I was tired after this adventure, very tired. It could hardly be called an adventure because it fitted so well into the pattern of my life. It was another attempt on the part of my troubles to disguise themselves as an everyday occurrence.

Hand in hand with my weariness, perhaps as a consequence of my weariness, I began to entertain the innocent hope that Vera would be as truthful as her name. I wanted to meet her when I was really cured. Meeting her would be a liberation for both of us. We would leave the sanatorium together and leave an ugly life behind us. We would begin a new life, healthy and free. The thought of meeting her, seeing and speaking to her as I imagined her with her long dark hair and her eyes large and frightened by her illness, overcame any misgivings I might have had because of her friendship with Marina and her presence in the bathroom. As a matter of fact this heightened my feelings of tenderness and protectiveness towards her, feelings that would give me strength when I came face to face with Marina's boldness. "Come then, my intruding Marina, offend me, hurt me, but my eyes don't see you. They look beyond that wall for that young girl you frighten, for that young girl I must save."

Marina must be an accomplice of Dr. Tortora, an associate sent to ruin me completely at the precise moment I'm using the sanatorium to help me get better and regain my strength. How did she know that I cried when they put me in the ward with the others and had refused to stay there? I had done it so that I wouldn't be exposed to infection. I had done it so that I would have some privacy and not always be under the prying eyes of the others. I didn't want to be distracted from the business of rebuilding my body and my spirit. Alone, I would be able to save myself. I could sleep more, undisturbed, in my bed with my window and my air, eating everything, without getting my food and dishes mixed up with the food and dishes of the other patients. It seemed as if Marina had tried to offend me on purpose with her advances and frighten me so that I would return to the ward. It was obvious that she was trying to infect me with God knows what incurable diseases. She was trying to discourage me from eating and getting well and leaving the sanatorium. My hope, Vera, whom I saw when I looked at Marina, was stronger than the evil artifices of Marina's black and white face. My hope, Vera, a girl who shared my illness and my need for help. That is why I never put a stop to the conversations from the other side of the wall. I endured the insults Marina hurled at me because I wouldn't go to see her or call any other men. She never dared come to my room again. Sometimes I would hear Vera laugh and say a few words in a low voice and, I thought, blushing. I was beginning to believe that they came because of me, to smoke a cigarette and talk to me. I supposed that Vera didn't have the courage to come alone and that this was the reason Marina came with her.

In the meantime my life in the sanatorium was going well. The chaplain's friendship kept me in a private room in spite of the fact that the doctors wanted to send me back to the ward. I hardly had any fever any more, and I had gained eight pounds. Nothing new had happened; the old Communist had left toward the end of August. He came to say good by and when I congratulated him on his cure he said: "People like us never get well."

He was paler than usual, and his pallor contrasted greatly with the dark suit he wore. They told me that he wasn't cured and that they were sending him away because of all the trouble he had caused during the days following the attempt on the life of Togliatti.

After the first day of anarchy I had stayed in bed. We heard the news on the stairs just as we were going up after our rest period in the garden. At first the news was more powerful than anything else, more powerful than those who heard it. The shock was so great that it registered as just news and was received with that sense of satisfaction that follows the announcement of a tragedy. This mood of fearful satisfaction was shattered by the old Communist who started screaming at the bottom of the stairs, running toward the garden: "Monsters, monsters, they've killed him. Don't you understand why they shot him, why? It's them, always them." His followers and friends gathered around him immediately. They too began to scream. They saw me standing still on the middle of the stairs. They all spotted me simultaneously. Their eyes rested on me for a moment, their mouths opened and one of them screamed louder than the others: "Yes, yes. It's them, and there's one of them." The whole group moved toward me. "No, no. You don't understand," the old man said from the door leading to the garden. "It's the big wheels . . . They are the ones who grind us down and keep us here. It's them, always them."

The others stopped for a minute because they didn't understand. They looked toward the stairs, and they looked at the ceiling. Since they couldn't find an outlet for their anger they kept pushing and jostling each other, looking at the old man, waiting for him to give them a signal. The old man said that I was just another patient, tubercular just like them. The cause of my illness was the poverty I had had to endure. I was another unfortunate, like them, even more unfortunate because I didn't understand the truth and I was a liar. He gave me a half-hearted slap that caught me between my ear and my shoulder. No one noticed the slap. It was more of a push than a slap but I understand that this was the old man's way of getting even with me for the stories about Russia. He knew that I had lied. I understood that the old man didn't consider me guilty, and because of this I did feel guilty; guilty of being on his side, the side of the many. I went upstairs and returned to my room.

One of the group glared at me and said, "Why are you in isolation?"

Yes, I thought only because I was in isolation I could still consider myself not one of them. Because I was in isolation I didn't do the things they did including the business with the women.

Now that I see things from a better perspective I realize that it was during those days that Marina arranged the meetings with the men who later came around looking for her in my room.

One night, not too long afterward, Marina knocked on the wall again. I waited a few minutes before answering to make her understand that I resented the fact that she had ignored me for several days.

"Are you alone?" she said when I went over to the wall.

"Yes."

"How are you?"

"Fine."

"They told me you were sick."

"No, I'm fine."

"You know, if you're sick you'd better stay in bed or you could get worse. Vera says hello, and she says that she hopes you will get better soon. Then you'll come to see us. In the meantime, stay in bed."

Right in the middle of this solicitous speech there was a knock on the door. Almost immediately someone opened the door for I didn't even have time to stretch my hands toward the sink and pretend to be sick. Three young men slipped into the room. Two of them were fully dressed, and the other one had on pajamas and a robe. They stood in the middle of my room.

"We're friends," they said quickly, and they smiled.

"We have to go over to the women's side and this is the only way we can get through. Please keep quiet. We're going to leave right away, but first we have to arrange a few things. They were the ones who called us." The three young men walked over to the window.

"How do we go?"

But at that moment they heard Marina's voice. They listened and then the three of them laughed and disappeared out the window. The last one said, "You can close it if you like. If we come back this way we'll knock on the shutters."

I certainly will close it, I thought, and I won't open it again for you. I threw myself on the bed and put out the lights. I got up for a second to run some water in the sink so that the group on the other side of the wall would hear that I was going about my business calmly and indifferently. I went back to bed, coughed, put out the lights again, and tried to find a comfortable position. I patted the pillow, and I slowly began to cry.

"Dear mother," I sobbed, "you did warn me. You always told me about the treachery of women. You who know how I've been betrayed. My room and my real bed are near you. Around you, dark and calm are our chests of drawers and our things. My shirts, my suits, my linen, and my jacket. You put all my things in order and you nearly dress me. You wear my things with me. Your mouth gives them life, and your hands guide them. I hear you calling me the way you called when I was in prison. I see you, young, as you were in the garden of our house in Avignon.

"It was a small garden, completely surrounded by the wall of a very old church. At one time, our house with its low ceilings must have been the sacristy. During the summer you used to prepare dinner in the garden for some Italian bricklayers who would come bringing their own wine. They came in the evening, and it used to be my duty to help you set the table and light the lamp that hung from the only tree in the garden over the table. I had to put a piece of paper around the globe to keep away the bees that flew in from the larger gardens and the countryside. Every day at the same hour father would fall asleep on the steps leading to the house or more often he would go into your room for his nap. The others stayed on after he left. The last one to leave was a young man who wore his jacket over his shoulders. He always stayed to talk to you. You would tell me to go to bed, and I felt inside me that you wanted to stay with him because he spoke to you and made you laugh.

"Even today this memory hurts and disturbs me. The young bricklayer was very charming, and I was afraid because I thought that he might charm you too. I was tempted to spy on you; but I was afraid to see the reality of what I suspected. I'm still afraid today, and I am sorry that I didn't look because if I had only seen you talking today I would have peace.

"Tonight I feel everything as if we were still in Avignon going up the stairs to my room, turning my head so as not to see the garden from the window; perhaps it is because I am sad that on the other side of the wall Vera is meeting the men who passed through my room. I know for sure that she is there because I heard her laugh, and I know that she is not innocent for she obeys Marina and she is tricky.

"This, too, is another blow dealt me by my troubles, but I mustn't surrender. I have never seen Vera. I only think that once I recognized her, so I mustn't be angry with her; I must only think about getting well."

It was August, and I thought that I had only a few months left to spend in the sanatorium before I returned to my house and the factory, cured.

Then I would immediately write to my cousin in France, inviting her to come for the holidays around the Feast of All Saints. Our countryside and our house are very beautiful in November. The lake is more tranquil and the water is calmly contained by the banks.

I closed the faucet and coughed again. I felt feverish in bed so I closed the windowpanes. I must have fallen asleep for a second, still straining to catch any sound that might come from the other side of the wall. I heard the knock on the shutters immediately. I made them knock again before opening. There were only two of them now, one fully dressed and the other with a robe. Both of them were smoking, and they told me not to say anything to anyone and to wait for their friend who hadn't finished yet.

"Don't come back any more," I said, and as they were still hesitating at the door I pushed them out. I went back to bed and began to think of the things I would say to Marina if she ever spoke to me again from behind the wall. I slept till morning and the third one never showed up; perhaps he used the corridor.

Unfortunately, they returned many evenings, and they weren't even the same ones; I found out that ten men took part in these reunions. Marina didn't speak to me anymore from behind the wall, and only once or twice did she try to insult me: "Watch the traffic, turn on the stoplight; there isn't room for anybody else." She didn't mention Vera any more. Once I told her that she had ruined Vera and that she would have to pay for her sin. "What Vera? Idiot, they're all Veras. And I have already paid, for everything in full, even for the future."

I never said anything to the doctor or to the chaplain. The fact that the visits continued and I was the only one who knew about them made me feel very special, and I didn't want to lose that feeling.

One night one of the regulars said: "Marina says she wants to receive you too." Another fellow who was with him was surprised: "You mean to tell me he has never gone?" and he stared at me. His stare made up for many humiliations, because I sensed a certain admiration in his look, an acknowledgment of my superiority. I held his gaze without moving a muscle; firmly and without bothering to get up I ordered them to close the door. They obeyed, and disappeared into the corridor.

Once in a while I would think that Vera was not with the others and that she wasn't the one I thought she was, the young dark one, the one I had seen in the hall outside the operating room. I knew, however, that the women were at least two, two every night. All in all, there were four or five who took turns.

One day I stayed on a little longer in the dining room so that I could look from the terrace into the garden under the cherry tree. I wanted to see Marina's friends, the women in her group so that I could recognize Vera and read her guilt or her innocence on her face. I walked slowly toward the railing. The sun was very strong, and it pierced the curtains of the glassed-in porch like a razor blade. I was alone, and when I walked out onto the second porch without curtains and paved with asphalt, flooded with blinding sunlight, I had the impression that I was in some unknown place without the possibility of ever turning back. I looked out over the railing but the view still seemed strange. The terrace was magnified by the heat, and it seemed to lean toward the hills, like something seen in an unreal world, like something about to fly. It must have seemed this way to me because I was very excited. I had to focus carefully before I looked into the garden. There were only a few people there, or so it seemed from the stillness of the place and the sound of a lone voice coming from the direction of the green sunshades and beach umbrellas. It was difficult to recognize and orient myself in that section of the garden.

Then I realized that I was overlooking the women's section. I looked for the cherry tree and found it in the farthest corner of the garden by the hedge. There was no one underneath. A few feet away in the shade of the building there were two or three umbrellas. I went nearer and I recognized Marina's voice. She was always present and always recognizable, like a symbol of evil. I saw a pair of legs, a young girl's legs protruding from under the umbrella nearest Marina. The legs were still and slightly spread apart. For a moment, at knee height I saw the shadow of a hand. The left leg changed position slightly; it moved closer to the other one. After another pause, the right leg swung indolently. It remained suspended in mid-air for a second, abandoned; then it crossed over and rested on the left leg. In the meantime the conversation continued in a monotonous murmur or so it seemed because the distance dulled the sound. There were long pauses in the conversation, pauses of boredom or indifference. Perhaps it seemed that way to me because I couldn't see the expressions on their faces as they talked.

The circle of conversation and bodies in the light under the umbrellas had a sensual quality. Like something alive though still, like an animal that sleeps and digests his food in the sun.

Those legs made me realize that the girl was guilty, indolent, subservient to Marina, an accomplice in the nightly merry-go-round with the men. I knew without a doubt that the girl was Vera because she was sitting very close to Marina with her legs pointing in her direction. The fact that I didn't see her face confirmed my impression. It was clear that I wasn't meant to see her. I was to be spared further confusion and humiliation. Then too, her face was forever hidden from me by her sin.

When I returned to the dining room I felt more tranquil, and that flicker of obstinacy that had induced me to look into the garden had disappeared.

That night I locked the door to my room, and I didn't open it when the men came and knocked. Marina was scratching on the wall, and I simply told her that if she didn't stop I would call the guards. When she began to insult me I didn't answer, and I merely made sure that the inner panes of my window were tightly shut. During the next few days I scarcely went down to the garden, and when I did go I stayed close to an orderly.

At night I would close the door and the window even though the heat was unbearable. I ignored the noises from behind the wall. I hoped that Vera would call me just once, and every night I would go over the answer I had prepared for her. This hope strengthened my determination and helped me put up with the heat and the other unpleasant aspects of the situation they had created around me.

By this time I was thinking of leaving the sanatorium, and every day I would ask the doctors if there were any news. I was feeling fairly well, and I even managed to curb my appetite. I would spend hours looking at myself in the mirror and I would console myself with the certainty that I looked well and tan. At the beginning of October I started to lose my hair. There was a bare spot at the top of my head, and by the light of the bulb hanging over the sink I could see that I was getting bald.

I wrote a letter to the company directors asking them not to prejudge me and to put me back to work. I also told them about the way Dr. Tortora had behaved toward me. After three days I received an answer telling me not to worry and to continue to take care of myself. The company would give my case the utmost consideration. They concluded by telling me to have faith in Dr. Tortora whose conduct was above suspicion. They assured me that all our troubles and misunderstandings would be cleared up to our mutual satisfaction.

I was very happy, not only because the letter had renewed my hopes but because I was positive the company had realized the enormity of their mistake and were now aware of Dr. Tortora's abuses.

During the weeks prior to leaving the sanatorium I became aware of many things I hadn't noticed during my stay. I decided to investigate the sanatorium section by section. During one of my tours I ran into Dr. Coltori, the head of the sanatorium.

"I know that you want to leave as soon as possible. I don't want to forbid it but I would advise you to stay here for the rest of the winter, at least—long enough to complete the first series of pneumothoracic treatments. Next year you'll be a new man. Will they take good care of you at home? And will you be able to continue the pneumothoracic treatments?" The Neapolitan doctor answered for me. He told him where I lived and where I worked and assured him that the company would certainly look after me, and he added two or three other things in a low voice. "But not before Christmas," concluded Dr. Coltori.

I returned to my room without answering and without paying any further attention to the other doctors including the Neapolitan doctor. I suspected that Dr. Coltori must have had his terrible speech ready ever since he talked to Dr. Tortora on the day I was first admitted to the sanatorium. I hadn't liked the doctor's speech about the factory helping me. Once I was out I didn't want any medical help from the company. I didn't want to fall into the hands of Dr. Tortora and his accomplices again. I had to wait till Christmas, perhaps leave on Christmas Eve.

The doctor's talk robbed me of all the joy I had felt at the thought that I would soon be leaving the sanatorium. I had looked at the front door and the gate in the garden with certainty. They were open, and I felt strong enough to walk the road I could see on the other side of the hedge. Now I had to find that certainty inside myself, for the gate looked like an unyielding barrier marking the limits of my freedom.

I managed to keep going with the help of the chaplain, whom I assisted at mass in the deserted church in the sanatorium. He told me, "In this illness I see many symptoms of rebellion against God and rebellion against yourself."

When the needle of the pneumothorax pierced my ribs I came to the end, and I no longer knew what to think. I wasn't even sure that I wasn't ill or that I was on the verge of being cured of an illness that had never been as terrible as Dr. Tortora had tried to make it. I felt alone; I realized it less clearly than I do today. Today I know that I am alone, but even then the hope of a better future could not deaden the sorrow of my knowledge.

Today I write this letter to everyone and to no one, but I know that this letter is primarily written to my past; to myself, still young and still hopeful as I left the sanatorium Christmas Eve against the advice of the doctors. I left in the evening. It was nearly night. I had been delayed because of another pneumothorax. I walked slowly, and I was afraid that I had made a mistake in leaving. If someone had called me back, anyone, I would have returned. I knew that my pain, that same familiar pain would be waiting for me once I went up the stairs to my room and placed my suitcase on the chair. I headed straight home. At the end of the driveway I found the car the factory had sent. The sanatorium was ablaze with lights, more so than the town; it was on the side of a hill facing the fields and the Mansino woods. It breathed, it was alive, and it seemed to be ready to walk off somewhere under the stars.

France, school, prison, factory, sanatorium; all of them seemed to flow through time, to the left and right, swirling like the sky in a sudden change of season.

IV

DURING JANUARY, FEBRUARY, March, April, and May I went twice a week to the tuberculosis clinic in the city for pneumothoracic treatments. I'm not ashamed to say so because there I was looked after with great kindness by Dr. De Saint Martin. I saw and I felt that he was taking good care of me, without considering my illness too important and making it the dominant factor in my life. As a matter of fact toward April he said I was cured, but he suggested I continue the treatments for a few more weeks to remove any possible doubt of my cure from the mind of even the most zealous doctor in the factory. In the middle of May he told me that the treatments were finished, that I was well, that I could go back to work, and that now I was like any other young man in good health, capable of living my life as I saw fit.

That same day, in the city before even setting foot in the factory, I paid a visit to the Department of Public Safety. I told the clerk who received me that I was completely cured, and I showed him all my papers from the clinic saying that my file with the National Insurance and Welfare Board for Civil Servants was closed. I told him to make a note of this and of the fact that I had been cured of an illness I had not wanted, from an illness that had been forced upon me by others. That evening in Candia I told the priest and the next morning the chief of police. They all congratulated me and wished me luck. And I told them, "If a doctor told you now or soon after this that I was sick, what would you say to him? If you are good Christians you would say that the doctor is a liar and that he is trying to kill me. Yes, wish me luck but above all protect me, by remembering what I have told you."

On the twentieth of May when I got on the bus to go to the factory, I was very frightened. I was as frightened as I was happy. It was the same feeling I had the night I left the sanatorium and during the holidays. That morning the bus seemed to be going very fast. The road was wet from the rain that had begun at dawn and had vanished before sunrise. It filled me with apprehension, or rather, rekindled the apprehension I had felt the previous evening. The rain woke me up as if it too had lain in wait for me all night. It had been a small shower exclusively for me, like the uncertainty of daydreams or an unusual sound. It had caught me at home to tell me not to go out, to stay in, to remain safe within myself and my house, surrounded by the familiar objects of many years. But I had to catch the bus; I had to get dressed because my clothes were ready and waiting for me on the chair at the foot of the bed. I found traces of rain once more on the highway, but the entire countryside and the lake were still, as if it hadn't rained at all. The traces of rain that I saw on the road and in certain streaks of lighter clouds in the sky sapped the force that had driven me to get dressed, get my documents, and leave my house to go once more to the factory.

At that moment the bus was traveling fast, and I couldn't get off. Once I arrived at the factory I couldn't turn back; I had to show everyone that I felt strong within my rights. In this state of mind I walked into the Personnel Department. I was received immediately but almost as quickly I was told by the clerk who was taking care of me that first of all I absolutely had to go to the infirmary for a checkup and a physical aptitude test to see which type of work would suit me best.

"But I work with the power saws," I objected, without mentioning the infirmary and my unwillingness to go there so as not to arouse his suspicion.

"You worked with power saws, and it's possible you'll work there again. But the doctor has to tell me what is best."

Then I understood that I shouldn't hold back any longer. "So, then Dr. Tortora is a better doctor than Dr. De Saint Martin? He cured me personally, and he said that I was fit for anything. What does the factory's doctor have to do with this? Ask the boss and not the doctor and put me back to work. Then come and tell me your troubles."

"Nevertheless, you still have to go to the infirmary. Then I'll be able to assign you to your new job." He called a guard and without another glance at me he said, "Please accompany him to the infirmary. Tell them that it's urgent."

I'll say right away that it was the same Dr. Tortora who examined me now in the infirmary. He was very quick about it; he admitted that I was cured and certified that I could begin to work immediately.

"In the power saw division?"

"Yes, yes, even there. But are you specialized?"

"No, I was waiting for my certificate when you sent me to the sanatorium."

"But then it doesn't matter what type of work you do. You could work in the assembly section or the store rooms, or . . ."

"No, I want to go back with Grosset and the power saws."

"All right, I'll OK it. But I think it would be a good idea to have Dr. Bompiero take a look at you, tomorrow or day after tomorrow. After all, he was the one who took care of you."

Here we go, I thought. Here we go again with the checkups; here we go from one to the other; they'll make me the same speeches, each one adding a final word of his own, a little nastier word each time, to the very end.

When I returned to the Personnel Department it was already noon. The factory noises stopped, and the noise of the voices in the halls and in the offices began. There was always somebody coming to the Personnel Department at that hour; they'd arrive silently, sit in the waiting room and avoid each other's glances. Pensions, change of work, sick leave, a job for a relative, fights with the boss—these were the reasons that brought them to those chairs in silence. Some of them would go faithfully once or twice a week or month, as if it were enough to talk. They used all the excuses they could find just to go and talk, especially if this could be done during working hours; they asked for information on health insurance, on school aid for their children, or they asked about living quarters, a loan, a raise, special food, a transfer. Pinna became one of these men. He began a whole series of inquiries about summer camps, menus, housing, to the point of boredom. Perhaps he even bored himself. Finally it got so that he didn't make a move without asking somebody for something, and he actually ended up by canceling his membership in the Socialist party. Others went to complain about some injustice, and I was one of these. I was one of the ones who spoke the most and was most ignored. It began that twentieth of May. I had to return that afternoon but not before five.

Then the clerk who had waited on me in the morning assigned me temporarily to a power saw division headed by the foreman Manzino. I said that I wanted to go back to Grosset, that my place was there.

"I'd catch it," he answered, and he told me to present myself to Manzino the next day at the C office. I stopped arguing, and walked out to the street. I waited for Grosset, and I caught him just as he was about to get into a car. I told him everything and asked him to take me back into his department. He was happy to see me, and he walked me to the café on the corner and invited me to have a drink. "Why didn't you want to see me when you were in the sanatorium?" he asked. He took me to the train and promised to do everything he could to get me back in his department.

On the way back I didn't feel very well because of the excitement during the day and because of the vermouth I had drunk that was now quivering between my stomach and my mouth. It was even worse because I hadn't eaten anything at noon in order to have time to plan what I had to say to the Personnel Department; speeches I hadn't been able to make now remained stuck in my throat like the vermouth, together with all the ideas I had lined up—ideas which in turn had been annulled by the outcome of my interview. Grosset was my last hope even though he had been the one who turned me over to the guards. I excused him with the thought that his respect for his work was such that it made it impossible for him to oppose the factory, even as a favor to me.

As usual I consoled myself walking along the road toward my house. There were blue mists drifting, not too high and not too low over the lake—only over the lake, like smoke. The sky was serene, and a small moon rode high behind the veil of day. "You see, Albino," I thought, "if only all your troubles were like that mist that the moon will have scattered by midnight."

Before going to bed I looked out the window, and I saw that everything was serene and that the Indian's silk turban was shining on the wall of the barn. It was late because my mother had delayed me. I was crushed that on days like these, days that were important to me, she had only talked about money, about the money that

Public Assistance owed me. And from the sanatorium I even had the chaplain arrange a power of attorney for her so she could withdraw the money I was getting from the factory. I was one of the poorest in the sanatorium, and I had to read the newspapers and books that the others bought. The candy I kept for Vera was candy they had sent me from the factory.

The whiteness of night streamed in the window, and even with its silent spirit it kept me company as it played on the window sill.

The next day I took the factory bus; they gave me a ride although I had to stand all the way. There were people I had never seen on the bus, many young men, many women and girls. I didn't respond to all those glances, and I didn't assume any poses.

I appeared before Manzino, Pier Mario, a skilled worker, feigning a calmness that I couldn't feel. He received me with great kindness, shook my hand, and told me to be frank with him and he would help me in every way he could. If I needed him for any reason whatsoever I could go to him at any time; it would be better, however, if I waited till I finished the work I was doing and stopped the machine, and even better if I waited for the rest periods. According to him there was one thing he couldn't stand: disorganized work, anxiety, filth and unnecessary chatter.

"Only shoemakers, ragged and ugly with long beards and messy hair, are the ones who curse and spit, not we who work for a company like this one. Don't keep photographs, newspapers, or vases with flowers at your work places and always put the oil can back on its shelf under the conveyor belt. That way we'll get along."

He wanted our uniforms to be spotlessly clean, and he wanted us to wear proper shoes instead of wooden ones. "As an antidisaster principle," he would say, "and because the noise is horrible. We're not milkmen."

"He has broken our b—s," muttered Gualatrone, one of the tallest men in the section, with the air of one who had heard Manzino's speech many times and understood its hidden meaning.

That morning when I went back to work Manzino interrupted me twice: "If you keep your head higher you'll be able to see better how the piece is coming out. Go easy on the motor, gently. Pretty fair, pretty fair."

I understood very quickly why Gualatrone and many others couldn't stand Manzino. "One of these days I'll give it to him in the john . . ." Gualatrone unfortunately was another one of the Communists in the factory.

"And what else would I be? It's as clear as day, as day," and he shone all over as if in those moments of faith day were really dawning inside him.

According to what Gualatrone said, Manzino was very reserved with him. "I won't argue, but I don't want him to work in his undershirt or talk too much."

Gualatrone and Manzino had the reputation of being two of the handsomest men in the factory. Manzino was a little bit taller and the effect was heightened by the long gray smock he wore buttoned all the way up to his chin. That is why Manzino had placed his work table in front of all the others facing the corridor and had stuck Gualatrone in the middle of the row of work tables where it was harder to find him.

This business was the life of our section; you couldn't talk, you couldn't read the papers, you couldn't move around. The life of our section were the girls who came around to be seen, Gualatrone's kidding, and Manzino's embarrassing little speeches, begging to be let into your confidence and always hanging around asking yes or no. The work, however, went well with the added advantage as far as I was concerned that our section was not united; that is, we had no interests or activities in common. Leaving or entering our department after Gualatrone finished his orations standing at the door, we would each go our separate ways and not meet again. Maybe we did it because Manzino asked us to do exactly the opposite.

At first I was always running over to Grosset to ask him if he had any news about the transfer, until he finally told me that nothing could be done till after the holidays.

I seldom met Pinna; he was the one who always came looking for me. My friendship for him had cooled ever since the day I returned from the sanatorium when he hugged and kissed me as no one else had done, implying that the others were still afraid of infection, and had said, "Just think, Albino; seventeen months, and you were well! After all, if you had really been sick how long do you think they would have kept you?" I hadn't liked his joke. The weight of the "if" fell heavily on the lid of my thoughts and reminded me of another measure.

Two days after I began working in Manzino's section I was asked to go to the infirmary for my checkup with Dr. Bompiero. Not satisfied with having thumped me, looked me over, and turned me inside out, the eminent doctor decided he wanted to take a new set of X rays. "Here we go again," I thought, "they'll begin to listen to my insides again and to plot against me."

That evening, instead of leaving right away I went back to the Commission of Public Safety and left them a note that said: "On the sixth of May, 1949, Dr. De Saint Martin stated that to all effects and purposes I am completely cured. A few days later, during which period the possibility of a reopened pathological inquest on the state of my lungs is to be eliminated, Dr. Bompiero maliciously wishes to carry on further investigations for the sole purpose of raking up the muck. What does the public security think of this? I ask for its protection."

I made the same speech that evening to the chief of police in Candia.

Only these efforts on my part and the promise of protection I received gave me the peace of mind and strength to go and have new X rays taken. In my heart of hearts I hoped that Tortora and Bompiero would show their hand. I wanted them to have the nerve to say that the X rays showed I was sick, and I wanted them to suggest that I be excused from work again. Then the trap would snap shut—but on them, with the help of the public security and the police in Candia. Unfortunately, as I learned later on, even the public security and the police, or at least the heads of both agencies, were already, as they still are, in league with Tortora, and perhaps even that very night they had rushed to warn him.

At any rate Bompiero had to be satisfied with pronouncing my case "doubtful" and because of his innate meanness adding, "Yes yes, doubtful," and again, so that his mouth would not betray the bitterness of his heart, "Very doubtful."

I didn't pay any attention to the anxious advice he gave me or to his instructions. I watched him closely, ready to shut his mouth.

He didn't say what I most feared. He merely said, "a period for precautions." Once I understood that I could leave and that his little speech wasn't going to stop me from working, at least for the time being, I passively accepted everything he said without screaming at him any of the accusations I had prepared.

I returned to my department relieved of many worries. I was the one who smiled at Manzino, and I ran my hands over the power saw as if it were the first time I had seen it. It was the same model as the one I had when I was with Grosset; it was newer and made less noise, and it was placed in such a way that you weren't bothered by anyone around you as you worked. This allowed me to resume my work without having to make an effort to disguise my mood. I could continue to be alone with my satisfaction. I didn't have to put on an act for anybody. No one here knew my story nor asked for news as Grosset and Pinna would have done.

Hidden by the motor of the power saw I arranged my thoughts; but as usual the order of my thoughts didn't help my situation because my thoughts, neatly lined up in a row, inexorably pointed to my troubles. Consequently, even then—the day of my victory— my thoughts at first multiplied in darkness, weakening the calm conviction of victory. Then they moved into a clearer perspective at the end of which there rose like an altar the vast colonnade of my troubles. How could I truthfully think that Bompiero was beaten? If already, only after a few days he had the gall to doubt Dr. De Saint Martin's proved and positive report, what wouldn't he have the nerve to say and do to me once a few months had gone by?

I tried to calm myself, establishing three immutable rules of conduct: to avoid visits to the infirmary; to go to Dr. De Saint Martin for frequent checkups; to keep the *carbinieri* and the police informed. Furthermore, to work well so that there won't be any incidents in the factory, to live in peace with my mother, and to pray.

On the other hand, I was uncertain about my intention of going back to Grosset's section. At least two people there knew about my illness, and their knowledge kept it alive. It was easier for men to give in to the doctors by recalling my previous history and dragging it out when the occasion demanded. And Grosset and Pinna had completely believed the doctors' story, which they had proved by their attentions, their visits to the sanatorium, their gifts of fruit and chocolates.

I was completely unknown in this department, and perhaps Manzino could really help me in time of trouble, as he always assured me he would whenever he talked to me. While Grosset guided and helped the work along with a look, Manzino came around too often with too many suggestions that only helped to confuse. Manzino was not as pleasant or as easy to take, but he had the advantage of not knowing anything about my illness, and his section was not united; no friends here and no curiosity.

It was wiser therefore not to push my demands for a transfer but to let it go as Grosset had said till after the holidays. In the meantime I could discover other advantages. The noise of the machines had stopped, and Manzino, who had already taken off his smock, called out to me to stop working.

As I passed him he asked me what they had wanted in the infirmary.

It was the first indication that I had not been forgiven, the first of many signs that the factory does not forgive; it doesn't forgive those who remain alone, those who will not bow to its power, those who believe in human justice and invoke its pity; the factory doesn't forgive failures.

I had the courage then to answer Manzino that the infirmary had only wanted some information. Bompiero needed it so that he could close my file on a successful cure.

Manzino looked at me still smiling. "Fine," he said, "I'm glad. Employees should be in good health so that they can produce to my satisfaction. I don't accept persons who are ill; it isn't fair. If you are sick you have the right to stay home."

Today I know only too well the meaning of the right to stay home; I know what it means to wait to get well or, better still to wait every day, every morning that the train goes into the tunnel under the hill to be taken back to work; to be able to go out, get down from my bed, get dressed, and go to work.

The right to stay home is already the beginning of death. That day, however, I was more impressed by Manzino's statement that he didn't want sick people. It seemed directed at me and already intertwined with Tortora's and Bompiero's bad intentions.

Gualatrone saved me at that moment by asking me, in a tone of voice that put an end to my thoughts, whether Manzino was trying to make trouble for me. "He is the type who always has to latch on to someone in order to feel important."

When I was near Gualatrone I felt protected. I envied the hands that he washed under the faucet; he would wash his neck and his shoulders, splash water in his armpits, which were narrow and buried deep in a mass of muscle. He smelled sweet, with an ever stronger smell, and he had the moist and sparkling look that carnations have. I didn't walk with him to the cafeteria because I was shy; I made some excuse and went another way.

Gualatrone could have been a good friend; but I lost even that in the factory.

The weeks before the holiday passed without further incident. It was very hot, and my suffering was even apparent to the others. Gualatrone made me a pretty cardboard spiral that turned slowly above the power saw: while I worked I imagined it was a tower or a flag. But it reminded me of the terrace in the sanatorium during June and July the year before when the wind gently swayed the curtains in the dining room; around two o'clock in the afternoon, the only sound you could hear was the rustle of the curtains.

In the middle of July, I was called to the Public Assistance Office. I already knew the office because of the money I had given my mother during my illness. Even when I began to work again my mother had urged me more than once to go to Public Assistance and ask for further subsidies. I only went once, and they gave me a small sum. They barely remembered my name and they knew only that they had helped me and my dependents during my illness. I returned to the office without the slightest worry. The clerk told me that my name was on the list prepared by the infirmary of those who could go to the mountains for their vacations, all expenses paid by the factory. His manner was so matter of fact that I immediately asked him, "What list is that?"

"It is the list of those who are sick or convalescing that we prepare, based on recommendations from the infirmary."

"I want you to know that I'm not sick and I'm not convalescent because I've never been sick in the first place. I don't need your recommendations, nor any seasonal stay in a sanatorium. I feel fine, and during the holidays in my house I'll even feel better."

"I only want to point out to you that we are not talking about a sanatorium but a hotel in Val d'Aosta, open to the public."

I told him that I couldn't permit them to place me once more on the sick list and that if they did I would ask for another subsidy. I wasn't sick and the infirmary (and by that I meant Dr. Tortora) had to quit trying to find ways to make me and the others believe that I was.

"Are you rejecting the offer?" the clerk asked me without the surprise I expected because of my behavior, not because my behavior was rebellious or unusual but because it was just and pointed directly at Dr. Tortora's trickery. The clerk showed that he didn't understand, and when I answered yes he bent his head over the table and drew a red line through my name. At the end of the line he wrote a capital *R*, the only one on the page.

The idea of that lonely red letter haunted me for several days. What if the doctors used my refusal as an excuse to begin the questions and the checkups? I realized that I had disobeyed the rules I had set down for my own conduct, rules that discouraged the doctors or anyone else from persecuting me. And what if the Personnel Department and the industrious Manzino should mistake my motives for refusing the offer and think that because of personal problems, I didn't feel completely happy with the factory and with my work? Wouldn't this further the plans of Dr. Tortora and his clique? Three days later I decided to phone the Personnel Department to ask them to ignore my refusal and tell them that I was ready to spend my vacation in the hotel.

They told me that my place had been taken by someone else and that they couldn't possibly put me back on the list. I then asked them to forget that I had refused their offer and to please erase the red line and the *R* from my name. I told them that since I really wasn't refusing any longer, as I had stated previously, I would at this point hold them responsible for my exclusion. So the least they could do was erase the *R*.

Unfortunately, my attempts were useless. A few days later as I was beginning to feel easier about the way I had managed to arrange matters, Tortora called me to the infirmary. I didn't go, but the same afternoon someone whose name is not important called Manzino to tell him what had happened. The factory and its total organization had reopened their attack on me. After the phone call Manzino called me to his table. "Dr. Tortora wants to see you," he said, "and you have to go; there is no way you can refuse. The doctor is the factory doctor, and in yours and the factory's interest he can make appointments for visits and checkups and so forth . . . He wants to get to know your capacity."

"But there is a difference between the factory and the doctor."

"What do you mean? There isn't any difference. Dr. Tortora decides certain things for the factory."

"But is the factory against me? Does it have any reason to harm me?"

"No."

"Well, Tortora does. Tortora has decided to ruin me. From the first day, at every opportunity. The factory doesn't have anything to do with this at all. As a matter of fact, it should help me."

"Why is Tortora against you?"

"I don't know. Meanness perhaps."

"I don't believe it. At any rate you have to go to him and tell him frankly your reasons for feeling this way. Then you can always appeal to the Board of Directors."

"The Board of Directors?"

"Yes, to the Board of Directors of the company. There they will be able to distinguish between the factory and the doctor. In the meantime remember that Dr. Tortora is expecting you at nine tomorrow morning. He only wants to talk to you. I'm telling you that if you don't go to him I won't be able to put you back to work."

I returned to my place, and I felt death on my shoulders, the end of everything. Gualatrone looked at me; he walked around his machine to get a better look at me, and he made a gesture with both hands, a hugging and lifting movement, a gesture of help. I continued to work, looking down at my hands and my arms often to convince myself that I existed. Manzino came over to me at quitting time and said, "Now don't forget Dr. Tortora tomorrow morning and keep cool; any of your well-founded complaints will be listened to."

On my way back home on the train, Giuliana, one of the waitresses in the cafeteria, came and sat down next to me. I didn't know her very well. Besides her name I knew only that she lived somewhere near me. Today I know very well what it was she wanted from that very first evening with her talk about work, the life of the factory, and the village. She sat close to me during the whole trip, so much so that her handbag kept bumping my knee.

"It's hot," she said. "It's hot. The heat is unbearable in the cafeteria. You people who work in the other departments are much better off. What section do you work in? I see you once in a while with Gualatrone. But how long have you been eating in the cafeteria?"

Her chatter was pleasant, and it distracted me from my fear of tomorrow's visit with Dr. Tortora. I looked at her arms projecting from the sleeves of her blouse, lovely and pink. She had the skin of a blond although her hair was darker. There was a curly strand of blond in her hair that she kept patting and rearranging while she talked, repeating her words. She moved her hands a great deal. After she patted her hair she would rest her hands on her pocketbook near my knees. Her hands were also very pink and the fingernails were broken. They looked like the hands of a fourteen- or fifteen-year-old boy, quick hands, neither a man's nor a woman's. No one could have dreamed that one day those hands would try to poison me.

When the train arrived in Candia, I shook hands with her and started to walk toward the village. I wanted to alert the priest and the chief of police once more about what was going on; but I couldn't find either of them. Finally I decided that it would be better if I spoke to them the next day after I had seen Dr. Tortora. By then I would know what he was planning.

Tortora received me immediately. "Good morning," he said. "How are you? How do you feel? Are you happy with your work? Why do you act this way with me and with the other doctors?"

I remained silent. I certainly didn't have any intention of falling into the dear doctor's trap. He continued with his nice round

[111

mouth and his ten enormous fingers drumming on the table.

"Now why don't you want to go to the mountains? What's this business all about? The men compete with each other, try to fool us in every way imaginable in order to have the factory pay for their vacation and you consider it an offense. Why on earth do you? I try in good conscience to help you. Once you were sick; today after treatments you are better, nearly well, and just at the most critical point of your convalescence you hold back, fight us. Now you must be frank with me; you must tell me what dark thought makes you doubt us, what torments you to the point of making you suspicious and afraid."

I couldn't tell him my thoughts; the moment I did so he would have thrown me out of the factory. I only said, "I am well, and I don't think it's necessary for me to cure an illness I haven't got. I can continue to work peacefully."

"That's for us to say, my friend, if you are well or if you are sick. And the tests we have made and X rays we have taken of you are more than the tests and X rays we take for an entire department. But I certainly don't have to justify Dr. Bompiero's behavior and mine. Our conclusions are irrefutable. I don't have to justify myself. And as a matter of fact I'm going to ask you to stop maligning me and the infirmary or else we shall not be able to be friends any longer. I have here the note you left the clinic. For the good of everybody they decided to clear this matter up and make me the judge of what is to be done. They could have given you some very unpleasant moments—made things very difficult for you: defamation of character and so on . . ."

"But Dr. De Saint Martin?"

"Very well. Now we come to the great man! Well now, I'll tell you everything. Did you know that Dr. De Saint Martin worked in this very infirmary before Dr. Bompiero? And did you know that because of his age he was judged incapable of handling the immense amount of work in the accurate and precise fashion demanded by the factory? This means that Dr. De Saint Martin has a grudge, and unfortunately he says white—and I'd like to think he does so in good faith—when we say black, and vice versa. If we had said that you were well, he immediately would have said you were sick. Put aside all your uncertainties, trust us, and go to the mountains. I'll have them give you back your place. After the mountains we will have to see you again and with our help . . ."

How could I answer a speech like this? I detected his deception in every word and in the kindness of his tone, and because of this I was incapable of answering back. I couldn't even pretend; he expected me to tell him the truth. The situation was based on such a lie, as well as the factory and everything around me, that if I had told him the truth I would have been automatically fired.

I didn't say anything, and I agreed to go to the mountains, to Valtournanche in Val d'Aosta. It wasn't a sanatorium; it was a hotel where the people from the factory occupied one floor. We slept two in a room, and we ate very well, breakfast, lunch, a snack, and dinner. We took short walks, but not all of us.

I would walk in the morning and in the evening; the rest of the time I slept or read. Before leaving I had taken some books out of the library, both in Italian and French, just to see if I could brush up on the language of my childhood. I had also taken out a book about the Val d'Aosta: *Le Lepreux de la Cité d'Aoste*. This book, which I read slowly, moved me so much that I would often find myself sharing the poor leper's tears and the cruelty of his destiny and wondering if my luck could be worse than it was already. When I came to the part where the leper's sister dies I couldn't control myself and my terrible sense of loneliness so that on that same night after warning the man who slept in the other bed I left the hotel and the town and returned home.

I arrived at my house filled with great happiness, with my heart open to everything, to the lane, to the trees, to the shutters. My mother received me with great surprise. She was amazed to see me and she kept asking such commonplace questions that she took the edge off my enthusiasm. As I looked at her so old and greedy, so suspicious of everything, I wondered if it was for her sake that I had left the mountains and walked so far to get to the railroad station? I looked at her for a long time, but I couldn't recognize in this old woman any of the images I had in my heart of my mother. That same day I returned to Valtournanche. I arrived when the others were just going to bed. My roommate, who as usual had gone to bed immediately after dinner, must have told the others that I had gone off to be with some woman.

[113

I was very unhappy. I went to bed holding the book about the poor leper.

Time passed very quickly in the mountains, and the rain of the last few days calmed me, filling my heart with the serenity and tenderness of autumn.

It was still summer in the city, and work was very tedious. There was some talk about shorter work contracts and a rumor that the mayor was going to ask for a minimum wage increase. Manzino had returned from the seashore all tanned and with his hair cut shorter. Gualatrone grumbled about the work contracts and Scelba. "The longer you let Scelba stay in office the shorter the contracts will become," he would say, punctuating his remarks with a belly laugh. "Go on," Manzino told him once when he heard him as he was leaving the department. "Go on. Scelba doesn't even know how long the contracts run." "Then he's pretty ignorant," answered Gualatrone.

That day I had an appointment with Tortora. He told me that my stay in the mountains must certainly have done me a lot of good and that he didn't think he had to prescribe any new remedies. Perhaps a little vitamin C before winter set in as a precaution against the cold weather. But all his kindness was once more proven false when toward the end of my visit he announced that it wouldn't be a bad idea if Bompiero looked me over some time around November. They had drawn their battle plans, and they were proceeding slowly with a malice that made their success inevitable. I decided to retaliate. Following the advice Manzino had given me before the holidays, I wrote a letter to the Board of Directors telling them about Dr. Tortora and his behavior toward me. I thought it was fair to write it at that moment of amnesty between Tortora and myself, at a time when there wasn't any specific issue between us, so that they wouldn't think the letter was a defense.

I had learned my lesson from the police when they had given my note to Tortora—of all people—and consequently my letter read, "And what if the factory's doctor makes a mistake? And what if contrary opinions exist? Who is to establish the truth about a case in such a way that those in authority are not the judges, especially when their judgment is colored by a desire to persecute the workers?"

After three days I received an answer which I still have.

DEAR MR. SALUGGIA:

We are writing in the name of the President of the Board of Directors, who has asked us first of all to tell you how much he regrets not being able to write to you personally. His busy schedule at present is rendered even busier by an imminent and prolonged visit to America that keeps him from doing so.

We can assure you that the President has given your case his most careful attention and expressed his amazement at the contents of your letter, together with his regrets for the unfortunate circumstances that prompted you to write it. We can further assure you that as a matter of principle our organization, based on a well-founded system of supervision and control—a system, however, which does not diminish the personal responsibility of the individual toward his work regardless of his position in the factory—excludes the possibility that there exist cases of injustice because of rank and even worse, judgments detrimental to the liberty of those individuals who participate in the life of the factory, dictated by a deliberate desire to harm and offend. However, there is the possibility of appealing to various levels of company authority whose function it is to correct any possible errors or unfortunate interpretations of the established rules that govern the behavior of each and every individual in the factory.

In specialized fields, such as the medical department, the judges can be supervised by qualified consultants as in your case, where scientific judgment has been passed by Dr. Bompiero.

We would like to add that even through means other than the usual channels of communication provided by the factory we have never received less than reassuring reports on the capacity and integrity of our doctors, especially Dr. Tortora, in whom the President himself places his complete trust.

We hope that our letter will give you the peace of mind available to all those who work for our company, and we ask you to place yourself with complete faith in the hands of Dr. Tortora and his assistants, with whose conduct, even in your case, we are in complete accord.

Our best wishes,

(Signed) OSCAR CARPUSI
Secretary of the Board of Directors

[115

I read this letter over many times with mounting fear. It seemed as if these very sentences, their meanings, their periods, commas, and indentations, were more of Tortora's traps. They resembled him. I don't know exactly how, but they resembled him. I had the urge to read the letter out loud.

The President, who was the one who was supposed to have answered my letter, was only mentioned twice, at the beginning and at the end of the letter saying that he had complete faith in Dr. Tortora. If the factory had already decided to mass against me, whom would I have on my side? No one or perhaps only my sorrow, myself, prayers, and justice, that sense of justice that even today keeps me from surrendering.

Two days later I was convinced that the Secretary of the Board of Directors had been ordered by Dr. Tortora to keep my letter from reaching the President.

By then I knew that Carpusi was Tortora's friend and that if I was to have justice I would have to knock at another door. Perhaps the Bishop's.

But Tortora didn't bother me for a long time. I kept on working, traveling back and forth, and getting tired. In the cafeteria I would eat only the soup. Summer continued even after September and from my window I could see that the lake looked very small. I would look at it at night, still clear with the moon high above, and on Sunday mornings while I was waiting for my mother to cook lunch.

All Souls' Day arrived, and they still hadn't called me from the infirmary.

The first of November, a holiday, fell on a Friday; Saturday was a workday; Sunday the third and Monday the fourth were holidays. The factory gave us Saturday and declared a long week end. The good weather was over. It began to rain during those four days and it kept on raining harder and harder. In the rain I weeded and trimmed the garden, so that the flowers and vegetables would grow strong and prosper. I shook the bushes, tied the tomatoes, and smoothed out the leaves from the wrinkles of summer. I arranged them so that they would catch the first rain, and while I worked I constantly thought about my troubles and the factory.

In the factory I would forget about my house and even my

mother, but at home I could never forget the factory or Dr. Tortora. On the fifth of November, after having thought and come to certain decisions, I went once more to Grosset to ask him to have me transferred to his department, and I asked him to do the same thing for Gualatrone, who was tired of Manzino.

Grosset said that it was impossible and that according to the latest instructions all changes and transfers were to be handled by another office.

I saw Pinna again; he was happy, as usual. He told me that he was waiting for his papers and that soon he would be moving to the Machine Tools Department. When Gualatrone heard about this he said, "They move up from the other departments but never from ours."

As a matter of fact, we felt and gave the impression of standing stock-still. The entire department had come to a halt. We worked and we moved about, but the way that Manzino made us work, the orderliness, the silence, the furtive glances, the exaggerated cleanliness, the very way he spoke, his way of approaching us, of addressing and of asking us questions, all these things seemed fake; everything was fake, but unchangeable.

Gualatrone was the only one in the department who fought this tendency. He would get excited and wave his arms, but even he was always the same and eventually he became part of the picture. You could talk to him better outside of the department. After work, all the others disappeared from sight. Gualatrone changed color and became more handsome the moment he cupped his hands under the faucet of the sink in the locker room.

During the entire month of November, while I was waiting to be called by Dr. Bompiero, I thought about the way we worked in our department. I began to realize that we were all being enveloped by a great sense of boredom, including myself who had always considered the factory my battlefield. I didn't like the factory as much as I used to; it was less beautiful, it was worn and stifling, and even the engineers and department heads who used to pass by in the halls like the light from a window and always alone, now were more accessible and often you would run into them at the elevators and hear them laugh and talk.

I didn't enjoy the work so much, and the machine didn't thrill me any longer: even its noise was unbearable. If I hadn't been there to run it, it would have gone on spinning uselessly for a whole day, without biting the steel or finishing any of the pieces. I had known this from the start, but the knowledge was only now beginning to disturb me. Everything seemed to be getting more boring every day, and even the machine was an added weight that I had to bear. The steel pieces to be cut, all lined up in their box, frightened me at first and then annoyed me. How many pieces were there? One exactly like the other, indistinguishable one from the other. Which would be the first piece I would handle and which the last, and why? How many times would I have to go back and forth, fit the pieces into the machine, start the motor, bend down, blow on them and put them back in their place? At the beginning when there were only a few finished pieces in the box, they looked like poor little orphans, dressed in gray with their mouths open, showing their teeth. The pieces to be finished were in the majority, they were arrogant and they reminded me of a regiment armed with swords. The swords established a balance between the two boxes and produced a continuous traffic back and forth between the boxes.

In the evening when it was time to quit, the box with the finished pieces sparkled in the light: they had won and they looked like proud polished officers in comparison to the surviving few from the other side. Some evenings I would let some oil from the machine fall on the finished pieces so that they wouldn't shine so much in their undeserved glory. Manzino saw me once and smiling, as usual, he said that I didn't have to do that since the pieces wouldn't be there long enough to get rusty: they were sent directly to the assembly line the next morning, and they didn't need all that extra care. He hadn't understood anything, and he didn't realize that I would have liked to follow the box into another department. Perhaps even with my promotion papers.

That's the way I spent my days behind the boxes of finished and unfinished pieces. This was the measure of my time, the knowledge that spread like a pale light over every object in the factory, as in a dream. My life was going by behind those boxes. There were many who had been doing the same work for twenty years, and they were still young. The work wasn't heavy, but it made you tremble because of the continuous fight with time, not just the factory's time but time in general.

Vacations are the days you spend waiting for other boxes filled with unfinished pieces. Even those who grumble about the number of pieces to finish, about the noise or the heat, shake their heads hopelessly in the face of this pretense: the real effort was to use up your time in the factory, in the same place, in the uselessness of work.

Those things that at the beginning had seemed like the advantages of factory life had slowly become its drawbacks. Those who worked in Candia, walking back and forth, fiddling with motors and banging doors, and who tried out the different paints on the doors and on the walls, were much better off. I would see them once in a while in the café drinking and talking; I never saw anybody from the factory.

I thought that if I got my promotion papers I would be able to go to another department and put an end to this situation. In the meantime I was getting to know my companions better. I learned to know them by their gestures during work, those who worked with their shoulders raised, those who worked with their shoulders lowered, those who bent completely over, and those who stood up straight, and all of them with their hands spread out in front of them as if to warm them and protect themselves.

And all their faces were twisted in some grimace the way you do when you stand facing a very hot fire. One stretched the muscles of his neck, the other would press his lips tightly together. Another would narrow his eyes, and still another would wrinkle his forehead. It meant that they all had one thought that beat inside their heads and bounced off every object in the factory and kept on beating. The factory didn't provide any distractions from such a thought: a tree, a bird, a word, a passer-by. It wasn't enough to raise your eyes from your work: there wasn't anything around that wasn't a piece of factory equipment.

The work itself didn't help. It didn't require any thought; it went on by itself pulling our hands along. Nothing else was possible in the factory. Even the talk became a habit; it was always the same. Only when work was about to end, while we cleaned our machines and put our places in order waiting to leave, did the talk change. It broadened, if only by a few words.

Only after most of the others had left did one feel that there were men working in the factory; these were the few who went to the cafeteria for their evening meal, or men on a part-time shift who worked better alone. Four thousand people cannot work together, all at once. That was why I had to get my promotion papers.

In the evening I would walk slowly out of the factory because I didn't want to run to catch the train and plunge myself into this other factory: get off the train, say good-by again to my companions and then immediately run home to dinner. Especially since my mother gave no sign of understanding my worries during this period.

Once I left the factory I would walk slowly toward the center of the city. I would go into the library for a minute and browse slowly among the books without ever finding one I liked. Then I would continue my walk, stopping at all the shop windows. There was a bar where they sold ice cream. I would go in and sit down for a minute and buy a fifty-lira ice cream. Often this was my only dinner because I didn't feel like going to the factory cafeteria. Afterwards I would go to the movies. As I bought my ticket I could smell the darkness and the calm of the auditorium. I would sit in one of the front rows toward the side where it was usually less crowded. There my thoughts would quiet down, till at last I could relax and pay attention to the screen. I would leave the theater around a quarter to ten. I'd pass the bar again and stop in for coffee; then I would go directly to the station. At the tobacco shop in the station I would buy a pack of twenty cigarettes, which had to last me till the next evening at the same time. In the movies I enjoyed searching for one of the remaining cigarettes in the half-empty pack without looking.

It was very cold as I walked from the station to my house at night, and I felt the wind blow on my skin as it blew over the lake making the water race from one shore to the other. I still hadn't started to wear my overcoat, and my mother would cry because she was afraid I would catch cold. Every night she'd ask me why I returned so late. But by then I would feel a long shiver of sleepiness and warmth run through my body, and I would go to bed without answering.

On the fourth or fifth of December I put on my overcoat. It was the same day that Bompiero called me to the infirmary for my checkup. Just at the time when I had nearly convinced Manzino to ask for my promotion papers. I had had three long talks with him; one evening I walked home with him, explaining what a change the promotion papers would make in my life.

But Bompiero ruined all my chances. "Come back to work after Epiphany. If you go on this way, you won't get through the winter without getting worse. Please listen to me."

The head nurse and a girl, the social assistant, were waiting for me at the door.

The social assistant said, "Don't worry about anything; we won't open a new National Insurance and Welfare Board file on you. You'll stay home on regular sick leave, like someone who needs rest. National Health will take care of everything, and we will add a clause in your report that will enable you to draw your full salary while you are away."

During the month of December and the holidays I went every afternoon to the movies in Turin; I would leave Candia at three o'clock, and at eight thirty in the evening I was back at the station. Twice I went to X just to look at the factory.

It didn't snow that Christmas.

V

I WENT BACK TO WORK on January seventeenth, and I immediately went to Manzino to ask him about my promotion. He said that it wasn't the right moment. I went back to him after fifteen days, and he turned me down again. He smiled all the time. "There's nothing to smile about," I told him; and for some reason I added, "Nothing at all," in Neapolitan dialect.

Manzino didn't let me go back to our section but sent me instead to the engineer in charge of all our departments, Mr. Pignotti. The engineer was very tall. He was pacing back and forth, smoking a cigarette when I arrived. As I came closer he hunched his shoulders and arched his neck the way chickens do sometimes; then he looked at me. After he had heard my story he said: "Come back in ten days."

They let me return to my section and resume my work. I deliberately gunned the motor of my machine, wishing it would break. Manzino didn't say anything because he hadn't noticed what I was doing. Any other foreman would have come over immediately to see what all the noise was about.

This made me think of Grosset. I went to see him and told him everything. I also asked him for the transfer. "I'll do everything I can," he answered. "It will be even more difficult now that Pignotti is in the picture. Be careful of him." We ate together in the cafeteria where he made me finish all my meat and urged me to take care of myself; being healthy was much more important than being promoted, he said. I answered that I didn't want the promotion because of the money but because it meant a change.

"Nothing changes," he said. "How many times I've wished I could change. I would have gone with Saragat; he's right about lots of things. But why should I leave the union, why create factions inside the factory? You have to be strong in many ways if you want to get along in here."

It was the first time that Grosset had ever spoken to me about politics and looked me straight in the eye, conquering that timidity that distracted him so at other times. Grosset's confidence consoled me, and finally the day arrived for my appointment with the engineer, Pignotti.

Pignotti told me immediately that he remembered me and that he had thought about my case. He was unfamiliar with Manzino's section and a large part of the other sections in the department. They were like a dark island in the middle of the factory.

"But let's get back to you. Why did you talk that way to Manzino? He is one of the best foremen in the factory, and I believe that he treats you all very well. That's what so hard to understand about you people; if a foreman treats you decently and politely you call him a hypocrite and you make fun of him. If he is firm with you, you say that he is presumptuous, you accuse him of being a jailer or the boss's pet; then you end up by siding with some foreman who is more severe than any of the others. This is one of the mysteries of the factory. I won't punish you this time. But I would like to know why you answered Manzino that way. Did he provoke you? Or has the unfavorable talk circulating in your department about the directors given you the idea that you can behave this way?"

He didn't give me a chance to speak, but sat down with his elbows on the desk and lowering his booming voice added, "Speeches are made outside the factory and even then you've got to be careful."

By the end of the interview I still didn't know what Pignotti had meant. He hadn't let me say a word; I had barely mentioned the promotion when he immediately said, "The promotion is nothing. It can be had as well as not. It's not the promotion that—"

The heart of the speech was in that ambiguous phrase that would keep me in doubt for days on end. But Pignotti sent for me again the next day. This time he was more conclusive. He began by talking about my life, the prison, the factory, my illness, my mother, and he concluded by asking me to become a spy in the department. Today I can talk this way because I have understood many other things; but then I was confused and I almost refused to understand the meaning of his words. It was difficult to understand him; the double meanings and the hints confused me.

Pignotti was embarrassed at the end of his speech. His glance roamed all over his desk, and he kept shaking his head. He wanted information that would help him to know how best to run the department. He wanted information about the morale, the talk, and the men. "Do you always pay attention to the talk going on?" At this point I realized that even unimportant talk was important and that my promotion was involved because Pignotti said immediately, "If you keep on working well, I'll let you have your promotion in a couple of months."

I must confess that when I left his office I was almost proud of the offer even though I wasn't inclined to accept it right away. I tried to convince myself that it was for everybody's good. Maybe I could even get a transfer for Gualatrone. But slowly I became very sad, and I understood that Pignotti was even worse than Tortora. He, too, had singled me out but in a way that was much more vile. I was certain that I was neither the first nor the last worker who had dealt with him. He didn't know me, nor could any of his friends have recommended me to him. Then why had he chosen me to be a spy? He had spoken about many of my troubles, and he seemed to know my history very well; he had even said, "Don't worry about Tortora; I'll take care of that." What was there so vile in me that could give him the idea or the impression that I would carry out his suggestions? I thought that perhaps he had interpreted my solitude as a sign of resentment against the others; but if he had misunderstood my story to that extent then how very low had the mighty Pignotti fallen.

Plagued by all these doubts, I went to confession to the priest in Candia hoping that someone better than I, someone with more education, would be able to understand Pignotti's speech and intentions. The young priest whom I greatly admired began by saying that it was a serious issue but not as serious as I had led him to believe.

"You know, Albino, governing men is always very difficult. We cannot judge. What if the engineer meant well? We have to fight Communism, establish order and moral principles; we have to settle everything well. The factory is a difficult place, and you know it. The seed of indifference to God is planted in the factory. Do you know that a short time after one of my parishioners is hired by the factory, he doesn't bother to come to church any more? The women become freer with themselves and the men more arrogant. Maybe Pignotti was merely referring to these issues that have to be faced. You must judge according to your conscience. Don't get alarmed right away. Try to talk to him again and see if you can understand his meaning better."

"But he wants me to be a spy."

"That's a pretty strong word, spy! Is there a war going on in the factory that you need spies?"

"Yes, there is a war," said Grosset as soon as I had told him everything. "That's exactly what there is, a war, and Pignotti would beat us to make us work if he could. What have we come to in such a few years? After the liberation our dear Pignotti was as meek as a little lamb; as a matter of fact, toward the end he even helped us to turn out machine guns. I guess all his old ambitions have come back. He wants to be boss, he wants to be boss at any cost. There really is a war; not till the factories belong to everyone will we ever work in peace. And even then we'll have to be careful. But you, every once in a while, go to Pignotti and tell him something. Tell him that the men complain about the food and the pay, and that's enough."

I didn't even have the courage to do this, and I didn't go to Pignotti again. A few months later they said that he had invented a new type of machine and after that, no one could see him anymore; they spoke about him as if he were the President. After a few more months he left the factory and Italy to go and take charge of some mines in Brazil. No one missed him. Once Manzino mentioned that Pignotti was a great organizer, and even Pinna said the same thing, probably because he remembered that Pignotti had gotten him his transfer.

"At what price, Pinna?" I felt like asking him, and I'd still like to ask him today, now that he's doing specialized work; but I'm not bad and I don't even want to think bad thoughts.

The whole affair with Pignotti had left me slightly depressed, with dark thoughts about the factory and this life. Not even Grosset's explanations satisfied me. He examined everything and ended up by minimizing the importance of work. Gualatrone remained a good friend, and every once in a while he would accompany me to the movies. One night when it was snowing very hard he didn't let me go back to Candia but made me spend the night in his house.

He slept in a small bed against the wall. It was hardly big enough for him, and he slept with his arms outside the covers as if it were summer. Before he went to bed I saw that he had made an awkward sign of the cross and kissed one of his fingers. Lying in the other bed I felt stronger and more protected than I felt at home. Roberto —that was Gualatrone's first name—Roberto's sleep was so peaceful and innocent that I felt I had returned to my boyhood in Avignon.

Three days later I was called by the social assistant. She only wanted to know how I was doing and if I had received my regular salary during my absence. When I was about to leave she asked me if I was planning to go home on the train right after work. I said no because I had to go to the movies. She was amazed and began to lecture me, but I told her quickly that I had to go to the movies. And that was that.

I kept working at the same job in my department, and I still didn't have my promotion. The work tired me now, tired me very much, and the weariness that I seemed to read clearly on the others' faces was like a dead weight on my shoulders. I didn't like the fact either that Gualatrone was having a messy affair with one of the secretaries. She was an older woman, and she had a husband. He had told me about it himself, and he hinted at the times of their meetings which took place nearly always in the factory. They would meet in the bathroom, one day in the morning, the next in the afternoon. Always at different hours which they agreed on the day before. When I saw him leave to go to those meetings I would be very upset, and it seemed as if I saw Manzino sniggering to himself because he was sure that Gualatrone would get into trouble.

One day while standing on line for the cafeteria I noticed that Gualatrone's girl friend was in front of me, full of smiles, flaunting her big rear end that stretched the black silk of her uniform. I managed to step heavily on one of the bare toes sticking out of her sandals.

I became more irascible every day, always in a black mood and so bitter that I couldn't even blame my troubles for my bitterness. I was this way with my mother but most of all at work. Everything made me angry and, I repeat, my anger didn't have anything to do with my troubles; as a matter of fact, it kept my troubles at bay and gave me another personality and other worries. But this couldn't really do me any good and in the end I would be left even more defenseless.

The carnival season with the ambiguous atmosphere it spread over the factory made me even angrier. I would kick over the box with the unfinished pieces, and that noisy flow of metal was like a signal, like an incentive to further destruction and chaos. So I would break everything I could, from the chain on the toilets to the water glasses in the locker room. I would snarl at my companions, and if I could I would have hit them. My work suffered; and my quota went down. Yet the more it went down, the more pleasure I derived from my humiliation and the less work I did.

Maybe all this was happening because I hadn't received my promotion, or because the work tired me and the effort of staying in one place was too great. My life at the factory didn't progress as I had thought it would at the beginning; as a matter of fact, any progress was hampered by many of the problems I still carried over from my army and prison-camp days besides other problems of a serious nature which were a natural consequence of my advancing years.

During carnival my companions increased their attitude of patient forbearance toward me, and that of course was a greater offense than any direct insult: smiles, unfinished phrases, gestures. My desire to escape from them was so great that I was driven to the point of throwing a hammer at an old fool named Borgofranco. The atmosphere of terror that spread over the entire department and the false generosity they all adopted in my behalf in order to cover up the incident were even more unbearable, till I reached the point where I felt like repeating the scene at the very moment when Manzino came into the room.

All hell broke loose. I was sent to the Personnel Department and

[127

they began an investigation. At last I had found the means to be heard, and I told them everything from A to Z, beginning with Tortora and ending with the promotion. The Personnel Department gave me a written warning, but they didn't answer any of my questions.

The days following were even worse. I absolutely couldn't bear the looks my companions gave me, for their glances seemed exaggeratedly curious and alarmed. Manzino talked to me as little as possible. I would look for any excuse to leave the room and go and talk to anybody who would listen to me, from the guards to the clerks in the Personnel Department. There I would always ask them for a promotion and a transfer; unfortunately I couldn't get the head man's assistance because I didn't want to appeal to Mr. Pignotti. I was tempted to do it several times and always with the intention of volunteering my services; but each time my resentment would melt away and I would return to my department thinking about Sergeant Vattino, lying sick in the concentration camp; Sergeant Vattino, who would greet me with tears in his eyes. It seemed as if he were telling me something now in addition to the advice he had given me then. He was telling me that there were certain things you just couldn't do, that it was unworthy to be a spy.

The Personnel Department had promised me a transfer, and they assured me they were waiting for a good opening for me.

The social assistant was the one who listened with the greatest interest to my talk. She would ask me to explain certain things and also ask me about events that had taken place in my life before I began to work in the factory. However, she didn't want to see me more than once a week and after a month or two she said that she could only see me once every fifteen days because she already knew the whole story and the only important thing from now on was to analyze any new developments and see what could be done to bring the whole matter to a satisfactory conclusion. I would prepare myself for these talks by carefully writing down in a little book every new event that took place; but I must confess that these weren't many because my talks dealt with my life and its very real problems: my troubles, Tortora's faked diagnosis, the promotion and the transfer.

128]

The days passed, and once again it was time for the holidays and once again I agreed to go to the hotel in the mountains.

Autumn would bring me my greatest suffering and the beginning of my downfall in the factory.

I can now say that in the course of thinking about myself and the factory I have arrived at several very sound conclusions that apply not only to me but to all the others who work with me. Only now do I realize that problems like minimum wages, production quota, this or that type of work, are all relatively unimportant and do not influence our life in the factory. The trouble is that the factories as they exist today slowly rob all those who work in them of the feeling that they are on this earth alone and with others and all the things of this earth. In this way one forgets the true destiny of man and this vision is replaced by an ever-increasing pride in the factory, in the machines, and in the organization that succeeds in doing things no man has ever done or dreamed of doing before. One can even go so far as to suppose, with a certain conviction, that the factory can change men's personal history and sentiments and fill them with other thoughts besides that of living in peace and freedom with their fellow men. One can even imagine a man no longer created in the image and likeness of God on this earth; but created in the image of a machine, tied to a machine, belonging to a different race. Now I can say, after having tried so many different roads, both inside and outside the factory, and after so many painful failures, that this is the problem of all industry in general, from the cities where it grows to the trains and buses that serve it, from its image in the newspapers to its workers, vast as an army, an army like my lake, always beating its head against the same shore. All industry should be controlled, for if it isn't it will no longer be a means toward a better life on this earth, but it will become an implement of sorrow and the way to a speedy exit from this life.

The men who have been lucky and have the better jobs in the factory feel this pride; in the end they are the most unhappy. There are also those who fall, those who cannot manage to keep up with industry, those who work in sorrow till the last moment when they are thrown out or they rebel. They are luckier, for they remain men!

I wanted to say these things that I know today but didn't know those first days in autumn. I made many speeches then that I will now write down. I made them when it seemed that there was no way out for me, no practical solution for my situation within the factory, when I was beginning to arrive at the conclusion I have already set down, when I was overpowered by the crushing burden of my sorrows and the world's injustice I could not and would not accept. Nor could those who hinted at these conclusions fully understand or explain them, for they were hampered by their position in the factory. They would have had to betray their function, which has always been to find ways and means where there are none and justice where injustice is the working principle upon which everything else is founded. And most assuredly they—the social assistant, the foreman, the Personnel Department, the syndicate—could not reveal their hand to me, but the most rotten apple in the barrel turned out to be Mr. Polverini, a lawyer from Milan. He was consultant supervisor, and I went to him, encouraged by his title.

After two or three visits during which he tried to make my case into a general case applicable to all who worked in the factory, after he had examined all its aspects, ramifications and complexities, after having practically admitted that by its very nature industry was an evil thing and that dissatisfaction with the existing situation in industry was not my personal monopoly, he concluded by trying to convince me and all those who talked to him about me that, contrary to Dr. Tortora's diagnosis, I wasn't sick but crazy.

But I might as well continue my story and describe how these things took place.

I had begun my routine of work and going to the movies again after a whole month's vacation during which I hadn't been able to go either to work or to the movies. A few days after I was back at work, the social assistant sent for me. Manzino told me that it was "just for a talk"; the social assistant had something to tell me, and he added that I didn't have to go if I didn't want to. But why should I turn down a talk about things that concerned me?

Manzino's uncertainty made me think that the news had something to do with my transfer or my position in the department, and for that reason I was all the more eager to keep the appointment with the social assistant. Besides I had some unfinished business with her that had been pending ever since before the holidays. I remember that she was still wearing summer clothes and it disturbed me because I had already plunged headlong into autumn, the resumption of my evenings at the movies.

She didn't have any news for me, only questions. How was I? How had I enjoyed the mountains? How was my mother? And I told her, "But these are all questions!"

"Why do you say that?" she answered.

"Because Manzino told me that you had some news for me."

"Yes, I do have something to tell you. But since we know each other so well I think it's very natural for me to ask about you and your health. I am asking you directly so you must realize that my questions are not unjustified."

I answered briefly and unwillingly, even though the questions reopened many of the old wounds and encouraged me to speak about my troubles and my transfer.

The relaxed feeling of the holidays was about to be swallowed up by the bitterness I felt toward my work, the same as before. Already after a month all the old troubles were coming back again. Besides, there was the heat spell that gave no sign of breaking. Every morning and every evening I would look at the lake to see if it was covered with mist, the mist that called the rain; but the lake remained shiny and small. One afternoon during the first days of October we had a storm with enormous bursts of thunder crashing the sky and a downpour of rain. It was during working hours and the storm seemed like a defect in the machinery of the factory, especially since it deprived us of electricity. All the windowpanes were rattling, and they looked as if they were on fire. Inside the factory the different departments and the machines were wrapped in a green darkness. The lightning illuminated the beams in the ceiling, the crossbeams, and the joints. The storm made us see the horrible skeleton of the factory, indifferent, tall, built and standing—but not for us.

[131

No one spoke. It was as if we had all landed together pell-mell in that one place, or as if we understood its monstrosity for the first time and realized that we were powerless.

That evening I didn't go to the movies but went home with the others. Everyone spoke about the storm that had exploded in the Val d'Aosta and plunged down into the plain toward the region of Vercelli. From the train we looked out at the damaged fields and retraced the course of the storm. The corn and the vines planted on Masino's and Caluso's hillside must be down. Walking toward my house I saw that the same thing had happened in Candia; but the lake was only slightly ruffled and just a little less brilliant than usual.

My mother got very excited when she saw me arriving so early, and it made me angry. I wasn't a baby, and it shouldn't have mattered whether I returned home at eight o'clock or at eleven. She cooked dinner in such a hurry that she ruined it, and I had to get angry again. I was sorry that I had hurried back to see my mother and my garden, as if the storm that had changed the countryside could have possibly changed me. I was sorry that I had come back early, and I couldn't even remember the reasons why I had done it—the only thing that remained was a feeling of annoyance.

But the trip had gone rather well, and I had seen Giuliana and her broad smile, sitting in her usual place at the end of the car.

My mother came over to me and stood leaning over the window sill by my side. She didn't say anything at first, but then she commented on the church bell and the damage caused by the storm and the good fortune of having a steady job in a factory. I didn't answer, and I focused my attention on the lake because I didn't want to make room for her in my thoughts. My mother added that I should try to hold on to such good luck. Her chatter annoyed me, and I didn't understand exactly what she said then about the social assistant, whether she had complimented her or thanked her, as if she had known her personally. I didn't try to understand my mother, nor did I ask her the meaning of her little speech. Instead I went to my room and closed the door. I undressed and began to read a book I had taken out of the library several months before. I stopped reading after a little while, and as I lay on my bed trying to get to sleep I saw my mother and the social assistant standing in a corner of my mind. I didn't know what sort of relationship existed between them. It was an enigma, unless I chose to think that they were another channel for my troubles.

For the next few days I made sure that things were quiet in the factory. I asked to see the social assistant but I didn't keep the appointment because I wanted to see her reaction and hoped it would force her into revealing her hand. After a week had gone by she called me to her office. It was a very short visit, during which we decided to resume the regular talks we were having before the holidays.

Her reasons for these talks didn't worry me. I was only interested in discovering everything I could about my mother. I wanted to know if she had secretly called the office to ask them for help or if she had talked to them about me.

It turned out that the social assistant's objective coincided with mine, for during our third talk she mentioned my mother. I must confess that I had done everything I could to bring her into the conversation. I had even refused to answer the social assistant's questions in order to make her think that I was completely dependent on my mother, my only source of comfort.

It's strange, but during all the talks about my mother I always pictured her as she had looked in Avignon, in the courtyard, or as she had looked the first time we walked into our house in Candia, when it seemed that we were the only ones entering the house, destined to live there alone, together. This was the only image of my mother I could speak about.

I suppose that is the reason why the social assistant and I had different pictures of my mother, and I suppose that this is why we didn't understand each other very well.

"You should go home early in the evening, like everybody else; that way the relationship between you and your mother will improve."

"But my mother and I love each other and our relationship is fine."

The social assistant said something about the way my mother and I loved each other, but she also mentioned that my mother was very worried about my behavior. I denied nearly everything, and at the same time I was aware of a strange feeling within me, a compulsion to lie, intensified by the knowledge that the truth was not sufficient. My lies uncovered a bigger truth, a truth that I had kept within myself for many years. Now it was coming out, together with my desire to hurt and my lies. My mother and I were emerging together under cover of a lie in a combined image that didn't correspond to reality.

The social assistant said, "Don't lie. You are avoiding your mother and you're trying to hurt her in every way." Her words gave me an almost perfect sense of satisfaction; they were true, intimately true. They gave me the joy of feeling someone understood me. They reestablished the contact I had had with my mother when I was a boy. I wanted the social assistant to say more, and I imagined that this sweet and terrible conversation would take place in front of my mother. So I lied again hoping that the scene I had imagined would come true.

The social assistant kept on talking almost angrily, and with every word she tried to minimize the truth of what she had said before as if she were sorry she had said anything.

"You should be kinder to your mother. I realize your mother is a bit difficult . . . her age, you know."

I didn't like this; she was supposed to talk about me, only about me.

"You can't seem to get rid of the fear you've always felt toward your mother; you can't handle a domineering person this way. You have to talk things over with her." She told me that I shouldn't try to put up with so much and then fight back. I would feel guilty about my rebellion and consequently I would fight the feeling of guilt. I was only enlarging the vicious circle.

I let her finish her speech to the last faltering words. Then I stood up and said, "I cannot accept what you have told me. I am alone with my conscience. I love and respect my mother, and she can say anything she wants. It's none of the factory's business, and it must leave me alone. I am a worker."

My words seemed to strengthen the social assistant, and she spoke to me again more firmly. "Why didn't you ever want to see your mother when you were in the sanatorium? Why don't you go home evenings? Why don't you talk to her? You even hid your mother's clothes so that she couldn't come to see us." It was true, in a more profound sense than her words revealed. It was true and right in a way that only I could understand. I felt that I was alone with my truth and my battle but that from that moment on I would not be able to be alone in the various situations still in store for me.

The social assistant paused for a moment and looked me straight in the eye, but I didn't move. I was waiting for her to say something else. Then at last I could be sure that my mother had felt all my injustices; I could be sure that she had borne them and perhaps cried over them as she told them to this woman. But the social assistant didn't say anything else. She only moralized a little, and that didn't give me any satisfaction or help.

"You shouldn't put up with your mother and then try not to offend her in every way. Try to understand her. If you keep on avoiding her as you are doing now you will only increase the distance between you."

I denied everything once again, but the social assistant didn't press the matter. She didn't know anything else that she could scold me about, and if she did, she had forgotten. It seemed incredible that my mother hadn't told her everything especially since she had already gone so far in her confidences. I was impassive, but the social assistant didn't say another word.

I went back to her several times during that month, but I was always disappointed because I didn't learn anything new. It seemed as if my mother had swallowed quite a few of my insults without noticing them. As I thought about this and listened to her speak, I realized that it was the social assistant who didn't consider certain facts important. They *were* important, and I would have liked to get them off my conscience.

In the meantime the situation between my mother and me continued as usual. I hadn't changed my habits. At home I was silent, and I didn't let anything bother me even though I was physically aware that in the evening my mother did more than wait for me and look at me; she spied on me.

Toward the end of October I noticed something when I started to go to eight o'clock Sunday Mass with her again. I had decided to go to show everyone, including the priest, that my mother and I got along very well together. I had decided to go because that first Sunday around the Feast of All Saints when I had accompanied her to mass filled with good intentions I noticed that my mother considered my presence another insult. On the Sunday of Advent I went to confession. The priest didn't know anything about these events, and when I told him that I was afraid that my mother and the social assistant were uniting against me he made it clear that all confessions on matters of conscience, which were after all matters of faith, were to be made only to him. "I will also tell your mother," he concluded.

This made me happy because I realized that I had isolated and protected my mother even further.

Returning home I noticed that a beautiful autumn was invading the countryside and surrounding the lake. It didn't seem like the end of the season. The sun was still strong and the air was sweet. It made you think that there were still grapes hanging on the vines. The vines were full of colored leaves, especially the vines surrounding the lake. Hundreds of larks still whistled in the sky without the fear that accompanies the flight of the remaining birds during that time of year. There were fewer birds that autumn. I was filled with an overpowering desire to remain in the country. I wanted to tend the garden, to walk along the most hidden paths, to gather mushrooms. Then, happy once more, I would go to Turin to the football games and the movies.

The factory seemed very far away, as if it didn't exist on this earth that I was admiring. Only the pain that followed in the wake of its memory brought back its existence and its threat against my life. The work and the men gave me that sense of pain—Manzino, Tortora, the unknown workers, the crowd, not the real factory with its glass face and its doors.

This meant that if I had found other people in the factory I would have been fine, just as I was fine in the country where no one bothered me. I decided to go back to work on Monday. I wanted to ask Manzino and the Personnel Department for a definite answer on the matter of my promotion. If they didn't give it to me or give me some assurance of their good intentions, I would pretend I was sick for at least fifteen days.

Around nine o'clock the next day I spoke to Manzino. He received me smiling, and he remarked immediately that interruptions in a job are harmful. I told him to forget the interruptions and tell me when I would get my promotion. He stiffened and circled his ugly desk.

"In this department I'm the one who decides what has to be forgotten. You can be sure that one day I'm going to tell you what I can forget and it won't be too long from now. I don't give the promotions; I can only present your name for consideration. In your case I don't consider it wise to do so for reasons regarding your output and the organization of my department."

I was silent for a minute because I had to conquer my desire to run away. "All right," I said. "Give me permission to go and speak to the Personnel Department and to the Board." Manzino looked around, and he must have noticed that many of the men were watching him. He stared at me, and I think he understood that I was strong in that moment of crucial importance.

He moved his arm as if he were about to make a threatening remark, but he said: "Go ahead if you think you can find others who are more understanding than I somewhere else."

I went out into the hall but when I reached the stairs I didn't have the conviction to go to the Personnel Department. Even I, like Manzino, felt something that was stronger than myself and my feelings. I felt the windowpanes tremble, and once more I wanted to run away. "Tomorrow," I thought. I went to take a drink of water, and I walked up and down the hallway twice before going back to my department. Manzino didn't look at me as I headed toward my place. Gualatrone looked up and questioned me, but I returned to my work. The pieces we were turning out were very small, and I concentrated my attention on them. All during that working day I continued to scrutinize them from every angle and aspect. Some pieces grew as large as mountains, and their ridges became streets. Others shrank, and together they took the shape of unknown creatures, like worms covering an animal.

I left the factory without any further problems and without

meeting anyone. I went to the movies and afterwards I went home peacefully thinking about the speech I would give my mother. I had to convince her to go to the infirmary two days later and tell them I was sick and to get the certificate I needed for the insurance. I wanted her to agree so I gave her the opportunity to go to the social assistant and tell her that I was sick. My mother didn't understand, and she began to cry; but I didn't weaken, and I managed to convince her. The next day I was free, and I went to the lake in the morning. But I wasn't as pleased as I had thought I would be on Sunday. "It's the first day," I thought. But the other days were all the same. I looked after the garden unwillingly, discouraged by all the difficulties that stood in the way of a job well done.

I went to the movies in Turin but the city was deserted. That emptiness heightened my uneasiness, and I felt guilty about not going to work like all the others. I wanted to comfort myself, and so I reasoned that my absence was not my fault; it was the consequence of my desire to escape the blows that the unfriendly organization had arranged to ruin me.

This rekindled my resentment, with a violence that was stronger than my anger in the factory. I couldn't find peace, and after a few days, now that the weather had gotten worse, I spent almost all my mornings in bed. I could only manage to calm myself at the entrance of the movie theater in Turin. As soon as I stepped out of the theater I was engulfed by the unpleasant prospects of the trip and the fear of missing the train.

Toward the end of the second week of my absence, on an afternoon when I was in Turin, someone from the infirmary stopped by my house. According to him he was in that neighborhood on some other business and he had only stopped by to give me a message from Dr. Tortora. It was obvious that they had sent him to spy on me. I was almost glad that he hadn't found me; this way whoever had sent him would understand the strength of my liberty. I was afraid that he would return so I didn't go to Turin again. My heavy days grew longer. I was overwhelmed by a complete apathy. I couldn't even stay in bed, and it robbed me of the strength to confide my thoughts to the Indian and the boot. The humidity from the rain that had fallen during those days made them stand out from the other spots on the wall. In this state, work seemed like a liberation from a pain that was even more acute than the pain inflicted on me by Tortora and his associates. On Monday the fourteenth of November I returned to the factory.

Manzino stopped me at the door of the department. He didn't have my health certificate so he couldn't let me go back to work. I had to go to Dr. Tortora. They had found another trick to capture me again.

Tortora made me wait a long time. Every year without fail, around the month of December, for one reason or another I invariably had to go to Tortora. His plans were so precise that they had succeeded once more, even though this time the initiative had been mine with my idea of pretending to be sick.

Tortora greeted me with a scowl, moving his enormous head from side to side and looking past me. He gave me a perfunctory examination. He told me that he would issue my health certificate so I could go back to work even though he hadn't been the one who had said I was sick and even though I was never completely cured as far as the more serious and persistent dangers to my health were concerned.

"We honestly try to help you, but you . . . I wanted to know something more about your illness than your mother told me, but the first time I sent someone to find out further details you weren't even home and the second time you didn't even open the door. You'd better change your ways or you'll be in trouble." He uttered this phrase as he was washing his hands, but he was even more guilty than Pilate and looking in the mirror he should have repeated those words to himself. "Change your ways, Tortora, or Saluggia will get into even more trouble."

I found Franco Robino at the entrance to the infirmary. He was the man who had come to my house to see me twice. The second time I had seen him through the window, and I had noticed that he hadn't waited for an answer. He had even knocked with his feet; he had circled the house and gone into the barn. Why was he waiting for me now at the bottom of the stairs? He had nothing to do, and I was sure that Dr. Tortora had called him and told him to spy on me. At noon I saw him again in the cafeteria. He was sitting two tables in front of me with his back turned to me so that I wouldn't recognize him. I watched him shaking his head as he chewed and leaned back to drink. Giuliana was serving a table near him and I saw him turn around and speak to her very confidentially. He grabbed her arm, and I half expected him to pull her on top of him. They whispered a few more words, and they both looked at me and laughed. What did it mean? Was Giuliana against me too?

I was sorry that I had come back to work, and I longed for my bed. A difficult bed where I had thought many thoughts but mine, far away from the factory and all the ugly faces. I broke the motor on the power saw, and I had several other accidents.

I left the department and refused to come back. I was ready for anything, especially now that Manzino had scolded me on my absence. He had been very stupid and mean to punish me, and he shouldn't have done it because I had been heavily punished already. This too contributed to my leaving the department.

Other incidents took place during the following days. Now that everything was lost I felt a satisfaction that was greater than my pain, a satisfaction that hid my pain and my usual troubles and urged me to take the opposite tack. I had a call from the Personnel Department but they didn't know what to say.

After Christmas I received the second call. They informed me that Manzino had released me from his department.

VI

I DIDN'T GO TO WORK for a few days while I waited for them to assign me to a new department.

I went to the library, to the movies at noon and to the language courses; anywhere that made me feel closer to the factory.

"They don't fire you, they don't beat you, they don't cut your salary. They know that you're not a good worker so they give you more assistance, more kindness and you can have more absences. The foremen leave you alone, and they even say that you're a good worker so that they'll transfer you to another section, and you get a raise in the bargain. You get to know all the departments in the factory, and you speak to more people. The only risk you run is that you won't be able to get rid of them, and you're even likely to find them swarming all over your house." The man who spoke was standing near me. He was called Cimatti or Rimatti. He was very lazy, and he said that he wrote poetry and was descended from a noble Roman family. Drinking was his specialty. And very often he didn't make it to the bathroom in time.

Since the first day he spoke to me I hadn't bothered to answer him. So he started pestering me and calling me "the thinker" and telling me vulgar stories, as vulgar as his face. He kept it up till one day, just a short time after I started working in the department, he reached for me with his dirty hands as if to pinch me or caress me muttering something with his mouth full of saliva. I was disgusted by that mouth, and I hit him with a fistful of metal. They took care of him in the infirmary, and he was out for many days, the noble Cimatti or Rimatti, shit of a poet.

They sent me a written reprimand and suspended me for three days. I went to Aosta to see the old walls of the city and the poor leper's tower. That winter the snow and the fog muffled the city and made it nearly invisible, and I felt as if I had gone to pay a clandestine visit to the leper who was still alive and hiding.

When I returned to the factory I was more tranquil and determined not to take things so seriously—so much so that I cannot even remember all the events of those days or the discussions in the Personnel Department. While I listened to them I merely thought that if you're a leper you're a leper.

Except for Cimatti, the new department wasn't bad, at least in the beginning. The change had helped me. I didn't have a machine any more; I sat in a row with other men and I had to assemble a funny metal fixture with two little arms that had to be screwed to a wheel. The people who worked around me didn't bother me. Every once in a while they would sigh and stretch their legs under the table. There were nearly a hundred of us doing the same kind of work. We worked on the second floor of the factory, and we could see several tall black oaks rising above the roofs of the outbuildings. The people who worked were all different—thin, fat, tall, short, young, or old—and when you saw them all together, even though they were all dressed alike, they didn't look like a group of workers who should be doing the same job. The pieces were in the boxes, and they buzzed like a nest of insects. Perhaps the floor vibrated because of the machines on the first floor.

The foreman sat at the end of the room and we didn't see him very often. The pieces arrived on the conveyor belts, all counted and checked: so many pieces an hour. After a week I managed to get the rhythm of the work and once in a while I even had time to raise my head. To lift my head as if I could rise above my troubles and the miserable plots against me.

Outside, the winter ran over the countryside and climbed the oak trees that rose above the outbuildings. At night I saw it lying over the white and narrow lake.

It didn't snow very much till late January. It snowed often, every two or three days, but the snow didn't stick to the ground. I watched the snow from the factory, and I realized that it was useless and that it could not last. In the meantime I continued to work with the others, in silence and without friends. I hardly ever saw Pinna and although sometimes I ran into Gualatrone in the cafeteria he was very busy with his love affairs and with the party. I hadn't seen the social assistant again after my transfer and suspension. I didn't go to the movies every night any more because even with my overcoat it was very cold that late in the evening.

In the Assembling Department everything struck me as new, and I didn't feel the resentment I had felt before. I suffered, but I suffered more calmly. The whole department, which was larger and lighter, seemed like a place that didn't exist, like a place that would soon disappear. We were a mixed group of people, and we didn't ask for anything, even of ourselves.

We were all a little dazed even though our thoughts burned within us. At certain hours they piped music into the department. I would listen to it, and it helped me. When the music played, the foreman would get up and walk up and down the rows between the tables. He didn't look or speak to anyone. His name was Salvatore, and he was a stamp collector. During the time I was with him he only spoke to me once or twice when he had a message to give me from the infirmary or the Personnel Department. His oral messages were accompanied by a written memo. I remember that when he signed his memos the pen would always catch on the paper a second before he wrote the capital *S*. His silence was the silence of the department, and his eyes were blank.

I stayed in that quiet department for a long time. I didn't care any more about my promotion or my work.

Assembling the pieces was boring, but it was also tiring. Weariness would take hold of me and stay with me all day, like a bad mood.

The heat began in May, and it got even worse in June. In June I received a memo from Salvatore saying I had to go for my physical checkup. I didn't see Tortora, only Dr. Steffino, the second most important doctor in the factory. I was happy because I didn't feel very well, and I thought that if a new doctor treated me for a while everything would be all right. But he too sent me to Dr. Bompiero.

Another note from Salvatore with the words "A must."

At the end of June, Bompiero said: "You cannot bear the summer in this condition. You run a fever every evening. You are not well, and I suggest you spend some time in another sanatorium or undergo a rigid cure under my personal supervision. But first of all I want to see the X rays."

[143

Nothing had changed. He spent fifteen days studying the X rays so that he would have enough time to plan every new trick. He said that if I didn't go to the sanatorium I was to stay at home. "When will I have a more definite answer?" I asked, trying to postpone this alternative. It was terribly hot and our vacation was only fifteen days away.

"This is the answer, and it is definite. You cannot work, for your own good as well as for everyone else's. You have to take care of yourself or it will be too late."

I crossed myself and began to recite the *Our Father*.

"What kind of act is this? Incantations are useless."

"Forgive them, for they know not what they are doing to themselves."

Bompiero threw me out of his office. I didn't go back to the factory; I went to look for the police lieutenant. He wasn't there, but his superior received me. I tried to explain everything to him. "But what accusations can you make against these doctors?"

I had to leave there disappointed. I walked through the city in the opposite direction from the factory. I went toward the river through the shadows in the gardens.

They looked for me in the factory and then at home. When the social assistant arrived I was in bed, and I didn't move as I listened to her speak with my mother. That evening my mother came into my room; she put on the light and spoke to me. The general opinion was that I was seriously ill. They could cure me at home if I stayed in bed. After two or three months they would send me to the mountains but not to a sanatorium. At the beginning of winter I would be sent home again for further treatment till I was completely cured. In the meantime the factory would pay for the treatment and my medicines and put me on a reduced salary.

That is what happened. I stayed in my bed. I often thought that in this way I was destroying my life. They didn't send me to the mountains because the weather wasn't too good after the middle of October.

It was already the middle of November of that year that ran so quickly through my soul even though the treatments had begun again with a vengeance. I was coming home from Turin where I had gone to the movies.

After the pneumothoracic treatment at the dispensary in X I had gone directly to Turin without stopping at my house. I was discouraged in my hopes of conquering my troubles and those who were the cause of my troubles. When Bompiero shook his head I decided to go to the movies. I was returning at the usual hour, around eight fifteen, and on the train I saw a man stretch himself, gesticulate, and yawn in front of the train window. As I watched, great flashes of lightning slashed the sky. I could see them very clearly because the lights on the train were dim. Then I discovered that it wasn't lightning but discharges of electricity along the track.

The man lit a cigarette, and by the light of the match and the electric flashes I saw him smile at me in a way I shall never forget. His uncombed long wavy hair shone in the glow of that smile; so did his teeth, including the four or five silver ones he had in front. He smiled again and greeted me. He offered me a cigarette and began to speak. He kept on fidgeting, and every once in a while he would get up without stopping the flow of words and without looking at me. But when he sat down again he always smiled and his face became increasingly comforting.

At a certain point while he was looking for the cigarettes in his pocket he said, "I don't have any money. I'm nearly all out of money. In three days I won't have a lira. Good-by, money of mine! What will I do without money? And to think I came up here looking for money."

I was afraid that he was going to ask me for money, and I was ready to give him some because his sincerity made it impossible to refuse.

"My father left me a beautiful house, and I sold it. I'd just come back from the war to Gubbio, my home town. Meanwhile, I had learned my lesson. The English and the Poles don't want Communism here, and neither does the Church. The monarchy falls, and the Church commands. So I began to sell religious articles— candles, holy pictures and missals. But I made a mistake because just at the moment the Church was going to take over they decided to put on a show of humility and they didn't buy anything. The priests didn't buy anything. I had to sell the entire sacristy. I had also gotten married so that the clergy would have greater confidence in me. So then I thought, who has won the war? America.

[145

Industry. Never mind the land owned by the good men in Gubbio! Fortune is industry. So when all the farmers went to Rome I went to Milan. I wanted to manufacture medical supplies, but I didn't have enough money. The only things I've saved are my wife's secret formulas. She got them from a Russian scientist who was a prisoner in a little town near Gubbio. Later they found out he was half German and came from Bolzano.

"From Milan we went to Varese, Novara, Vercelli, Trino Vercellese, and I was reduced to treating rice farmers with our miraculous medicines. The Virgin of Oropa has appeared often in my wife's dream to tell her that her work is blessed and her medicines can kill any pain. It was the Black Virgin who suggested her moving to X and her association with Dr. Fioravanti. It was quite a coincidence because the doctor was just about to leave Turin. By now he had invented the X-3 serum, which cures cancer and tuberculosis. All diseases come from a definite source, and our medicine is blessed in being able to go straight to that source. There can't be any science without religion and faith, or you'd only be curing dogs and making atomic bombs. But we don't have any money, and Dr. Fioravanti is hounded by other doctors, like all true scientists. My wife also advises; she reads the future."

This was a very long speech because when he had finished we had come to Candia.

"My name is Virgilio Palmarucci, and I live at 27 via del Distretto. It's a lovely old building. Ask for my wife, Signora Eufemia."

I was moved by the meeting, and I felt that the Virgin of Oropa had set me on the road to freedom. Dr. Fioravanti is persecuted by the other doctors because he is honest and cures people. Medicine is religion. This would be my salvation.

I nearly ran all the way home. The front door was open, and the light shone through. Inside, the atmosphere was pleasant and the table was set for dinner. My mother was tranquil, and I hugged her with tears of happiness. That night I had trouble getting to sleep, and my bed was sweet and warm as it had been when I was a boy.

I would most certainly go to via del Distretto and to Dr. Fioravanti. But in the morning I was hesitant, and my soul was undecided. During the night I had not dreamt of the Black Virgin. The good thing about these thoughts was that they blotted out all thoughts of the factory, the doctors, and the professors who were plotting my ruin. I imagined that Dr. Fioravanti was still a young man, small and kind.

I should have gone to the city sooner; then I would have gone to the Palmaruccis' house. Palmarucci—palms of the resurrection. I felt better, and I stayed in bed most of the time. I would get up to watch my mother prepare the meals and set the table, and I would crouch close to the stove like a cat. I was anxious to go to the city; the third day I couldn't wait any longer. I went to church and to communion before leaving, and I asked my mother to come to church with me.

The priest asked me how I was, and I answered that I was better and that I had great faith in Divine Providence. "Good. You must obey," he said, and I understood that I had to obey the will of the Virgin of Oropa. I was hopeful even though I had not dreamt about her or received any direct sign. And I thought, "Isn't this new desire to get well, this peace, already a sign of her protection and benevolence?"

On November twentieth, during that period when my troubles usually led me to Dr. Tortora, I was on my way to the city filled with hope. I was not calm, and my arm shook in the grasp of the nurse who had to give me my injection in the dispensary. My arm was white, hairy and thin with a blue spot in the center that marked my veins. It was the arm of a sick person, and I felt as if I were looking at it for the first time. It looked deteriorated, a part of me that had been abandoned, as if the lack of an autonomous force that resisted, like the force of my thoughts, had allowed the sickness to enter my system and nest under my skin. It was imperative now that a doctor like Professor Fioravanti should help me. When the nurse had given me my two injections I sat for a half-hour on a bench in the dispensary.

The noonday bells rang through the clouds when I crossed the doorway of the Palmaruccis' house. I found their door after I had crossed the hallway and gone up three wide steps made of light stone. The door was open, and something compelled me to go in. I immediately ran into Palmarucci who was working in the kitchen.

[147

There was a lighted cigarette in his mouth, and it seemed as if he had not put it down since that evening when we met. He was still smiling, but he hadn't recognized me.

"Welcome," he said. "Please come in. Do you want to see Signora Eufemia?"

I asked to see Professor Fioravanti. "Professor Fioravanti is not here. He is in Turin attending a conference at the university. Did you want a consultation? But please do speak with my wife." And the wife arrived immediately.

Signora Eufemia was all black and I could hardly see her in the darkness of the kitchen. I caught a glimpse of her neck and the low neckline flecked with white beads. She smoked like her husband, and when we were in the hallway her breath made me cough. She looked at me and took me by the hand to lead me to her rooms.

The dark hallway led to very large rooms with high windows. The ceiling was very high and painted gold with garlands of little angels and roses coming down in loops to the middle of the wall. Behind Signora Eufemia on the wall directly in front of me was a picture of Palmarucci in evening clothes, with the eternal cigarette. Next to it was a picture of a child who I imagined must have died some time ago. He was leaning like a sick person against the legs of an unseen woman. A hand caressed his head, but when you looked closer you noticed that the hand was holding the little head steady for the photographer. How many times I've looked at that child and how many times I've thought of how much we resembled each other. I mean to say that our luck was the same. The mother, the woman with the hand, was very mysterious because the photograph chopped off her head.

Signora Eufemia made me sit down. She walked around me, touching me on the shoulders; then she sat down in her chair and adjusted her position and her neckline. She got up immediately to close one of the shutters at the window. "You suffer," she said. I remained seated, and she stared at me. "You suffer a great deal. So much so that I don't know whether we will be able to help you. Look into this mirror. Do you recognize yourself? What do you think you have? Tell me, how would you like to see yourself?"

I was dumbfounded, and I didn't know what to say or think. I looked into the mirror. It wasn't a trick. I saw myself even though

148]

my face seemed to be far away. "I want to see Dr. Fioravanti. I am sick." Why had I said immediately and for the first time: "I am sick"? Why did my face look so sad, the way my arm had looked in the dispensary?

"It's obvious that you're sick. Why don't you wear a wedding ring?"

"But I'm not married."

"Yes, I know. And this is one of the reasons for your illness. There are so many good girls around . . . your cousin . . ."

What did she know about my cousin? She said several other things that I didn't hear. How could she speak about my cousin? I was afraid, and I thought that Palmarucci or Fioravanti were coming to attack me. But I was cowed and powerless in the face of an inevitable attack.

Signora Eufemia looked at me closely. "Who opposes it? Your mother?" How could she say these things? I was so confused that at that moment I thought that my mother had written my cousin telling her not to come or that she had hidden the letters I had received from France.

"You must really get well so that you'll be able to make sensible decisions."

"Yes," I said.

"Your troubles are exhausting, very exhausting. The country doesn't help, all those chores . . . Where does it hurt? Is it mainly your bones? Your legs? Your back? Or do you have headaches?"

I admitted that the cause of my troubles was uncertain and that I felt their pressure on my spirit and on my chest both inside and out. I told her that the doctors had plotted together and said I was tubercular. They had decided to make me sick with that illness. I had resisted, but I was in a terrible state and that is why I needed Dr. Fioravanti.

"Don't worry; tomorrow you will meet the doctor. He will cure your illness with his serum, and I will help you bloom again. I will rejuvenate your body and your spirit, and I will reveal to you the plans and secrets of those who have plotted against you. Bring me the photographs of all your family. We will begin our search with them."

"I'm not accusing anyone," I said.

The woman looked at me: "We have to find the door. You mustn't be afraid. You must accuse, and you mustn't spare yourself or anyone any pain. If you want to vomit you must stick your fingers all the way down your throat. After we find the right person, I'll take care of everything."

Once again I asked for the Professor. "The Professor knows my methods. He will cure your body only with injections and massages. Bring me the photographs . . . first your relatives and the women."

At that point Palmarucci came in with two little cups of coffee, one in each hand, and offered them to us. The woman drank her coffee in one gulp, and I swallowed mine because I hadn't had the courage to refuse. Drinking together without knowing each other had all the earmarks of a pact. The mumbo-jumbo had begun under the angels and the roses.

"Can I leave? If not I'll be late for the cafeteria," I said.

Together they answered yes, and as Palmarucci led me into the hall he said something about luck and the cafeteria, something I didn't understand very well because his wife was talking to me at the same time, arranging our appointments and my meeting with Dr. Fioravanti.

Palmarucci disappeared at the end of the hall, and Signora Eufemia held me back for a minute. "Don't worry," she said. "You'll see; we'll straighten everything out. Fioravanti will cure you, and I will help him. Come to me as trusting as a lover." She squeezed my hand and kept on looking at me as she slowly closed the door.

It was raining when I got outside and via del Distretto was already full of mud puddles. There was a strong smell of wine coming from the local wine shop. The street was one of the oldest and ugliest streets in the city, inhabited by immigrants from the south and by old pensioners. No one who worked in the factory would have lived there, and already many of the houses were abandoned and falling apart. But not even this made me realize the truth about the people I had just left. Instead I thought that since they were hounded by the doctors they were in as sad a condition as myself.

The only part of Dr. Fioravanti's office I had seen was a high door in the middle of the corridor. It was shut and pasted on the front was a large red paper cross. During most of the trip back I thought about that door, but I couldn't make up my mind whether it frightened me or attracted me. I was uncertain of everything and weak. And Signora Eufemia had made me even weaker with all her questions and with her presence. I wanted to see her again, feel her interest in me, feel her looking at me, watch her sitting down gracefully for me and extending her arms toward me.

That night, toward daybreak, it stopped raining. I had dozed and I wasn't sleepy. I looked out the window without opening the glass panes, and to one side I saw an enormous bright moon shining over the roofs of Candia. The town and the lake were covered by wisps of white fog. They looked like trenches or waves, and a light wind whipped the foam higher. It seemed as if the town and the lake were isolated and on the verge of being swallowed up by the live fog. Slowly it would vanish, and there would be nothing left. I was the only witness to the miracle that was about to take place, a miracle that hovered in the glow of my window as if it were dependent on me and my thoughts. I felt strong and like a king with my blanket over my shoulders. I decided to put my faith in the vivid moon that had returned to mark the beginning of my liberation. It was the last full moon of autumn.

My nights of little sleep and magic, when everything talked to me, began. The short naps brought me periods of exhilarating clarity: I resolved all my problems in a second, but in the morning I couldn't remember how.

That first night after I went back to sleep under the dawn moon I dreamed about Signora Eufemia. I was meeting her in front of the factory; while getting off the bus I saw her clearly reflected in the glass of the window but then it wasn't Signora Eufemia any more but a strange woman who beckoned me to follow her. I saw her from the back, and I didn't recognize her. She walked toward the infirmary. There was a hedge and a country road where the steps of the infirmary should have been. The road was dusty and full of flowers like a painting. I thought, "This dust—where does this dust come from?" The dust would settle and shine over the countryside. In the meantime the road climbed uphill, and the woman changed. Her clothes were different, but above all her figure and her neck were transformed till at last she turned around and looked at me and I recognized Signora Eufemia again. She smiled at me with a very sweet smile. Then she started going up a flight of stairs without touching the steps. Her dress and her body changed again till they nearly disappeared. Then for a second I saw her standing still, but her face was no longer human. It was expressionless. It was a face made of metal, a shining, sacred face. Then the whole figure reappeared and it was the Virgin of Oropa, black and resplendent. As I huddled and tried to pray, caught in a maelstrom that robbed me of speech, the woman once more became Signora Eufemia. Her image was less brilliant, essence escaped in rays of light through the windows of her house. Everything lost the sacred look it had had before. The woman smiled at me and gave me her hand. I couldn't reach her because I was far away. Then she retreated even farther to a corner and began to undress. I was offended by her immodesty, offended and disturbed, but then in a flash everything disappeared. At the end of the dream just as I was about to wake up I had the distinct impression that she was going to betray me with another man. It was this feeling that woke me up.

The dream removed any doubt I might have had about going for my cure, and when I awoke my decision was reinforced by the image of Dr. Fioravanti's door with the cross. However, in my heart of hearts where the impressions of the dream still lingered, I felt that it was precisely to Dr. Fioravanti that Signora Eufemia went to hide and betray me.

When I went for the second time to her house, Signora Eufemia greeted me with smiles and compliments. People hadn't treated me this way for a long time. She wanted the photographs, but I only gave her one of my mother when she was young. She didn't realize it was my mother; she was confused by the dress and the enormous braid wound around the head of the woman in the picture. When she learned it was my mother, she said that I had nothing to fear from her, at least not at that moment and if there had been any little meannesses in the past they had long since vanished.

She asked for other photographs, even group photos, and she

began to ask me about my youth and love. The room was very cold, and it was pouring rain outside. Palmarucci came for a second to bring a brazier that Signora Eufemia set down on the floor close to her legs. We were so close that I didn't dare move my legs for fear of touching hers. The woman lit a cigarette with one of the coals and continued talking to me. She had a woolen blanket over her shoulders, but her neckline was still very low and I could see the lace inside her dress. She asked me about my love life, what it had been and what it was now, and she would get excited in her speech because I wouldn't tell her the things she expected to hear. I accepted her flirtatious manner, and it enveloped me with the curiosity of an accomplice. It covered me and dispelled the cold in that unfamiliar room. Every now and then Signora Eufemia would unconsciously brush against me with her knee, and I understood that the gesture was an added incitement to the conversation, a gentle prodding that would bring forth the fire she felt I had and I felt I had lost.

Palmarucci returned with the coffee and told me that Fioravanti was waiting for me. I found him in the hall while he was still talking to a client. He was nearly as tall as Tortora but much thinner and paler. He had two long hands, identical, like two blocks. He was smoking, and I always saw him smoking even during our consultations. While he gave me my intravenous injections he would put down his cigarette on the edge of the table next to my arm.

He ushered me into his office. There were two glass shelves full of bottles and instruments and another glass shelf painted blue in the middle of the room where he kept his famous X–3 serum.

As I turned my head I saw a sink in a corner and a small white bed partly hidden by a screen, a small table covered with books and more instruments and, to complete the picture, a large blue divan. There was a strong and disgusting smell in the room. It wasn't as cold as it had been in Signora Eufemia's room because he had a little electric stove and the shutters were tightly closed. Two lamps were lighted, one hanging from the middle of the ceiling in the center of the room and the other next to the little white bed. The smoke exhaled by Dr. Fioravanti was blue and thick, and it consumed all the air in the room. Fioravanti smiled at me and sat down behind the table. As he talked to me, leaning

[153

close, his breath smelled of toothpaste. He made me take everything off except my trousers and he began to prod me. At the conclusion of a silent examination he said that there wasn't any doubt that his serum could cure me. He asked me the name of my doctor and I answered, "Dr. Tortora."

"He is unknown," he said, "at least in university circles and in the clinics. But I'm sure that he is a fine doctor." Then he said that the patient had to choose the cure himself because the patient's intelligence and instinct of self-preservation were driven by the very illness to discover the cure. In this way the spirit and the body were united in battle, and the doctor had only to interpret the patient's choice, comfort him, and that was all.

Everything he said was true. He didn't comment on my illness. He looked at the cavity left by the needle of the pneumothorax in my side and shook his head. Once I was outside, Signora Eufemia smiled at me, and Palmarucci chatted with me as he walked me to the door. How many times he told me that I didn't know how to live like so many other people around me and that this part of the country was much too depressing! He smoked—everybody in that house smoked—and as he talked he would lean against the window pane while I stood and waited.

I would often wait until Signora Eufemia was free and until Dr. Fioravanti returned from the university.

Signora Eufemia would smile at me and touch me. She wrapped me in her own blanket all winter.

Fioravanti gave me many injecions of X–3 serum. They made my lips warm as they penetrated my veins with their magic. I would raise my head, and all my thoughts went flying off like a flock of blackbirds darting here and there in the sky, each thought sharp and logically in place like the wings of birds that beat close to each other in flight but never touch.

I still went faithfully to the dispensary, but after three months Fioravanti told me not to go any more.

"Do you feel tubercular?" he would ask me.

"No," I answered.

"Well, then, no more pneumothorax."

At home things weren't going too badly. I spent a lot of time in bed reading and listening to the radio. I would fight openly with my mother every time I needed money to pay Professor Fioravanti and Signora Eufemia. Signora Eufemia's cure was a complement to Fioravanti's treatments, and it gave me the strength to fight with my mother. Once a week we talked about my future, huddled close together around the brazier, and each morning I had to drink a liquid made out of herbs before I ate my breakfast.

This too was part of the witchcraft that kept me tied to them and made me pay out good money as if I were a bank. Not once did Palmarucci forget to ask me for money, including a few hundred lire for himself. Once he started crying just to get more money out of me, and he accused his wife of meanness. Signora Eufemia arrived and threw him out of the kitchen; she put her arm through mine and smiling she led me to our room. Every once in a while she would go and turn off the fuses so that Fioravanti's stove wouldn't consume too much electricity. Toward the middle of February we started sitting on the bed, both of us wrapped in her blanket to keep warm. She would lie down, but I sat up with my feet dangling over the side.

"I was born in Africa," she would say, blowing her nose. "I am so cold." And she would take one of my hands and place it on her shoulders or on her thighs. Later on she used to place it on her bosom.

Once when he was drunk and crying, Palmarucci told me to be careful because his wife wanted to make me her lover and ruin me and shut me up in a room like poor Professor Fioravanti. He said this was the reason that the Professor hadn't finished his internship. But I only put my hands under Signora Eufemia's dress and I held her close to me so that she wouldn't be cold. In those moments she would interrupt her talk with a spasm that was like a sob.

In the meantime winter kept getting colder and whiter. It seemed like an endless period of time and I abandoned myself to the idea that the cures would last forever. I felt far away from the factory. It was a gentle school without exams, days in bed and days in the Palmarucci house with coffee and the injections that made me feel well and that atmosphere that took me far away from all

[155

my old problems. I even felt far away from the city I was in. Silently I would hug Signora Eufemia on the bed and feel a sweet pleasure inside of me. It was a marvelous game.

"Be careful; Fioravanti is jealous," Palmarucci told me one morning. His eyes were as red as a rabbit's.

I went into the consulting room, and I found Fioravanti washing himself. The smell was more unbearable this morning than any other morning. The bed in the corner was unmade and as usual a cigarette was burning on the edge of the table.

"Get out," he said, and he called Palmarucci. I found Signora Eufemia crying in her room. She was half naked. I went back into the hall, and I ran into Palmarucci who was carrying a chamber pot. A woman arrived, another client, and she immediately went into Fioravanti's consulting room. I waited for Palmarucci to reappear. He had a handful of money. He straightened out each bill and put it in his wallet; then he took an umbrella and left.

That morning Signora Eufemia asked me when I planned to go back to work. She obviously could read the future very clearly because two days later I found an invitation from Dr. Tortora at home. I was supposed to go and see him. I didn't go, and I told Fioravanti everything. He told me to go and see Tortora and have him give me my X rays.

When I went to Tortora he sent me to Dr. Bompiero at the dispensary. Bompiero had even managed to get that job as soon as Dr. De Saint Martin had retired. He told me that I was better but that I had to continue my treatment. I said I would, and I asked him for my X rays. He answered that he didn't have them. I insisted, and he told me to go and ask about them in the infirmary.

That same day I went to the infirmary, finally getting hold of a nurse after waiting around for a bit. She went upstairs to find out about my X rays and gave me a dirty look as she left. When she came back she said that Dr. Bompiero had my plates at the dispensary. Then I asked her to write down her answer and sign it because it was Dr. Bompiero who had sent me to the infirmary to get my X rays. The nurse tried to get out of it but eventually she had someone take me to Tortora. The doctor sighed: "Is it possible that everything has to happen to you?" But I was adamant.

He sat down and with a terrible effort he wrote out a note which he then handed to me. It was for Professor Bompiero. As I was leaving I saw the nurse running with a package under her arm. I was sure she was taking my X rays to the dispensary. I followed her but she must have noticed me because when we had reached the corner she got on a bus. I was positive that she was carrying my X rays.

I ran to Signora Eufemia to tell her everything. No one opened the door. I knocked again, and then I went into the street and looked up at their windows. A pale light was glowing in one of the rooms, but no one answered my knocks.

The next day at the dispensary they gave me my X rays, and they were folded the same way the package the nurse was carrying the day before had been folded. Bompiero himself gave them to me saying, "I don't want to ask you what you plan to do with them. You have a right to have them, but be careful, my friend. You can't fool around with an illness like yours. Stay in bed during this terrible weather and come here twice a week for your treatment, including the pneumothorax."

When I left I was happy because I felt I had upset part of Tortora's and Bompiero's plans by forcing them to give me the X rays.

The season was a beautiful spring, a delicate spring. The earth was slowly waking, with several hours of sun and some light showers that fell on the leaves and in the ditches. The sky was enormous. The wind scuttled and bloated it, driving through the countryside and scattering the blue air.

VII

THE LAKE WAS RESTLESS, and so were the poplars and birches that surrounded it. It was like the spring of a courageous year, and I hoped desperately that it would be the year of my victory. It seemed a good year for the farms and the countryside. It was beautiful, especially in the small towns that lay narrow and clean amid the green of the fields with the sun shining on the rooftops and the front of the houses that lined the wide streets open to the winds of the fields. It was a difficult year in the factory. There was more work in the fields, more liberty in the countryside, and later, in the evenings, in the towns.

Even in the city I could feel the air of that beautiful month of March as I walked to Fioravanti's house with my X rays. He looked at them, first by the light of the window and then he put them with his yellow hands against the light near the bed.

"Nothing terribly serious," he said, "at least not for my serum. There are many scars. School life, military life. But just so you won't have any setbacks, keep on with the pneumothoracic treatments." Then he gave me an injection of his serum, and I left drunk and free.

I passed by the factory. It didn't look good under the light of the sun. It was getting dirty like a piece of broken glass. It was ready to burst and croak like a frog in the summertime. I didn't see anyone, but when I thought about it I realized that I wasn't looking for anyone. I wasn't interested in meeting anyone, not even the people I knew.

On my way home the train was half empty at that hour of the afternoon, and I looked out the window at the farmers and the blades of green grain no taller than a hand span. There was a farmer sitting on a stone.

Two days later Palmarucci came to answer the door with a

priest's hat on his head. "We have an apostolic benediction for all the inmates and for the entire company if I am included."

A priest had come to see Signora Eufemia. Fioravanti was busy with the same woman I had seen there last time. I waited, and I went and drank some coffee with Palmarucci in the kitchen. I didn't speak to him because I was worried about having to return to the dispensary for the pneumothoracic treatments. I trusted Fioravanti, but I would have preferred a more open war with Bompiero instead of having to submit to his medications, if only for the sake of convenience.

The priest came out whispering quietly, and Palmarucci put his ear to the door so that he could hear what he was saying as Signora Eufemia led him down the corridor. After the priest had left, Signora Eufemia told me to wait just a little longer. Then she came back and opened the door smiling. When we were in her room she sat on the bed and said, "Something very wonderful is about to happen to us. The religious authorities are interested in our medicines, and they want to use them in their hospitals and to help poor unfortunates who cannot pay for their treatments." She looked at me closely and said: "How well you look, dear Saluggia! When will you stop coming for the cure?"

Her words were like a betrayal, and she didn't make me sit on the bed as she had done so many other times. Instead she sat down in a chair facing me. "Albino, little dear." She lit a cigarette and smoked half of it. "You aren't afraid of going back to the factory, are you?"

I felt even more abandoned. "Of all people, why should you say such things to me?" I said. "You know very well that I'm not afraid, that others are afraid of me. You of all people, you who know everything. If you don't stop I'll throw you on the bed." I had never addressed Signora Eufemia with the familiar "tu," and when I had finished she looked at me smiling.

"Bravo, Albino! You've made up your mind when it's too late. We've been on that bed so many times. You always make up your mind when it's too late. Don't be angry; no one is going to abandon you. Come here. Give me a little kiss, Albino, little dear." She offered me her cheek, but I refused her silly invitation. I wanted to beat her and hug her and never leave her again. She

got up and took my arm, and she led me toward the door. Fioravanti was waiting for me.

Signora Eufemia hugged me against the door. "Give me a kiss,"
she said. I didn't despise her any longer; so I kissed her on the
cheek as she had asked me to do at first. She laughed, took me by
the hand, and pushed me outside. "Albino, Albino, what do you
want to do if you don't know how to do anything?" Palmarucci was
watching me from the end of the hall.

I went into Fioravanti's consulting room. He was smoking and
looking out the window. He sat down behind the table. It was one
of the few times I had seen him sitting down. "My supply of serum
is getting very low. I have had to send many samples to the Vatican
and to Switzerland. In order to manufacture more serum I need
certain organs of live animals, and they are very difficult to find.
I'm hoping that they will build me a factory in Switzerland. Now,
if you want to finish the cure you will have to book ahead of time.
I must be sure. If you decide to book for further appointments
you will have to give me a hundred and fifty thousand lire: a hundred and twenty for the injections I have already given you and
thirty as advance payment for the rest of the cure."

After he had finished talking he stood up again. He was baring
my arm getting it ready for the injection. He looked at me and
said, "Yes, yes, we can still give you another one today, but within
the week I want either one hundred and fifty thousand lire to continue the cure or one hundred and twenty thousand for the injections I have already given you. Five thousand lire are for today's
treatment."

The injection made me feel more drunk than usual and in the
end I promised him all the money. The doctor wrote down my
answer in his diary and said, "There's no need to give anything
to Palmarucci."

I found Palmarucci standing near the door. He walked outside
with me, but after a few steps he waved at me and disappeared into
the local wine shop.

I would often find him sitting on one of the benches of the shop
during the days I waited for Fioravanti and Signora Eufemia to
return from Rome, where they had gone to submit their project to
the Vatican.

160]

They had left a few days after I had taken the entire sum of one hundred and fifty thousand lire to Fioravanti, plus twenty-five thousand lire to Signora Eufemia for the sessions and the herb tonic. The social assistant at the factory had lent me the money. I had had to fight to get it, but I got it. I had asked for two hundred thousand lire because I wanted to buy a present for Signora Eufemia, but I didn't get her anything after all because she asked me for the twenty-five thousand lire. She had seen me put some of the large pink bank notes in my pocket and her eyes had nearly popped out of her head. Once I had given her the money she looked at me with one of her old sobbing looks.

A few days later they had left together without a word to me. I'm sure they hadn't said anything to Palmarucci either.

During those waiting days in a city that was always empty during working hours, I often ended up at the movies or sitting next to Palmarucci on one of the benches in the wine shop. He drank and complained continuously. He wasn't happy in Piedmont.

"Is this a city? There isn't even a promenade where people go walking to see and be seen. And where are the cafés and the groups of friends? All you see is old men in the taverns with their noses dripping snot down to their trouser legs. They don't say two words to each other. Even the women are ugly. In Gubbio at this time of day there are at least five cafés filled with people and at least a hundred tables where they are playing cards. All of them men, students, storekeepers, landowners, clerks, lawyers, doctors. Here there are only three old men who drink more spit than wine. Everyone is in the factory, and it's not even in the city. It's outside the city where we put our jails and our cemeteries. When you walk by it frightens you. The only people you see around are women, old men, and invalids. On Sunday there isn't a soul to be found. I don't even know where the churches are. A small town in my part of the country, any small town, is better than this. There is more life in the Cat Tavern than there is here. At least people know where to go. Even our wine tastes better. This *Barbera* has been decanted so many times that it sits on your stomach like a lump. Look at these drinkers. There's more sobbing than drinking going on here."

Palmarucci's complaints were true, and this truth made me want to go back home and find protection in the life in Candia. Even Candia wasn't what Palmarucci was talking about, but when I thought about my town, sitting in that wine shop surrounded by the disorder of the city—not even sure of what I was looking for, I thought about it as a quiet, comfortable place, with a large main street and two cafés always open, the main square and the church and on each side lanes that led down to the gardens and the lake or up toward the vineyards and the woods filled with chestnuts.

If I had become a farmer and stayed in Candia I wouldn't have gotten sick. I would have been able to buy more land, buy a tractor and start a stable. I would have been able to live as I wished and decide what kind of work I would do each day, free in the fields. The stars mark the seasons, and you know when you have to plant, plow, or cut the grain. The rains bloat the seeds and open the furrows to the sun. I could have stopped my work to go after a rabbit or follow the furrows to the confines of the land. I could have shaken the fruit trees or sat down and called out to other men working nearby in the fields. I could have worked only for myself, saving, selecting the animals, the wood, and the fodder, leaving everything else for the winter and spending very little money.

Instead I chose to work in the factory. Other people and their plans forced me to do it, and I was their victim, a victim who works by the hour, one minute after another, one hand after another, back to back in the different departments of the factory. I was dependent on people I didn't even know; I was just another faceless worker. All the advantages of the factory in the end become the cause of sorrow. On top of all this one has to put up with injustices.

At this point, I got up. Palmarucci was still talking, addressing himself to the people at another table. The smell of the wine was too strong for me, and it had an acid tang that made me think of certain places in the factory.

I left, and I walked slowly toward the dispensary. That day I was only supposed to have an injection. The usual people were sitting on the benches in the waiting room. I didn't know them, and I'm not really sure if they were the same people I always saw when I went there. But in that place everyone looked alike. Perhaps it was because we never managed to break the silence that the dispensary imposed on us. It always seemed as if the voices and the noises had nothing to do with the people there.

I was impatient and more thoroughly convinced than usual that these treatments were useless. Once again I rested my naked arm on the little bed, and as it happened sometimes its nakedness made me pity myself and love myself as if I were a child. I was excited, and they had to puncture my arm three times before they found the vein. I felt the liquid flowing into me, and after a moment my teeth were on edge. They felt terribly sensitive as if they had changed places in my gums. All this gave me a sensation of sin and immodesty. I left in a hurry, and I walked quickly down the street. After a while I realized that I was walking toward the factory.

I knew that I was doing it out of force of habit and perhaps too because I had a desire to be there. This discovery didn't displease me. When I raised my head to see where I was going and to break the spell completely I saw Pinna crossing the street. He tried to start some banal conversation right away, but I stopped him. "I'd like to be in the open air too," he said, "in the open air."

I asked him if anything new had happened in the factory. "Nothing," he answered. "Nothing. The work gets harder, that's the only news; and there are always more people."

"But you," I said, "how do you manage to live in the city?" He looked at me seriously and gave a long sigh as he thought about his answer. "I live with debts," he said, and the heaviness of his burden seemed to increase. His sadness stopped me from telling him that he hadn't understood what I meant. But then he added something that helped me. "Sick or not," he said, "try to stay away from work as long as you can."

There was nobody in front of the factory, and I thought about Palmarucci's speech, but when I saw Pinna disappearing quickly into the factory I envied him.

When I returned home I told my mother that it would have been better if I had been a farmer. She didn't understand. "Who would have cured you and paid you? Have more faith and take care of yourself. You could be well by now. Why do you always stay out so long?"

I ate without answering her, chewing on the answer word for word and thinking bitterly how I could hurt her. When I got upstairs I started writing her an anonymous letter. "Where does your son go? He is always running around, and he has fallen into the hands of some very bad women. He is ruining his health and spending his money. The fault is yours, too, because you're always hammering at him."

I decided to mail it a few days later from the city. Now she would understand that my problems deserved more attention than she gave them and that the situation was more serious than she imagined it to be or than her words one after another implied.

A few days later Fioravanti and Signora Eufemia came back from Rome. Signora Eufemia had a different hairdo, full of curls. She smiled at me and hugged me. She lit a cigarette. She ate a piece of chocolate, gave me one, and asked me how I was. After a while, and she did all the talking, she told me that things hadn't gone the way they had hoped they would. The Vatican wanted proofs that they couldn't give. Other doctors had plotted against Fioravanti. She began to cry, hugging me and telling me in the midst of her tears that she understood me, that she saw the difficult situation I was in and the tricks of which the doctors were capable. Fioravanti had offered to cure the Pope with his serum, but they hadn't let him. They needed millions to bribe the doctors and to have the serum named "Healing Jesus."

Hugging each other, we threw ourselves on the bed, and I waited for her to calm herself. Afterwards Fioravanti gave me my serum injection with his usual scientific indifference. I looked around, and I saw three new shirts on the divan.

"Toward the middle of May the cure will be completely finished. I already see signs that you are nearly cured. You're not absorbing all the serum."

The promise of my imminent recovery didn't make me very happy. I had been sure I was going to get well quickly since the day I had forced Bompiero to give me the X rays. As a matter of fact, it irritated me to think that I had to wait till the middle of May to get something that had already belonged to me for a long time. The days would pass with spring and Easter but to make them pass well I would have to learn something so that I could be sure of myself when I went back to the factory and found myself facing the doctors and working in God knows what department. The annoyance I felt at having to wait till some future specific date for something that was already mine suddenly vanished with the suspicion that Fioravanti wanted to save his serum, and I was filled with the fear that he wanted to abandon me just as we were reaching the end of my cure, just as I was on the verge of complete recovery.

I asked him then if he planned to keep on giving me the injections till the middle of May. "Certainly," he said. "For above all the cure is important to you. Don't let them take any more X rays. From now on they have to judge your case clinically."

The injection affected me more than usual, and I left swaying from side to side filled with the pleasure of my lightness. I left swaying on my faithful legs keenly aware of their presence. I was like a small bird in the springtime that skirts the thorny hedges along the road and is curious of every leaf.

Palmarucci called me from the tavern, but I answered no with a wave of my hand. I was alone, I was well, and I was enjoying the afternoon. All of a sudden my legs gave out on me, but I began to amuse myself with my face, all the way up to my ears. I felt each feature distinctly. I felt them as if I could hold them in my hand in front of my eyes, one by one—first the nose, then the cheeks, and the lips. I thought that it was as if I were rebuilding myself and getting to know myself. No Tortora was going to confuse me now.

When I got to the station, I thought about the letter I had written to my mother. I decided to reread it before mailing it. I wasn't so sure about it any more, perhaps because I didn't have any reason to offend her at that moment. I liked the part about her hammering at me, and I realized then that it was really time for my mother and everyone else to change their attitudes toward me. I didn't mail the letter; I put it back in my pocket. I wanted to save it for other moments or, better still, as a reminder of the necessity of telling others to watch how they treated me. Resentment against my mother seemed impossible, the way I felt now. I was full of tenderness about my cure and full of desire to run and hug her.

Easter was very balmy. I had prepared myself for it, and I had even bought myself a gray-blue suit that made me look younger. I bought a silk handkerchief and some cologne. The sky was filled with enormous white clouds, and they made the earth seem very small and shiny. Even though there were so many clouds the sun always managed to break through, and it shone over everything, clear and vibrant.

I saw Giuliana at noon mass in Candia. She had a veil on her head, and it gave her a homey look, much sweeter than the way she looked in the factory. She saw me too and she smiled at me. She left with two older women, and the three of them turned into the lake road that led out of town. I thought that Giuliana must live in the country, on the other side of the lake, on the shadier side that faced the north. At home from my window I looked in that direction, and I saw a house barely touched by the sun. I thought it might be her house. Perhaps Giuliana got off the train at the next stop after Candia and in order to get home she would cut across the base of the hill and walk halfway back toward Candia along the muddy little road half lost in its wanderings around the lake.

In the afternoon I went back to town. I was sure that I would find Giuliana there again. It was the happy day with its sunlight that made me so certain, but I was wrong. I was depressed for a couple of hours, and I wandered around from one place to another. Now I know that it was better that way, but in those days I not only looked at the Indian and the boot, I also looked at Giuliana's house. These things comforted me while I waited for the fifteenth of May to arrive. It was the day I was to be cured.

The treatments in the dispensary became more and more difficult. I was afraid that Bompiero wouldn't think that I was cured, and I dreaded the thought that he might refute Fioravanti's opinion. The closer I came to being cured—that is, the closer I came to being cured of the blows others had given me—the more doubtful I became about my work in the factory. You have to live in the factory day by day and poison yourself little by little. Once you free yourself from the factory, even if it's only for a little while, you immediately realize the full horror of the situation.

But I was attracted by the idea of returning alive, cured and victorious, and of making Tortora and Manzino finally understand that I was a man capable of resisting their abuses. If I reappeared in the factory I would be stronger than Pinna, and I would have a stronger character than any other person who was tied to his work with resignation and who hadn't fought the battles I had fought.

Together with these thoughts I had other thoughts of abandoning the factory and going into business. I dreamed of opening a tobacco shop, or buying some land on the lake shore, irrigating it, and growing vegetables for the markets of X and Turin. I also wanted to keep some dairy cows and calves. The tobacco shop would have been more suitable for me, and today I still think about the comfortable and easy life I might have had.

Those spring days made me feel victorious, and on the first of May I decided to go and spend the day in the city of X. The town was deserted. There had been a meeting of the Federal Trade Union at nine thirty and afterwards everyone had gone to the country or to some of the small lakes nearby.

There was only one automobile in front of the factory and a great swirl of white air, whiter than the air that drifted over the rest of the countryside. It was an enormous block of luminous air, false and metallic. The factory rested on the ground as if it had only arrived a few minutes before. You had the same impression even when the factory was occupied and men scurried around it like ants. That morning it was dazzling in its unnatural silence and under that strange column of air.

As I wandered away I had the distinct impression that I would return to the factory, that my fight wasn't over because I had not obtained the victory I deserved. Then I thought that I had never felt better than I felt at that moment standing before the factory. My health conquered every doubt and fear. Three days later Bompiero smiled at me and gave me to understand that I would soon be cured. Fioravanti said that it couldn't be any other way because I had only one serum injection left and then my treatment would be over. I greeted Signora Eufemia hurriedly from the doorway. Her wiles didn't convince me any longer, and she didn't even try to use them on me.

When I got home I wrote down the hour that would mark the

last week. I decided I wouldn't say anything to Bompiero till the day after the fifteenth. On that day I had to go to the dispensary for my usual treatment. I watched my mother carefully during those days because I didn't want any unpleasant surprises once I returned to the factory and took up the business of my life. She asked me if the doctors were as sure of my cure as I was. The difference between us was that she could be a victim of their plotting and once she fell into their hands she would drag me down with her. It was useless to try to convince her that she was wrong, and any discussion on the subject would have ended in arguments and tears. I reassured her about the doctor's opinion.

The morning of the fifteenth I opened my closet and took out the money I had hidden to pay Fioravanti. I put on my new suit, winked at myself in the mirror, and left to get my last injection. The weather was just what it should have been. The bus was half empty and we traveled quickly.

I drank a cup of coffee in the most elegant bar in X and as I drank it I felt as if I were doing something extraordinary and lucky. The smell of the coffee, like my happiness, overflowed my soul and permeated everything around me. I walked toward via del Distretto without stopping and without noticing the streets I passed. At last I faced Palmarucci's doorway in its reality, and it was another source of joy like the ray of sunlight that illuminated the paint and softened the brass fixtures of the shutters.

My arm was still, and Fioravanti gave me my injection. He was smoking, and on that last day he was also smiling. I had given him the money, and I hadn't minded. I was happy to pay. Signora Eufemia came to the consulting room to say hello and to invite me to her room. The air in her room was still cold even though the sun shone on all the brushes and bottles she used on her hair. Signora Eufemia told me that now that I was a happy man I would forget her and her treatments and that I would make a lucky marriage because I was a young man who had not abused himself. In the meantime the morning sun, subtle and silent, beat on her dressing gown and on her neck. It made her body seem as old as her face and her hair. Everything had the look of a winter fruit that had been removed from the store window. The entire room gave me that impression because my memory was tied to those ugly winter days, that wrinkled bed, and the stove. I gave Signora Eufemia the remainder of the money, and I walked out into the street.

Spring met me with its veil of sunlight and walked with me through the old streets of the city filled with the smell of cooking till I got to the warm shimmering square beside the river.

The next day I went to the dispensary, but I only had some minor medication because Bompiero wasn't there. On that day in May the weather changed, and once more we were engulfed in fog and rain from the Val d'Aosta. It was a thick fog, and it ran quickly in and out of the patches of light. The rain was already tinged with the dirt and the smell of summer rain. The weather tired me and sent a shiver down my back. It was so easy for Bompiero to tell me that I still had to have further treatments just for a short time, just to round out the cure.

"There's no hurry to get back to the factory. After the holidays?"

"No," I said, "before."

"All right, before. Just as you wish."

How could I trust a doctor with whom I could negotiate the date of my recovery? Still, I wasn't uncertain any longer, and I was happy to get back to work. It was a matter of pride. I was happy to begin before the holidays because the vacations that followed would give me a chance to rest and evaluate my reactions after I started work.

I wrote a letter to the Bishop asking for his help in my fight against my persecutors, and I decided to go and speak to Grosset. He came down to meet me near the guard's office inside the factory. At the end of a long talk during which he urged me to get back to work—"either inside or outside"—he told me that now it was his turn not to feel well. This annoyed me, and I was convinced it was an excuse he gave me for not wanting to understand the full measure of my situation. His statement showed a great lack of consideration for my feelings. It was an unfriendly joke.

After my talk with Grosset I went to see the social assistant. It was a wise move because she immediately reserved my room in the mountains for the month of vacations.

During those days at home I wandered from room to room but

[169

I didn't stay in bed or lean out the window and talk to the boot and the Indian as I had done before. The Indian's appearance was changing. He looked as if he were really getting old. My problems were so real at that time that now the boot and the Indian looked at me silently as I ran around the lake with my thoughts. I would catch them looking at me during the brief pauses when some movement around me would break my train of thought. Then I would see their old faces, each in its usual place, forever turned toward me and ready to begin.

As I wandered from room to room I had so many suggestions to make to myself and so many real ideas that I was kept quite busy as I waited out Bompiero's last days.

My anxiety diminished and lost its intensity as it spread over everything I did. I started looking at the house as I had never looked at it before. I wanted to fix it up, change the furniture, change the staircase, and widen the windows. I would often run into my mother, and I began to notice how she spent her days. We didn't speak to each other very much even though after every encounter we would follow the other's every movement, warily full of pretenses and suspicion. A speech should have followed every word and every look should have been full of memories and allusions. When I couldn't stand it any longer I'd go out into the garden. I had begun to smoke again. This was something else that bothered my mother. Every time I left the house or every time she went outside she would find the malign strength to begin to mumble under her breath so that I could hardly hear her.

"Speak up," I'd tell her. "I can't understand you."

"It's useless to speak up; you don't want to understand."

"What?"

"Everything. Why have you started smoking again? Why don't you take care of yourself?" This wasn't what was really worrying her, but this she could scream out with some justification.

"Tell the truth," I told her.

"What truth? You don't take care of yourself. What have you spent all your money on? You run around with bad women, and that's how you have ruined your health."

"I'm cured, and I'm going to start work again soon," I told her the last time we spoke, the day before I went to see Bompiero.

In the morning I found that she had ironed my new suit and had gotten everything else ready. She was waiting for me in the kitchen. I opened the door, and I looked out into the garden as I had my breakfast. My mother cried silently while I ate. Then she wanted to hug me. Breakfast had agreed with me because even when I got to the city my stomach felt full and warm, and it wasn't tied in knots with fright like the other times, even though the emotion this time was the strongest I had ever felt because I was waiting for Dr. Bompiero's answer. The warm weather helped me too, and I felt tranquil, wrapped in a gentle stupor. When I arrived at the dispensary, I sat down in the waiting room with all the others. My face didn't reflect my feelings, and out of a sense of discretion I didn't say a word, out of a delicate sense of discretion that made me more sensitive to the others.

They called me, and I saw Bompiero. He looked all new and shiny. His shirt sleeves were turned up, and his wrists showed black and hairy. He looked me straight in the eye; he smiled and made a brief speech that had the ring of hope.

"I'm sure that I am cured," I said.

He examined me carefully, touching every delicate place on my back and on my chest. He felt my stomach and my lower belly. He got up and looked out the window. He then raised my arms and lowered them again. He took a blood specimen and sent it on to the infirmary. He tapped my knees to test my reflexes. He even made me urinate in a glass. Then he made me lie down. He lit a cigarette. I could feel my heart secure and clean, beating on the little bed. My heart was more tranquil than the rest of me. Bompiero kept me lying down for a few minutes while he studied my X rays. Then he made me get up and fluoroscoped me. When he had freed me from the machine, he made me get completely undressed and he began to look at my back and prod it here and there all the way down to my legs. He kept poking me in the spine with a pencil and telling me to take care of myself or stand up straight. Finally he looked at my throat.

"Yes," he said, "you are better. Several more weeks of injections and rest and then back to the factory."

"Two weeks," I answered. Bompiero looked at me steadily but then he seemed to be persuaded.

[171

Two weeks later to the day, I stood at the door of the Personnel Department. I was alone and sure of myself and everything was as it should be. I didn't feel surrounded by the atmosphere of conspiracy I had felt at other times. My interview with the clerk was brief. He couldn't put me in Grosset's section; so he sent me to the Assembling Department.

Ten minutes later I was at my new post. Mr. Milione, the foreman, asked where I had worked before. Grosset's name made him smile. He told me to take my place at the end of the line.

The department was almost entirely filled with women; it was known for the beauty of some of the women and for the sharp tongues of others. After a few days I heard someone say that when one of the prettier girls went to the bathroom Milione would follow her and peer at her over the toilet partitions. They had nicknamed him "Toilet-paper Milione" and "Pull the Chain." I decided that I would not get involved in these discussions and that I would do my work and avoid troubles.

The work in the Assembling Department was simple, and the allotted time was adequate for the work. I managed to fill my quota easily without straining myself. The only thing that bothered me was the fact that the work seemed unworthy of a man and especially of a man of my ability. I felt the strength and the desire to build something important. But it wasn't the right moment to say anything to anybody. The women in the department eyed me with curiosity, but they didn't ask me any questions. The other men in the department were also isolated and consequently they didn't take any initiative or ask anything of anybody. Occasionally Milione would get up, walk around, and nod to us, but he didn't make any comments on the work. Our department was at one end of the factory and during the lunch break we had to go through a lot of empty sections before getting to the cafeteria.

Pinna and Gualatrone were in the cafeteria, and they came over to see me. Pinna was well dressed, and as usual he was smiling with his nice round mouth. He told me that he was interested in sports and wanted to take a course on how to be a referee. Gualatrone was still very handsome. He wore light blue overalls and carried a red handkerchief in his pocket. He wore his hair cut short over his forehead, and while he ate he read the newspaper. He was still working in the same department but not under Manzino. He had been promoted to desk work. Gualatrone was engaged to a girl from Viverone; her father was a hotel keeper. He showed me her photograph, and he said he still wasn't sure about the wedding date. Pinna and Gualatrone didn't ask me many questions about my life and my health. As a matter of fact, they assumed immediately that I was well and able to work in peace.

I didn't see Grosset in the cafeteria, and one day I went to look for him in his department, just after twelve o'clock. He was putting on his jacket, and he greeted me affectionately. He folded up his newspaper, and he told me that for some time now he had been going home for lunch because he couldn't digest the food in the cafeteria. He had to eat very little and rest a while after his meals. He didn't lock his desk before leaving, and he didn't turn around to give one last check to the machines. "If you've begun to work again, take it easy," he said, but he said it in a different tone of voice than the others did.

It was late when I arrived in the cafeteria and Giuliana waited on me. She made a sign as if to say that she couldn't talk to me, then. After lunch I went to sit down in the garden under the trees as usual.

I would get up to leave when they blew the second whistle because I knew a short cut to my section. It was an enclosed passageway that led by the room where they kept the inflammable materials. So I could stay outside a little longer, and I didn't have to follow the others. This little extra liberty gave me a feeling of relief.

Every day I would break up my afternoon in three ways. Till about four o'clock I would fight a feeling of drowsiness and the heat, working very little, below the quota, and thinking about many things including the plans I had made for a change of department and a promotion. I would examine each piece I had to assemble, and I would play with them to make the time pass. In the meantime I would smoke three cigarettes. Around four o'clock I would go to the bathroom and stay five or ten minutes. I would wash my hands and face over and over and I would walk up and down the hall taking very small steps, stopping whenever anything caught my eye, even a nail on the wall. Afterwards I would return to my work. I worked very quickly, and I'd fulfill my quota. I kept this up for about an hour. For one hour I worked at top speed without getting tired.

As I worked my thoughts flashed through my head, inarticulate and almost without any meaning. If you wanted to work at that speed your mind had to be active as well. If I thought of something sensible while I was working, I mean, if out of the tangle of thoughts I discovered a sensible combination of ideas, I would be forced to think about it seriously, and this of course would interrupt the rhythm of my work.

After this hour of work I would get up and go get an orangeade. I would drink three swallows standing next to the machine, and I would take the rest back to my place. This gave me the excuse of walking slowly back to the department in order not to spill any of the drink. I would finish the rest of the drink in intervals of a quarter of an hour while I looked out the window and watched the changing sky, waiting for the light to wane. I would always see some clouds, or a streak of color, or a current of wind, or else the sky would be covered over by an impregnable sheet of metal that looked like a continuation of the factory. Time passed like this till an hour before closing time. Then, since I had already caught up with my work, I would begin to feel the relief of my approaching liberation. I kept on working, but I would follow the happenings in the department which at that hour was full of bustle and talk. Already some of the women were getting up from their places to comb their hair or to make some future appointment with a friend. After another half hour nearly everyone stopped working. They pulled out their purses and newspapers, mirrors and combs, and little groups began to form. Some girl behind one of the tables would pull up her stocking and smooth out her slip under her uniform. The bolder and more calculating women did these little adjustments in front of Milione, who would keep walking up and down the entire length of the department. I kept on working in the middle of all these distractions, but I wasn't bored or anxious to see the hand on the clock slowly come down and point to six thirty.

When it was five minutes before six thirty, I would put away the last piece of equipment and stretch my legs for a minute. Then I would run my hand over the table and get up. I'd light a cigarette and smoke it slowly as I left the department, and I wouldn't throw away the butt till it was time to punch out for the day. I would dress quickly in the locker room and wash my face and hands. I would go to the station in time to catch the six forty train. It was difficult to get a seat at that hour, and I would stand in the passage looking at a view that had already become a part of me. But this was better than chattering stupidly in one of the compartments.

On the evening of the day I had spoken to Grosset I noticed that one of the girls from my department was traveling on the same train with me. She was standing with her legs slightly spread apart at the end of the corridor. After that I saw her nearly every evening and always standing with her legs slightly apart or with one leg hooked behind the other leg. If she was sitting down she always had her legs crossed and her skirt pulled tight above her knees. You couldn't avoid looking at her legs, and she would often look at them too and move them around as if it were a way of expressing herself. Her hair talked as much as her legs did, and she kept shaking her head from side to side almost continuously. All her gestures were imperious, and she was really beautiful. Her coloring wasn't particularly good, nor was she especially sweet, nor did she use lipstick or other feminine paraphernalia but the more you looked at her the more you became aware of her beauty, a serious persistent beauty, a beauty that grew stronger every time. I watched for her every evening, and I would stare at her in silence. She recognized me, and she would look at me with a questioning glance as if surprised at the dare in my eyes. There were always a lot of men around her, and she treated them with indifference. Once I noticed that she was wearing a wedding ring. During all that time, up to the day vacations began on the twenty-eighth of July I never saw Giuliana on the train, nor did I see her get off at the station.

I spent my vacation in the mountains in the time set apart for convalescent workers. During the first days of my stay the other men bothered me with their attempts at friendship. I would go off sightseeing by myself on foot or by bus, and I visited all the surrounding towns.

The mountains did me a lot of good: I slept, I ate, and I took walks. I would also drink large quantities of water with a high iron content from a nearby spring. My thoughts were few, and they had nothing to do with either the doctors or the factory. Most of all I thought about my mother, and I hoped that eventually we would understand each other completely. I knew that my hope was impossible, but I continued to hope with reservations. In my heart of hearts I continued to be on very good terms with her, and I remembered her in all her bygone sweetness. I couldn't accept the reality of her complaints and her old age and consequently I would offend her, and the more I offended her the more painful it was to recall the memory of the two of us, both of us younger and more affectionate.

None of these things had anything to do with the work that I felt was so important to me the moment I stepped into the factory. As a matter of fact during the days following the vacation and for the rest of that year the factory became the most interesting thing in my life. My life was my work. I was constantly seeking to understand my place in the factory and to convince myself of its beauty and its immutability. In the meantime autumn was approaching and the countryside became bare. It spread out in enormous puddles and huddled in the rain while from the great canyons in the mountains the cold and the fog advanced on the plain, bringing misery to the farmers.

At that time the only thing that seemed wrong and at the same time was a proof of particular beauty was my relationship with the factory. It was a unique relationship, an unspoken relationship, mine alone, and it had nothing to do with the people in my department or any of the others who worked in the factory. The factory remained insensitive; it left every initiative and decision up to me. It enchanted me, and it made me as delirious as a boy. Then I tried to observe the other people's attitude toward the factory and to discover what the factory meant to them. Nearly all of them merely put up with the factory. They worked and that was all, trying to get as much money and benefits from the factory as they could. Their real life took place outside the factory, or at best any life they might have within the building was merely a matter of chance. If not, why did so many, including myself, go on living in the country?

Perhaps the girls, or to be more specific the girls who came from the city, behaved naturally, but even they had a very matter-of-fact attitude toward the factory, an attitude that you don't have if you are doing something that really interests you. In other words, for everyone concerned, the factory was only a corridor, and to make matters worse it was always the same.

I, on the other hand, was still searching for the way to a complete life, maybe because I was the one who was farthest from the possibility of having one. I didn't have any friends, and I wasn't attached to any particular town; consequently it was only natural that I should try to find my place in the life of the factory. And those who thought that they could live their life outside the factory, what could they bring to that life except their old habits and memories? Cigliano, the man who sat in front of me, would often point to the girl sitting next to him and say, "This girl is more familiar to me than my wife, who has borne me three sons."

I also thought about something the clerk in the Personnel Department had told me the last time: "You must pretend that the factory is a town, and a man must accept its laws. If you want to live in this town you must circulate, make friends, and so forth and so on."

But how could I pretend that the factory was a town? In Candia I could live in many different ways, but in the factory there was only one way to live: under orders. In Candia I could have picked my friends, changed from group to group, speaking to everyone according to my thoughts of the moment, but I couldn't do this in the factory.

I was firmly convinced of all these things within myself, and yet I went on looking for a better way to live within the factory, to search for a bond that would bring us closer together. Perhaps I felt this way because I was even more afraid than the others that the factory would reject me again, and then too I was hoping to find within that bond the means to revenge all the injustices I had suffered. In any case it must be difficult for everyone to divide their lives between the factory and the outside world.

Even the beautiful girl from the train and her lovely legs lived a strange life in the factory. She was one of the most courted and popular girls around. Whether she was in the factory or the cafeteria or the train she was always surrounded by rather important people, designers or department heads. Often I could see that she was intimidated by their attentions and she responded to their presence with a meek little half smile. When she got off at the station in Candia many of them would wave at her from the train windows, and she would walk away smiling her meek little smile, but her gestures were always dignified and imperious. Her smile would vanish immediately, and once she was surrounded by the darkness she didn't toss her head any more. Very often I would see her standing alone with a young man from the student center. In the evenings he would get off at the station with her, and then he would run to catch the train again. I suppose that is why they traveled in the first car. It usually was the most deserted car and it stopped a little outside the station, on the other side of the small fountain hidden by tall rose bushes.

One evening toward the end of October the girl got off the train with the young man, and I got off right behind them. He gently pulled her hair and gave her a little push toward the darkness. She smiled at him and watched him climb aboard the moving train. Her hands were clasped together. I followed her out of the station. At the door of the station a tall young man approached her and called her by name. It was her husband, a tall dark farmer. He was smiling and talking but I realized that he was making a tremendous effort. The wife had lost her beauty and that meek look that lightened her eyes. Her face was set tight and straight like the face of the old women in the country. Her head was also rigid, and her hair didn't swing about her shoulders—it merely lay quietly down her back. I followed the couple for about two hundred yards along the road that led to my house. At first the wife was silent. They were both silent, but then I heard the girl speak. She was telling her husband not to go and meet her at the station, to wait for her near the motorcycle; in other words she was telling him that she didn't want anyone to see him. I understood from the husband's reaction as he stood there in the darkness like another tree in the country night that it wasn't the first time that they had had this argument. I knew that the husband suffered and that the wife suffered; both of them were ashamed.

I continued to analyze the factory. The Assembling Department was an uninterestingly stable place that didn't inspire your ambition or initiative. It was full of women. I was the only one at all interested in the work. The other men were nearly human leftovers, and they had been put to work with the women doing the simplest kind of assembling. The factory was their school uniform. They didn't even talk about salaries, or promotions, or bonuses; they were in the factory and that was that. There wasn't any feeling of camaraderie among them, and they only talked about the most superficial gossip. The younger girls kept to themselves, and the prettier ones even more so. I suffered, but I had decided to wait a year before requesting a transfer.

December arrived and the days were very short. The day ended quickly but working hours didn't, and it was difficult to stay in the factory for two or more hours after dark until it was closing time. It seemed as if you and the factory were plunged in darkness, a damp darkness reflected in the neon lights of the buildings, a heavy darkness of muffled sounds. There wasn't any bottom to this darkness. They had turned on the steam heat and I breathed with difficulty, aware of the infinite possibilities of contamination around me, much more so than during the summer when everything had an acid tang. You could smell the stagnant odors, especially the odor of human beings. I breathed the smell of the girls that rose in waves from under their blouses.

Christmas was not far off when Pinna came looking for me. He was terribly upset, but he was still smiling. Fear made his smile seem even more insolent than usual. I would have liked to pull his lips above his gums the way you do with dogs to see what he was hiding between his teeth. It was his smile that made me want to laugh at him just to make him understand that his air of self-assurance didn't fool anyone but himself and because I felt that between his teeth shone the vice that he wanted to hide. His eyes shone like his lips.

He started telling me that he was sure that I was rich because I was on the side of the priests. His leg started to twitch in a spasm of imaginary gaiety. But he understood immediately that I wasn't having any part of his joke. "Help me, Albino," he said. "Lend me some money." He needed half a million lire. The smile vanished, and he stood waiting in front of me like a dog. His lip had really curled up.

Even though I knew what my answer would be, since I didn't have any money, I told him in a low voice, almost as if I were speaking to myself: "Come back day after tomorrow."

"What?" he answered. He hadn't reacted and he was still waiting.

"I'll see what I can do," I said. "Come back day after tomorrow."

"I can't; give me the money tomorrow."

What he said seemed to be really true. I had answered him as I did because I had wanted to get back at him and make him pay for his grossness. I wanted to make him wait in order to make him suffer just one day, while I had been waiting and suffering for nearly twenty years!

Once I had decided there wasn't any chance of getting the least satisfaction out of Pinna and his problems, I became apprehensive about what would happen to him. My superiority was assured by the fact that no one could have banished my troubles in two days, no matter how much money they used.

Pinna was dazed. One of his lips was thicker than the other, and they were glued together with spit. Every once in a while he would begin to laugh and force his eyes to laugh but he was a hypocrite. We found out that he had tried to steal some money to repay all the IOU's he had handed out for his luxuries and the good life he led. He had more than a million lire worth of IOU's and he owed other money besides. He had to account for four hundred thousand lire that he had collected from a group of workers for the purpose of buying them clothes wholesale. But he hadn't paid the wholesaler, and he had only distributed half of the merchandise among the workers. He was on the point of going to jail. The union fired him, but the factory saved him.

"They have already transferred him to another department," said Gualatrone. "They have sent him to the Checking Department, and you can be sure that he will be promoted to operator. People like him who sell out to the company are too valuable to lose." I had gone to look for Gualatrone to see if the two of us could help Pinna. I was upset at what he told me, but he added simply, "Haven't you understood anything yet? The working class is being destroyed, and every climber, every thief, and every idiot prospers."

The certainty in Gualatrone's voice dismayed me. It relieved me of my worries over Pinna, but it filled me with other more confusing worries about myself. Why couldn't I see things as clearly as he did? While this question was forming in my mind, Gualatrone said something that provided the answer, "But you are only interested in your own business."

Did they attack me because I kept to myself? Even Sergeant Vattino had considered me a loner. "I can't stand seeing you always alone like this," he said to me one day while we were standing in the middle of the courtyard surrounded by thousands of soldiers.

Perhaps Tortora had guessed or found out that I was alone and that is why he had begun tampering with my fate. But how could I find any friends in any of those departments? How could I find a true and sincere friend in the midst of all those people who were content to stick together out of fear or because they shared a common boss? Their talk moved steadily on like the conveyor belts in the Assembling Department and it was even timed to the speed of the moving pieces. Their faces fled my memory and disintegrated over the machines and their parts, or else they glared down on me with false smiles like the very lights in the department. Even the gentler souls convinced themselves that they had friends and that they really knew someone in the factory. They convinced themselves, and that was enough. Maybe the man who worked in my section and had compared his wife to the girl who worked by his side no longer knew his wife, but he really didn't know the girl either. He was fooling himself just because he saw her beside him for eight or nine hours a day, blondish, pale, with swollen hands, just because he could smell her faint smell of powder and hear her breathe and hear her sneeze and hear her talk, saying the same few words over and over again, always the same, always the same. The man who worked with me really didn't know anybody any more in the true sense of knowing someone: to talk and sometimes postpone the talking about things that we really believe, to share

[181

something in the full honesty of conscience and above all to share one's conscience. He didn't really know anyone any more either inside or outside the factory. The rest were all the same. I was the only one who wasn't satisfied with this pretense, and I left them to themselves the way that some newborn chicks who have wandered away from the others try to climb the steps of the granary.

That same day I went to see Grosset, but he was at home, sick. Christmas was very near, and I was full of my own thoughts and these disturbed me greatly. They even affected my health. They renewed some of my old pains; or perhaps they had reappeared because I had begun thinking about them again. I had begun to think about all my old fears concerning the doctors. Would the old year end without Tortora interfering and ruining the new?

When I arrived at Grosset's house, his wife came and opened the door for me. She was very vague and she didn't say much. She was pretty but the makeup on her face was applied in a half-hearted slapdash fashion. She had on a long bathrobe and the lace of her nightgown protruded from the sleeves and the hem of the robe. She took me to her husband who was lying down in a room full of couches and cushions plus two chaises longues and two easy chairs. She went over to Grosset and shook him as if she were waking him up. She kept on shaking him with one hand and with the other she picked up a package of cigarettes that was lying nearby. He followed her with his eyes as happy as if he were enjoying the most courteous treatment. He shared his satisfaction with me, and he seemed to have found a more comfortable position in his easy chair.

"How are you?" he said. "You are the only one who has come to see me."

I answered that I wasn't feeling very well.

"The same old troubles?"

I told him that I had some new ones.

"Is it the doctors' fault?"

"The doctors and the factory," I replied.

"But what are you still looking for in the factory? What section are you in?"

I didn't answer him exactly and of course my answer didn't convince him.

182]

"You shouldn't hope to find everything in the factory—only work and your salary—and you should try to better both your work and your salary."

Then I spoke to him about the country.

"The farmers are worse off than you are."

I told him that I was talking about the whole country.

"And what do you mean by that? You're always speaking in general, whereas I'm convinced your troubles are all personal. Your town, the factory, your work; think of yourself in relation to these things. I know that the factory is bad, but you can't die because of that. One must try to control oneself both inside and outside the factory. You work honestly, you go to union meetings, you have fun on Sundays, and you read. I'm sick too. Well then, shouldn't I take my medicine? You're Catholic. Go to mass and confession; join the right-wing unions."

I told him I was alone.

Grosset gave me a long speech, and many new ideas sprang from his words, but the ideas were vague and confused and not at all like his old self. Now he made longer and more passionate speeches, but he had lost the clarity of former days when he had been a man of few words. He said that this business of feeling alone was as old as the world and that you didn't get any satisfaction in saying that even though it still might be true, that you're only alone if you think you are. "All of the unions in the world, not even all Russia, is enough to make you feel that you're not alone. The answer comes from within. You're at that stage now," he concluded.

He got very excited and a smile appeared on his face that was the proof of his convictions. I told him that I had always been willing to do the right thing but that the doctors had plotted against me.

"I have never been able to understand why. It's true that doctors often make mistakes. They are the most ignorant lot of all the scientists. I know I have cancer of the intestines, but they say I don't, and they won't operate. But tonight I'll tell them: either they take a look inside of me or they stop bothering me with their medicine. Something strange is happening to me; exactly twelve hours of pain and then twelve hours of respite and weariness, punctually every day."

[183

In the meantime his wife had come to the door. She smoked and listened to us. She asked me, "Do you work in my husband's department?" At the sound of her voice he turned around and looked at her with love.

"Sit down," he told her. "No, he doesn't work in my department. His name is Saluggia."

The woman left the room for a second and returned with a drink for her husband and a vermouth for me. Grosset drank, but he raised his head from the glass for a second and said, "I am a Socialist and I know how bad the factories can be. Still I would have liked to become a director."

At that moment his wife turned on the light, and I watched the intensity disappear from Grosset's eyes. His eyes couldn't sustain the meaning of his words, and they lost their significance in a smile that was as weak as water. I noticed his pallor. His body, sunk in cushions, already seemed to have been deposed and broken by the awkwardness of death.

He made some further comments on doctors in general, and he told me not to be afraid, not to fear things that don't exist. But I couldn't pay any attention to his advice in the presence of his death.

As we were going downstairs, his wife confirmed what I already knew. "Poor Grosset," she said. "They have left him all alone. He will die, poor soul. He will die."

Grosset's fate saddened me profoundly, and it presaged one of the ugliest winters I had ever had. I stopped at Grosset's department, and there was someone else in his place. Christmas and New Year's Day arrived but I couldn't echo the festivities. My loneliness increased, and I hardly ever bothered to say hello to anyone in my department any more. One day Gualatrone came looking for me to invite me to a New Year's Eve party they were giving at his fiancée's hotel. He invited me out of friendship even though he knew that I wasn't very interested in company. As a matter of fact, I refused.

"Find yourself a girl," said Gualatrone. "Try to talk to someone and have fun. Get your head out from under your wing."

I waved good-by and left him.

I spent Christmas thinking that my wave meant I hadn't been able to give him an answer. The last Sunday of the year I took a walk beyond the town by the road I had seen Giuliana take at Easter. I hoped that I would find myself before a little gate and see her at the window. I hadn't gone that way for years, and suddenly my walk took on an air of mystery. In the meantime the appearance of the lake was changing. It looked smaller but fuller and much less luminous. The land was squared off by many tall and naked poplars whose sparse dark leaves looked like birds huddling in the taller branches. They covered the tops of the trees like an immovable and silent flock of birds. The ground was frozen, dark and green and shining with drops of frost that lay in the hollows of the fallen leaves. My steps were the only things that disturbed this carpet that seemed to have been lying untouched for years.

Halfway down the hill I had left the road to avoid the long way around. I figured that I would get back on the road if I kept going in a straight line across the lower level of the hill near the shores of the lake. Here the land was terraced; trying to find the easiest crossing, I had inadvertently come nearly to the shore of the lake.

I kept running into little canals where the water filtered and purified itself as it ran through the bearded roots and granulous earth; strange ice shapes sparkled in the hollow, shady places. The canals were no deeper than a meter but the small waterfalls, the grasses, the roots, the grottoes, the ice and the movement of the water had such a mysterious and convincing look about them that they assumed gigantic proportions in my eyes. I was so taken by this magic that I could very well imagine being hurled about by a cascade of drops and grass tendrils and falling into a cavern of ice. The clear air, the clean water, and the ice gave me a spasmodic desire to drink and absorb them. All of a sudden I saw something jump in one of the canals. It was a bass as big as a man's arm, and he had caught a smaller fish. The bass was still for a moment while he devoured his prey. I could see him almost emerging from the water. I looked directly into his eyes; they were the eyes of an assassin who has been taken by surprise but who will not remove the knife. Before he could escape he had to eat the other creature. In that second the only thing that remained of the other fish was a slight movement in the water. The bass stayed still for another second, his eyes rooted to mine, breathing with exhaustion through his open sharp-toothed mouth.

The scene frightened me, and that pale distant sky where you could neither read nor write anything served to reconfirm my fear and my solitude. There was nothing I could do, not even for myself. I could only thrash the water like the dead fish, destined to die. Everything was like a dream, and my walk was spoiled. Before me ran a wider canal, and I couldn't cross it. I turned in toward the hillside, but walking was difficult because there were many thorny, violet-colored bushes growing in my path. I picked my way out of that patch of ground with difficulty, but I again found myself surrounded by water. I had reached the lake. I realized I had wandered onto some sort of small peninsula and I imagined how it must look from my window.

The view was unfamiliar, and the lake was still and white. I stopped and looked at it for a minute, lost in my thoughts. I heard a loud noise that seemed to fill the end of the day. Thousands of crows were screeching in the sky. They were returning from the Val d'Aosta to settle down for the night in the fields and in the poplar groves. High above, their singing was beautiful, and it remained high above without falling to earth or diminishing. The crows were flying beyond the lake to where the plains spread on indefinitely.

Another noise came from the lake. A man was standing on a long flat boat pushing it along the shore with a pole. He moved slowly with his eyes fixed in the distance. He didn't have any fishing gear or fish with him. A thin cold fog followed in the wake of his boat. I cried out suddenly and instinctively, like a force of nature. I was afraid because I was alone and dreaded being left there, alone, forever. I felt alone the way I felt when I was a boy, the way I felt in my dreams, and the moment I screamed it seemed as if all my wretched life had inexorably led to this destiny.

The man in the boat came toward me. His face was hidden because he had bent his head in an effort to concentrate on his rowing. He landed on the shore where I was standing, but he remained a stranger to me contrary to the senseless hope that I had felt within me, sparked by his air of mystery and his gesture of help.

He wasn't one of the ones who could ever have helped me or could help me now.

Silently I got into his boat while the man spoke only the necessary words to guide me through the reeds and sudden drops under the grass bridges. I stood behind him, and I could smell the wool of his jacket; it was a fatherly smell. How had he understood that I had wanted his help when I screamed? Was it so obvious even to those who weren't looking that I was alone and lost? He was a just man, and he headed straight across the lake toward Candia. If Tortora had been in his place he would have left me in the swamp.

It started to snow on the last night of the year. You couldn't see anything from my side of the lake, but you could hear the wild ducks. Perhaps two flocks were coming together, or perhaps they were getting ready to leave. I could still hear my scream mingling with their screams because the snow preserves noises and sadness the same way fear does.

VIII

IT SNOWED TILL AFTER EPIPHANY, and the deep snow made travel difficult, even by train. Both in the mornings and evenings the train was often late, sometimes as much as a half hour late. The mood of the passengers was strange; they traveled either in a state of great excitement or in complete silence.

During these trips I kept meeting Giuliana. She wore a blue wool scarf around her head, and her blue eyes seemed even larger than usual. One evening she got off the train in Candia. Besides the scarf, under her coat she wore a pair of tight toreador pants and white overshoes with a blue fur or wool lining. This strange way of dressing was an instant revelation of Giuliana's boldness, and I felt as if I had discovered her in an intimate moment, as if she were offering a hidden part of her body.

I wasn't surprised when one evening I saw a man step out from the shadow of the trees toward the end of the station platform away from the stream of people going home. He took a few steps toward Giuliana, and then he stood and waited for her. She ran the rest of the way toward him, and her arm was raised as if she were going to offer him something. I heard his voice while I watched him put an arm around her waist. They walked along the shadows, as indifferent to everyone as the shadows or the trees, without once turning their heads to look around or look back. His voice fell on the snow and remained alive for a second as if it had been some sort of light.

I had to follow them because they took the road that led to my house, but I also followed them because I was attracted by their sureness and their indifference. The road was empty, and after they had rounded the curve and the station was out of sight they started walking and bumping against each other zig-zagging along the road. Giuliana had opened her coat, and the man had stuck his hands inside it. They kept pushing each other, and then they kissed and hugged in the middle of the road, risking a fall because she kept bending under the man's pressure. They didn't speak any more. Every once in a while I heard their sighs and her short bursts of laughter. It seemed as if the road and the night were getting warm and lighting up even though there was no moon or stars in the sky. I was filled with a strange desire to interfere and scream at them to stop, but this desire overwhelmed me and blocked all my impulses except the impulse to follow them and watch them. Suddenly the man threw himself on a snow bank and pulled Giuliana on top of him. Then she broke away and ran toward the parapet of a little bridge nearby. She stopped, leaning on her hands against the side of the bridge.

Slowly the man emerged from the shadows of the snow bank and, always slowly, he walked toward her, even stopping to light a cigarette. When he reached her he threw the cigarette into the middle of the road, took off his coat, and put it on the parapet. He took Giuliana's hand and pulled her after him down the incline that led to the stream under the black arc of the bridge. When I reached the place where they had been standing the cigarette was still burning in the middle of the road. I leaned against the bridge on the same side where they had disappeared. My hands were near the man's coat. I thrust my head forward, and I heard them. I could hear the sound of their impure kisses, the murmur of their sighs, and I could hear them move and ravage each other. Sometimes the man kept quiet but not Giuliana. I took the man's overcoat and out of spite I started to squeeze it. The cloth was heavy and rough; the lining was light and smooth. In the meantime from beneath the bridge I could hear that desire was conquering the man and the woman. I listened up to the very end, wanting to scream, but the scream would spend itself within me. For the first time I felt in my guts that a bridge had formed connecting my throat, my stomach, my belly, and my male organs. I heard them come. The man lying six feet below me seemed to bump against something, seemed to lose the rhythm of his breathing and then tear himself away, get up or fall. I heard Giuliana slide and empty herself like a vase; her voice slowly grew weaker. I was leaning on my knees, and I held the man's coat in my hands.

Then, below me, they had found their voices again. I heard their feet searching for a foothold in the darkness. I went away from the bridge and left the overcoat. Now they were talking and laughing and climbing the bank. I started walking very slowly, and I wasn't afraid of being seen because I felt as exhilarated as they did, or even more. As a matter of fact, they were the ones who pulled back when they saw me. They had been talking when they reached the road, but as soon as they saw me so near, walking calmly in front of them without turning around, they stopped talking and stood quite still. I didn't turn around, but I heard Giuliana and the man turn and walk away in the opposite direction.

I hoped that Giuliana had seen me, even though I feared that such a meeting could be embarrassing. But she would have realized that I was better than that man, more honest, and that I wouldn't have taken her in a ditch. Giuliana had seen me and recognized me. Some time later I had to admit that she behaved very well toward me considering the circumstances.

I kept on walking toward my house, feeling nauseated by that encounter and yet so exhilarated that I could still feel real desire. I saw my mother leave the barn carrying some eggs. They were startlingly white in the darkness, whiter than the snow that the night hid beneath all the other things, trees, bushes, fences, and stones. On the crest of the hills I saw a streak of luminous snow that marked the tiny boundary of the vast desert of the sky.

The next day at the factory I looked for Gualatrone. I wanted to tell him everything, but after a few hesitant remarks I only asked him how many women he still had. He smiled and said that he was bored with all the complications, so much so that he was ready to get married even though he didn't like the mentality of his fiancée's family. "It would be better to run around free," he said contradicting what he had said a minute before. But we couldn't continue our talk because suddenly I felt very shy and because Gualatrone had started to think about something that seemed to have made him sad. We left the factory in silence.

At the exit I caught a glimpse of Giuliana. She was leaving in a hurry as if she had something terribly important to do. One hand was over her breast, holding on to her coat. She was so busy with her thoughts that I couldn't tell from her face whether she had seen me or not. She was supposed to be serving in the cafeteria, but instead she was running out of the factory. Her coat flapped as she ran up the steps of the infirmary. Why was she going to the infirmary at that hour? I would have liked to wait for her, but Gualatrone walked to the newsstand and called me over. After that, he wanted to stop a minute in the café, and then he said that he would go with me to the cafeteria.

"How do you make out with women?" he asked me, returning to our former conversation. I was thinking about Giuliana, and his question was so pertinent that it frightened me. I was even more frightened when I saw Giuliana standing in line, serving. She was no longer excited, and her face was still and rigid like the face of a machine. Her eyes traveled automatically from one pair of hands to the next down the line of people waiting to be served. Giuliana was serving on the line opposite to mine. Gualatrone was ahead of me, and I followed him. He talked and laughed, and a little drop of his spit hit me on the chin. That fresh drop of spit on my skin gave me the sensation of a reality other than the one that was destroying me. Giuliana was no longer the one who had shortly before betrayed me in the infirmary. Now she was smiling at me and helping me to cross the railroad tracks; she was drawing me toward the lake. In this new reality I was the head of the union. Gualatrone was my opponent but I was better informed and more popular than he was. I was freeing people from the factory, and I found a place for everyone. I helped many of them return to the country. I even got Giuliana back to the country.

When I was about to reach out and take a plate from behind Gualatrone, who was sniffing at the spaghetti, I saw Giuliana go round the column that divided the lines and come to serve on our side. She was carrying a plate of something, and it ended up on my tray. It was a plate of soup. Then she served me the other dishes without looking at me. My second reality stopped me from being entirely conscious of the first because the events of the second reality were more important. In the calm light of this second reality I moved with confidence, and I was a different age. I was much younger. But perhaps it was I who continued to weave these tender, transparent fantasies and tried to hide the terrible truth in order to accept my fate with resignation, in order to make myself completely miserable till I reached the point where I thought "I know that you are ruining me. I can see it. I am more intelligent than you are and it is I who is allowing you to do it, and if I didn't want to go along with you I could upset all your plans." I was sure that Giuliana would try to poison me, so sure that I was waiting for Gualatrone to notice it too. If he noticed, his accusation would carry more weight than mine. I couldn't find a place near him. He had squeezed himself between two blond girls and there was hardly any room for his tray.

I stood behind him for a few minutes waiting for the gravity of the situation to make him come to his senses. He was eating from the plates of the two girls so that he could forget that someone was about to be poisoned from his own plate. Then I went away. I only ate three spoonfuls of soup so that I would have a slight attack of stomach poisoning and so that I could keep the rest of the poisoned food as proof. But they grabbed the plates away from me as usual, and they threw me out of the cafeteria.

In the meantime my stomach was burning. In the infirmary where they had prepared the poison I found the usual goalkeeper who stopped me from going in. Then I had to run to the café and drink lots of milk as an antidote to the poison. All these betrayals, one after another, gave me the time and the strength to react. I decided to denounce all of them. Then once again they read my thoughts, and the doctors sent for me. Dr. Tortora asked me to come and see him the next day. Before I went to see him during recess I ran out to find Dr. Fioravanti so that he could honestly confirm the fact that they had tried to poison me. I had gone to look for him the previous evening, but the door in via del Distretto had been closed. That day, however, all the doors were wide open; the door to the apartment, the doors to the other rooms, even the door to Signora Eufemia's room was open, and when I went into the room I didn't see either the bed or the photographs. The door to Fioravanti's consulting room was closed. It seemed narrower and higher than before. While I stood in front of the door I heard a noise inside the room as if someone were slowly unwrapping a newspaper or were opening a parcel full of food. I knocked, and the noise stopped. "Dr. Fioravanti!" I cried. "Please open the door! I need your help."

After a second I heard Palmarucci's voice, and it frightened me.

"Go away, Albino. Go away. We are all sick. The others have gone. You go too. I'm worse off than the others; I can't open the door. I'm contagious."

"When is Fioravanti coming back?"

"There are great things happening to him. He has injected himself with a sickness. I don't know when he will come back. Maybe at the end of the week." There was no help for me. In the meantime I could hear Palmarucci's voice saying in that tone of wisdom that he knew how to use so well, "Then you will all be free . . . and those who have been as free as I have been . . ."

I ran out into the street, and instinctively I headed toward the police barracks. I stood in the middle of the square. The pavement was newly washed by the snow, and I remembered the chief's face, his hard exterior, and I remembered that the last time this had happened Dr. Tortora had immediately been informed. I might as well go directly to him.

I left the cobblestones of the old city, and I took the asphalt street that led to the factory. The snow was nearly all gone. The siren was blowing, and its terror pierced to the very core of my being. "Enough," I said. "Enough. This time, this time . . ." It was as if I had been going to see Tortora every day and as if I had gone, driven by some strange desire within me. As if I went willingly, to assert myself and my motives and to condemn every trick that had been played on me. I was going. Yes, I was going, and I would go every day.

"Doctor," I said, "someone tried to poison me and you know who it is. Call that person. It's about time we put a stop to all this. I won't say anything to anyone if you confess and you finally decide to free me. Everything within these limits. It all begins with my mother. This chain must be broken. I am well. I must be well. Even Bompiero has said that I am well. And the Holy Ghost said it before he did."

I heard the door open, but instead of a penitent Giuliana I saw only a nurse. She withdrew at a nod from Tortora. I looked at his great red hand and the blond hair on his wrist protruding from the sleeve of his smock. "You, big hand. You, why do you hold me back with your hands? Use them to ease pain and help your neighbor."

Tortora was smoking, the electric light was on, and the blue smoke was quickly sucked out of the room as the door opened for the second time. The nurse reappeared. She was carrying a glass of water on a white tray. A glass filled with water that reflected the blue light and the white tray. The water was alive and blue. Immediately I was thirsty. It was like a divine inspiration, and I drank the whole glass of water. The nurse left the room, and Tortora began to speak. While he spoke he came and took the glass from my hands. I wasn't listening to him, but I was sure that he was agreeing with me. Then I left.

Tortora had told me to stay home for a few days. There was hardly any snow in the country, and it lay over the land in patches of varying shapes along the furrows and the edges of the fields. The lake was round and turgid, and it was entirely surrounded by an icy star made by the rivulets and canals that penetrated the land. The crows would pass over the lake each morning and return each night. I had rediscovered the Indian and the boot, and the thoughts within me were more turbulent than the lake. What could I hope from the doctors? I had read that the doctors in Russia had plotted to poison Stalin. Their plot had been discovered.

The priest came to see me one morning, to talk to me. How did he know that I was home? He ended his speech by begging me to have faith in the factory and in the able doctors.

I spent the remaining days thinking. What does having faith in the factory mean? How can a Christian, a son of God, a precious man of flesh and blood, submit to the will of the factory, of an organization where not even work is respected? And as Grosset said, what if the factory itself is bad? What might one think of the doctors then? The factory denies you any satisfaction. When you are in the factory it is as if time never passed; time, brother of mankind. The factory is a closed organism made of iron. The hours pass from seven in the morning to seven at night but everything is at a standstill, the same way that everything is made of iron. The factory that was built for speed, built to beat time, is instead always at a standstill because man's time beats any artificial measure of time. The factory is built in one place, and it will always remain in the same place. The factory will never come into town. It will never have a market or a fair in front of its doors. It will never be surrounded by people, or flowers, or fountains, or arcades. No one will stand in front of it—only those who are not well, those who work in the factory, or those who want to work there. But there are certain things you mustn't say. Consequently you have doctors.

On the last day I went to see Gualatrone. I asked him to take me to his union. A very tall man with bushy hair sat facing me. I told him everything.

"Your problem is a personal problem. The union can help you, especially your morale, but it can't do much for your illness."

"But I'm not sick. The Communist union must help me fight the doctors. It has to denounce them."

"The union is not Communist. It deals with the general problems of the workers. What can we do for one man? We have often said that factory doctors are the tools of management, tools for discrimination and oppression . . ."

"No. In this case the doctors are my personal persecutors. They are aiming directly at me. Tortora . . ."

"I know, but they can always maintain that their diagnosis is accurate, that you are really sick, that you must really take care of yourself and stay away from work. You see, Comrade . . ."

"Comrade hell! You speak like a priest, and then you call me Comrade. Tell me what can the union do for me? Can you force the Internal Commission to intervene?"

"No. We can only have you examined by an impartial doctor, by a serious doctor, and then . . ."

The fever that had already overpowered me, the fever of a series of hands on my chest, locked around my throat, frightened even the man from the Communist union. He looked for a minimum of space on the surface of a white sheet of paper he held in his hands. He looked for a way out for his thoughts. "Then we cannot do anything," he said, "but our fight to improve the factories also applies to you. Ultimately if you suffer so much you could always leave, find another job. It has happened to so many others . . . All of them from this factory."

"You're siding with the doctors."

"It's not true, but I can also see how they could be right."

I fled, pushing my chair back from the table, leaving it with open arms and mouth to continue my conversation. A lot more could have been said in that union hall that reechoed like a church. Those poor chairs and those two huge rooms knew the truth even though the man didn't want to know it. I nodded to Gualatrone who had remained outside, outside of everything, and I walked toward the station as I had all the other times that I had been mistreated by the doctors, the factory, or the dispensary.

I was drinking a cup of coffee and milk when I noticed that a woman was staring at me. She shook her head, and then she came near me, very cautiously, without saying anything or looking at me. When she stood next to me she murmured "Dr. Fioravanti." Then she looked at me and walked toward the exit. When she reached the glass door leading to the tracks she clearly motioned to me to follow her.

I caught up with her near the tracks. Everything was imperceptible and in pieces. The bells were muffled; they sounded like a hurried and futile prayer. I wasn't expecting anything hopeful to happen, nor could I read any sign of hope on the woman's minute face. "I recognized you right away. You don't know how I've looked for you these past few days, even in the factory. Do you know that we have been betrayed, that they have fooled us? Fioravanti has run away, and so has Signora Eufemia and her husband. They have all run away. First Fioravanti and Signora Eufemia, and then last night or this morning Palmarucci. They didn't leave anything. Ten days ago, after more than a year of cures they weren't satisfied with money any more, and they even made me give them a bed spread of mine. They didn't finish my cure. Once I heard them fighting and beating each other, the three of them, locked in Fioravanti's study. Now they've run away. I have been at the station since this morning to see if I can trace Palmarucci. He was drunk last night, and no one knows for sure whether he has left or not. The others, taking the cure like us poor souls, have posted themselves at the bus terminal, those who could, that is. The rest are at home with even greater troubles."

I had finally recognized her. The woman's speech, punctuated by the bells and the tinkling of the entire station that lay broken under the wind and the February sun, told me things that I had

always known; or so it seemed to me in that moment full of betrayals, as still another betrayal was revealed to me, lifting the
covering that I had spread over the sharp angles of the truth in
order to protect myself. Why was this woman telling me these
things now? Had the time arrived when everything would be revealed to me? I didn't fear the unmasking of every fraud as much
as I feared the knowledge of the motives that had made Tortora
and his clique turn against me. And what if the motive stood and
was still present within me? Not that I admitted my illness, but
I was beginning to be afraid.

I was saved by a small crowd of people who were crossing the
tracks. It occurred to me to ask, "How many are there?"

"Who?" answered the woman.

"The patients being treated by Fioravanti."

"About ten of them."

Just like those poor bundled-up souls crossing the tracks.

"Good-by," I said smiling.

"But aren't you going to do anything?"

"What do you want to do? Do you want to catch him so you can
finish the cure? He's a cheat! It's a good thing they ran away."

"And the money?"

"And the suffering?" I said, and I got on the train. My question
followed me all the way home. It was mouthed by Signora Eufemia
whom I imagined standing before me with her head full of curls,
the way she had been when she returned from Rome.

When I got home I looked for my mother. I saw that she was
dozing after her dinner. Her sleep was heavy and noisy as if she
had had too much to drink. Then I woke her up to see if I could
talk to her. She immediately scolded me for waking her up. Her
tone was almost threatening, and I wanted to hit her. I scolded
her for having drunk too much. She dragged out her handkerchief
and blew in my face to prove that I was lying, then she started to
sway from side to side and cry.

There wasn't anything I could do, so I went into town. The town
was deserted except for a tendril of life made up of old men. If you
weren't at least sixty years old you were alone. There was no one
in the taverns or in the café, at least no one new. In the café there
was a man talking loudly and excitedly about the weather and the

[197

drought we would have in the spring because there had been so little snow that winter. He was alone and he spoke because as soon as he had finished his coffee he wouldn't stay another minute in town, or because speaking about spring was another way of leaving.

Who could help me? I didn't have any family; my mother didn't understand me and wouldn't let me understand her. I didn't have any friends; the town didn't count. The priest wasn't sincere, and my religious aspirations disturbed him greatly. He denied them with all the spit of his thin, fasting lips.

I had walked to the end of the street, and there I saw the old cripple I had seen that morning at dawn on the day I had gone to the factory for my first checkup. I greeted him, and I went over and leaned against the wall surrounding his little garden. His illness kept his face turned in my direction, and it almost forced him to return my greeting. His illness dictated all his movements. It even commanded him to live. I asked him how he was, and I told him that I too was sick.

He didn't seem surprised. As a matter of fact his attention increased. He opened his mouth. "Why?" he asked me.

His question forced me to examine my feelings deeply before answering. I wasn't satisfied to confess the usual twists and turns of my soul and repeating the same conclusions, so I answered, "A group of people have decided to ruin me."

"Go to the police."

"It's difficult to explain things to them because these people are very subtle and tricky."

"Against the fox use the hounds. Go to the boss, theirs or yours. Go to the boss." At the end of the conversation he asked me my name.

The days in February were already getting longer at least outside the factory, and that day I still had time to go and do one of the things the old man had told me to do. I went to the police. I didn't want to go to the chief of police in Candia because he was in league with the priest and Tortora and the Commission of Public Safety; so I decided to go to the police station in Caluso.

I realized immediately that even this police chief had been warned against me a long time ago. I don't think he remembered the facts very well because he acted impatient and annoyed at not remembering and perplexed by the confusion of my thoughts. In his face I could read the determination to ignore everything. Then I changed my tactics. I wanted to defend myself against his decision to ignore me, and I wanted to upset him. So I told him about the swindle. I told him the whole story about the healers. I saw him hesitate. I saw him try to trap me by confusing "doctor" Tortora with "doctor" Fioravanti, but I explained things very clearly to him.

"Why have you come from Candia to Caluso to denounce these people?"

"Because I think the chief of police in Candia is in league with the doctors."

He got up, and because he didn't understand he lighted all the lights in the little room. He got angry, and he threatened me with jail. "It's always you people from the factory. You're the most difficult," he said, but I answered that I wanted to sign a complaint. He told me that he would decide when the complaint would be signed, and then he threw me out.

I went to the railroad station in Caluso, and I watched the workers' train arrive. I looked into the car I would have ridden if I had taken the train with the rest of them at X. The car was nearly half empty, and it didn't show any particular signs of my having ridden in it or not. But there was something of mine in the polished wooden corners, something alive, and I knew this for certain as I watched the train pull out. Another part of me was in the sanatorium behind the hill. I thought about the exact place on the stairs where I would be standing at that moment on my way down to eat. I knew precisely what was going on at that moment in the sanatorium, and I knew precisely what would have been going on inside me if I had been in the sanatorium.

I left the station surrounded by the smell and the darkness. Another ugly day had gone by. There was a piece of me in so many places. I had lived in pain in so many places, and I had left traces of myself behind me like a snail. How much was there left for me? I was afraid of wasting myself again as I had done on that ugly day. I was afraid of dying.

The night passed, and in the morning while I was getting dressed

[199

I found that I was thinking the same thought I had been thinking the night before as I was getting undressed with my eyes always rooted to the window sill. I didn't look out toward the countryside or the lake or into the room at the table or the company of chairs.

My thought had been to go back to work and to go to the Personnel Department or even to the president of the company. I passed by the infirmary, and then I went to the Assembling Department. I started to work frenziedly; one piece after another, one piece after another. I got a new box of pieces, and I worked even more rapidly. As I had planned, I had asked to be excused for half a day starting at eleven o'clock. At eleven I went over to Milione and asked him to check and make sure. He looked at me blankly and said, "I believe you."

"I want to go and talk to the Personnel Department, and you will have to tell them what I have done."

"Do you want them to lynch you?" he said, pointing to all the others in the department who kept on working and bobbing their heads up and down over the pieces.

"Send me to the Personnel Department."

He picked up the phone, looked around, and asked the Personnel Department to see me immediately.

When I got to the Personnel Department, I told two persons sitting behind the same desk what I had done. They began by apologizing for the fact that there were two of them; then one of them asked me what significance I attached to the exceptional effort I had made in my work. I answered that I had done it to prove that I was a good worker.

"Just for that reason?" the same man asked smiling. "Didn't you do it for some other reason? To get a transfer or a promotion?"

I said no, that my only reason had been to show that I was a good worker.

"Thank you," the same man continued. Then changing his manner and the position of the light that shone on his glasses he asked me, "Do you realize that your action could harm the department?" I answered that I didn't care and that no one in the department had ever worried about me.

"But we think about everybody. We have to think about everybody, our impartial justice . . ." I told him that there was no justice and that I had done what I had done to show that a good worker was being persecuted and forced to act alone. The same man said that just because they hadn't given me my promotion some time back I couldn't really consider myself persecuted. "Other reasons . . ."

I wasn't talking about any promotion or "other reasons." I was talking about the attack of the doctors, the phony illnesses, the sanatorium. That is what the Personnel Department had to take into consideration. It had to declare once and for all that my health was good and that I could live within the factory without any reservations and that my work was satisfactory. The other man spoke, and he told me that my case would be thoroughly investigated.

"The doubts you have, actually the accusations you have made, will be carefully examined. We will not limit ourselves to talks, but we will conduct actual tests and produce affidavits. You will also be called, and you too will have to undergo these examinations."

"More medical examinations?" I asked.

"I cannot tell you anything more now. We have to study the case and then decide upon the procedure. Don't worry; you will be kept well informed. At the right moment you will have to assume your responsibilities like the rest, if you want fair and conclusive results."

The noise of the factory gave a ring to these words that made them seem larger than their meaning; they were larger than the two men or me, even larger than the room. It reminded me that I was listening to a piece of the factory and that the sound of those words was only a fraction of the entire sound. I left, and I had the sensation that the talk wasn't over, that it was impossible to put a stop to anything, that it was impossible to put a period along that wave of sound that continued as usual to permeate the atmosphere, going up and down and all over the place. I had to speak to someone who could decide and put an end to this business. I must speak to someone, as I had decided to do at home the evening before and that morning. I had to speak to the president of the company.

If I wrote a letter how long would it take me? Would it get lost among all the other papers? Would Dr. Carpusi intercept it? I had to talk and explain everything in person.

Once in a while I had seen the president of the company, Professor Ratto-Ferrua, driving by the factory, sunk in a corner of his big black car, where he seemed actually to be suffering. His mouth was always twisted by a grimace of pain, and he sat with his head hunched between his shoulders inside a fur collar as if he were always cold. He had a long face, made even longer by great vertical furrows on either side of his grimacing mouth. He always wore smoky lenses on his glasses. Maybe he did it to heighten his melancholic appearance and to hide a crooked eye—an eye that hid under his forehead and turned upon itself exposing all the white of the eyeball like a hardboiled egg with traces of rotten mucus. They said, however, that he was very kind and that after justly reproving someone he would settle everything sternly but fairly. He received one worker a week. If I had gone to his secretary for an appointment I would have had to wait for more than ten years.

I knew that there was someone in the factory who could help me: the head supervisor in the cafeteria, the only man in the factory who behaved as if he were free. He spoke in a loud voice and laughed and always talked about plants and flowers. This man had been Professor Ratto-Ferrua's personal servant for many years. He had been a waiter on a transatlantic liner, and he had been brought to X by the Professor. The Professor had the habit of writing poems that Leone, his servant, had to learn by heart and recite in the mornings while he was helping the Professor wash and dress. Pinna had told me that there had been a time when the Professor had shown other weaknesses concerning Leone. It had been Leone who had helped Pinna at the time of the theft and gotten him an interview with the Professor.

The Professor had dealt severely with Pinna, but toward the end of their talk he had said: "How hairy you are, my son."

I went to Leone, and I asked if I could speak to him. "Very well," he said, and he dragged me into his office in front of the storage rooms. He ordered two cups of coffee. He drank his coffee without any sugar, and laughing he showed me his plants and his flowers, which he kept on his desk and on shelves around the room.

He asked me to go ahead. He listened attentively to what I had to say. "Poor soul, poor soul," he kept saying and he often made me repeat what I had said so that he could show even greater concern the second time he heard my tale. "Poor soul," he said at last. "What terrible people there are in this world. I thought I had heard everything, but the things that go on in this factory! Poor soul. And your case is very difficult because the Professor has great faith in doctors. That Tortora is always hanging around with his great big eyes, his pills, his messes and syringes. It's a difficult case. But what can Tortora have against you? He made a mistake in the beginning and then he didn't want to admit it, or maybe he was offended because you have always been rude to him and you have never recognized his authority, even his right to love you and save you. What can I tell the Professor? How could they have switched X rays? You know, once I had a touch of tuberculosis, and I spent three months in the hospital in Casablanca . . . I'll tell him about the healers, about all the money they stole from you, and in the meantime I'll tell him a few things about Tortora."

I showed him Carpusi's letter. "The Professor hasn't even seen this letter," he said. Then he gave me a lot of advice that put me completely at ease.

Two days later, on the wall in front of the station I saw the announcement of Grosset's death. Michele Grosset, forty-four years old.

To me, his death seemed to have taken place a long time ago, during the worst period of my troubles. Now I was on the verge of salvation. I was going to be freed from the hostile time which included the period of Grosset's death. This feeling of remoteness and the contrast between the announcement of Grosset's death and my days of liberation moved me profoundly and tenderly, the way you are moved by a sad event that you suddenly recall in the same spirit of innocence in which you lived it. My emotions made me cry, but my tears lightened my heart by the mere fact that I had shed them.

During those days everything happened very quickly. The trips, the working hours, the night, and everything else were all very casual and painless. I traveled, and I looked both outside and inside the train. I looked in an orderly fashion, one glance after another, without any annoying confusion of glances. Everything was in its place and each thing ceded its place to make room for the next. Everything took place without hidden meanings, unlike the other times when I couldn't tear myself away from the vision of a plant or a bit of scenery even though the train sped on and I suffered as if my body were really splitting in two and my eyes were remaining behind. I would arrive in X after so many painful wrenches, and little things that had happened a few minutes before, things I had glimpsed and not fully understood, weighed heavily in my memory—useless things like the flight of a bird, the branches on a hedge moving by the train, the window of a house, and the shape of an unformed cloud. I would carry these images into the department with me, and there I continued to pursue them, adding words and sounds. I lifted these images out of the context of the speeches I made to myself, lifted them out of the sea of sound around me, and I kept them bottled up in me till they had completely lost their meaning. I didn't even bother to give them any meaning. It was like a chore I had to perform unwillingly, an effort not to surrender, and I thought about the sadness of that real life that was robbing my days.

All this had stopped after I had spoken to Leone. I had begun to lead a more simple life, even though the days flew by so quickly while I waited for another meeting with him and for his answer. I felt more religious, even though I didn't go to the priest any more because he had shown that he was in league with the factory. I felt kinder, more convinced of the existence of Divine Providence, more hopeful that it would deal kindly with Leone's interests and mine. Meantime, in the cafeteria Leone always greeted me with great friendliness even though in those moments he was caught in a flurry of work that kept him running from one place to another. Once in a while he would come over to me and put his arms around my shoulders and ask me how I was. At last the day arrived when he grasped my hand more urgently than usual. He had seen Professor Ratto-Ferrua, and he had many things to tell me at five o'clock in his office.

I managed to work quietly till five o'clock. If I felt a momentary feeling of impatience all I had to do was look at the others, benches full of people who were different from me, people who could communicate their insensibility by the sight of their curved backs. The department seemed to be split in two by the light. The upper part of the room was filled with drifts of artificial light while underneath I could see the crude and clearer light that came from the window. Even this seemed to be a good sign because it kept my attention focused on something other than my own thoughts. It reminded me of the division made by the light in all the religious paintings on the altars and of the division of light and shadow in the painting in front of which Father Caligari made us pray when we were boys. Then every once in a while I would see a little bird, riding the wind, come and perch on the roof of the factory. This had always seemed incredible to me, but that day the sight comforted me. It was a sign of youth and freedom, many signs because the birds came often that day.

A little before five I went to the foreman and asked him if I could have the rest of the day off. I told him that from that day on I wouldn't be needing any more permits or passes either for the Personnel Department or the infirmary. I got dressed in a few minutes and went to Leone's office. He too was getting dressed. He opened the door and asked me to sit down indicating with a gesture that he would join me immediately as soon as he arranged his shirt.

He began to talk even before he sat down. "I spoke to the Professor. It was difficult at first because he wasn't paying attention and he didn't want to hear anything new. He called me to check his clothes. This mild winter irritates him, and he doesn't know what to wear, what type of underwear to put on. 'But the doctors,' I told him, 'haven't they told you to wear woolen underwear?' 'Oh, the doctors,' he answered. 'They don't know anything about these things, even though they're most important.' I told him that often doctors got themselves in that kind of situation, but he didn't want to pursue the subject and he started talking about science. He said that people always betrayed everything. 'That's right,' I said. 'Science is limited, but there are a lot of doctors.' He looked at me in silence with his big crooked eye and when he looks at me that way without getting angry I know that I have caught him by surprise and that I can continue. As a matter of fact, at that moment in similar situations, he has always asked me for a glass of water. I gave him his mineral water and I continued. 'Do you know that with all the science there is in this world and with all the new developments, there are still magicians around?' He didn't drink his water and he said that magicians and charlatans are thieves and that they have always existed and will always exist. I told him that as a matter of fact one of his employees had been cheated out of three hundred thousand lire and had suffered the pains of the damned to boot. I had barely finished saying these words before he interrupted me and said two things. One: that you should fire anyone who worked for a company like his and still went to quacks. Two: why hadn't this employee gone to Tortora? Why hadn't Tortora done something about this? Then I told him that you had gone to see Tortora and that he wanted to force you to leave the factory to take care of yourself but that you didn't want to because you were attached to your work and because you had to support your mother. So he said that he would resolve your case. He doesn't want to help you. He wants to resolve your case. He said that he would get all the information from the social assistant and from Tortora, that he would look at your X rays and talk to all the doctors. He added that if you are ill he will have you cured, and if you are well he would let you work without any more troubles. I told him that you were very well and if he wanted to see you . . . 'I am not a quack,' he answered and he gave me back the glass of water he had been holding. When he gives back the water it means that the conversation is ended. Now, I can assure you that everything went fine and that the matter will be settled."

Leone told me everything including his evaluation of the Professor's feeling and his own opinion of the whole affair. "You're lucky," he said every once in a while. "You're lucky. If his woolen underwear hadn't itched, how could I have approached the subject?" When he noticed that my face didn't reflect his happiness, he was almost offended and he stopped talking.

"You're thinking that the Professor will talk to Tortora and will accuse him," Leone said.

Once he had regained the initiative and his right to evaluate and express his feelings on the matter, Leone's expression changed back to normal and he continued, "Of course he will accuse him. Tortora has already been hit. Everything he has said about you will have to be retracted, and he will have to start all over again. He will have to go through everything again, and this time under the eyes of the master, or I should say the Professor," and he laughed. He got up, and his body shook from his shoulders to the waist. He wasn't wearing his jacket and his thin belly quivered from his side to his waist. It was as clearly delineated as the belly on a doll. I noticed these things so that I could relate them to a thought that had just occurred to me. "In whose hands have I placed myself? Why have I turned to this person whom I don't even know, whom I see for the first time?" So I watched his shirt and his belly, and I was sure that I had never seen them before, that this was the very first time that I had ever laid eyes on them and that they were very special.

Leone continued, "Now the Professor knows your story, and now he must be kept informed of everything that happens to you both inside and outside the factory. If someone wants to hurt you he'd better watch out."

This was really the only advantage of the situation. But this speech also applied to anything I might want to do. I could no longer defend myself alone, and my defenses, seen from a different point of view than mine or seen by someone who didn't know all my reasons and motives, could always be mistaken for attacks or betrayals. But the thing that completely demoralized me was the fact that the doctors would have to visit me all over again. More checkups, X rays, diagnoses, and once more Professor Bompiero. Once again this chain of troubles like winter days, one after the other, when the tree is bare and it stands dying from day to day, like the different patches of scenery I saw from the train window, one after the other and always the same, from Candia to X. Things would be the same, like my mother and her eternal words. Where could I find another way, another direction? I stood up and asked Leone to come with me. He couldn't; so I thanked him, and I promised him that I would keep him informed about everything that happened to me. He had asked me, and I couldn't refuse.

The direction during the following days was always the same. Everything was monotonous, the way it is on a long trip when you abandon yourself to the automatic movement of your legs, and you don't want to stop thinking; all sorts of puns and rhymes pop into your head. Words like "travel" and "evil" and "think" and "brink" completely occupied me and acquired a life of their own independent of my will. Eventually the will is dominated by these words and it becomes passive. So words like "enemy" and "surgery" and other words ending in "emy" or "ery" and the "whirring" of the wheels of the train ran through my brain as we sped along the monotonous countryside and watched it double back on itself and form a semicircle like a scythe that curves toward the center, toward an ideal stalk that one has to reach and overcome but instead always disappears just at the moment when it should have risen and revealed its shape or at least its shadow. The words stopped me from thinking and lulled me into a train of abstract thoughts that completely separated me from reality. I would make up poems. I'd start off with a well-known poem that fitted the rhythm of the train, and then I would substitute my own words. I'd think about these poems during the entire trip and during work. While I was making them up I thought them beautiful and suggestive, full of meaning, especially words like lake, suffering, countryside, leaving. These were the most recurrent words. Every once in a while something would interrupt my game, a noise or some other manifestation of reality. Then I would go over the last poem I had on my lips before waking up and I would realize that it was meaningless and that the meaning was not in the words but in some dark corner of my being. This is what made it suggestive. But as soon as I repeated the words, that dark corner would expand and become my suffering. Then I would begin again. My suffering was not mine. I couldn't control it, and it forced me to blindly pursue any means of escape at my disposal. My suffering no longer drove me to personal animosities.

The social assistant sent for me during one of those days in March. The president was giving me a hundred and fifty thousand lire and asked me to remain calm while I waited for the doctors to reexamine me. The examination was to be a general consultation so that they could decide my case once and for all, without trickery or ill will. I asked if Tortora was going to be one of the doctors.

"I think so," answered the social assistant.

"Then I am doomed. It only took one out of twelve friends to betray." I was deeply moved, and I cried. I too was in my little garden.

The social assistant left me alone. She came back after a few minutes and gave me the money. She told me that she couldn't speak either and that she only wanted to say she hoped I would prosper.

I walked along the street and kept my hand in the pocket with the money. I would have given all of the money to Signora Eufemia if I could have spoken to her again in her house, if I could have felt once more the warmth of her stove glowing in the red light that recalled other times, enclosed in the space between the dark window and the edge of the bed. The roses arched down from the ceiling, and that day, I decided, as the social assistant had said "once and for all," that they were real. I went home early but my mother wasn't there. I ate whatever I could find, one thing after another without sitting down and with the door wide open. I ate as if I had just broken a long fast and everything I ate was new, the very essence of its kind. The open door made a strong draft, and I could feel the change in the air that blew over the lake. I felt the roofs of Candia spreading under that clear light that precedes a change of weather during the month of March. I, too, waited for the wind, and I prepared myself with a shiver. The rain was coming from the valley and sterile yellow clouds had already gathered over the hills. I thought, "the new leaves," and I went out to look at the garden. But why should I think about them? I went back into the house, closed the door, and went up to my room. It began to rain and when I looked out the window the boot and the Indian were shining together in the rain. The Indian was laughing so I turned away and concentrated on the boot. This time the boot didn't remind me of anything real. It was just a shape that could have resembled anything. That day it didn't remind me at all of my youth, those brief, intimate moments of my youth that had fallen within me like so many insignificant bits and pieces, moments when the particular instant of my living them had not brought me any special happiness or relief, moments that only in memory gave me a sense of joy and innocence, of sweet communion with myself as I was when I was young, when it seemed as if I could be my own protector and lead myself by the hand. None of these thoughts and feelings came back to me that day.

The boot shone perhaps too brightly, so that its light revealed the sham of its memory-inducing mechanism. The light made the boot real, no longer a springboard to fantasy. This reality was so cruel that it completely destroyed my order of things. The light, the lake, and the rain were the tools of this cruel reality, and they held me in their grip. I closed the window, and I tried to go to sleep lulled by the sound of the rain. I couldn't sleep. I heard someone knocking at the door, and I realized it must be my mother standing in the rain. I was waiting for her because I had locked the door on purpose. I wanted to shut her out. I went down to open the door, hoping I could get angry at her, but the sense of reality that made me see things so clearly, contrary to all the other times when I had been driven against my will by a feeling of resentment that swelled within me like a cough, showed me my mother suffering in the rain, and at that moment she really seemed to be my mother and the mother of all my sorrows. I told her everything about the impending examination, and I gave her all the money the president had given me.

We sat on either side of the table and we talked. My mother comforted me and spoke about my illness as if it really existed. I didn't react. I accepted her conviction and the idea of my illness. In the meantime I kept thinking that Tortora had won, but the thought didn't interrupt our conversation. The thought didn't upset me or fill me with a sense of rebellion because it was only a judgment on something that had already taken place. Tortora had won; whether I had been sick or not before, now it was true that I was sick.

I didn't go to sleep, I didn't get up, and I didn't go to work. I didn't do anything because I had done what I could and now I only waited for things to happen. After three days they sent the usual messenger to my house. I made him come in, and I told him that I accepted their invitation to appear in the infirmary.

There were four doctors. Tortora, Bompiero, Pietra, the head of the hospital in Turin, and Gherardi, the director of a sanatorium in Saronno. The last two doctors examined me. They were what they were, and they behaved like what they were. I had never seen them before, and I didn't know anything about them. Their eyes and their hands were as implacable as surgical instruments. I felt their cheeks and their ears on my back; one doctor was warmer than the other.

They didn't say very much to each other, but they spoke a little more to Tortora and Bompiero who were standing two meters away from me. Pietra, from Turin, spoke as if he were continuing a previous conversation, alluding to what had gone before by a phrase or a word. He said that "that" illness often affected the emotional balance of the patient. He said that it was a form of self-punishment, a desire for self-destruction or a defense mechanism used by the patient in order to escape responsibilities, a wish to remain an infant, a means to attract the sympathy and attention of other people. Tortora was very enthusiastic, and he said that at last he understood everything. Pietra spoke to me in the name of all the doctors present. He said that I was tubercular and that I had to go to a sanatorium immediately. "And if I don't?" I said, but without meaning to ask a question. Pietra answered anyway. "If you don't, then good-by factory, good-by life; one year, twenty months."

"Suicide?" I asked.

"No, tuberculosis."

The sanatorium was in Lombardy at the foot of the Alps. They drove me there a few days after the examination. The company gave me a package that contained pajamas, undershirts and shorts. It was a large package and it seemed as if they wanted me to know that I would be in the sanatorium for a very long time.

I remained in the sanatorium for more than two years.

During that time nothing happened to me. I was almost always alone. I often thought about my house, the lake, the countryside. I couldn't even bring myself to look at the garden, or the park, or the view around the sanatorium. I thought with pain and nostalgia about my countryside, but I didn't look at the countryside around me. It was as if the fields and the trees were different from mine. Even the changing seasons didn't interest me; only days passed, one at a time, in that sanatorium. Every day was a funeral in that laboratory of death, that monstrance of death, that censer of death!

I pursued words. Their sound was more important than anything else, more important than their meaning. I would put words in order, I would search them out or invent them because of their sound without bothering about their meaning or the true image they evoked. In this way I discovered a different level of words full of emotion. I discovered words that spoke my language. I didn't even go to the priest any more because my soul was already open to me. Without moving, I would follow my words with my thoughts even though I would relish every word between my lips and my teeth, and I would pronounce my words over and over again in all their rhyme as if they were a series of sweet chains. I would invent and sing the litany of my sorrows and of my victory. Some days I would replace the words with a musical phrase or a popular rhyme and for hours I would swoop and sway in their wake, like a kite. The tail of this kite unraveled in my mind and pulled my thoughts behind it in its flight. My thoughts left my head painlessly; they circulated in the air like the continuation of the blood in my head without wrenching anything from my heart, from my core.

> I am a drop
> the first or last drop of a rainstorm
> fallen from the eaves
> when the air didn't smell of rain
> and no one expected even that one drop.
> My drop is gone,
> it helped no one,
> Tortora despised it,
> and mixed it with the dust.
> There was no meeting,
> no other drops came;
> my sorrowing mother
> has given up hope.
> The freedom-giving water didn't come,
> the other drops of water didn't come,
> they didn't follow me
> but they came alone,
> each for its own sake.

God for all
excepting frauds.
The other drops are divided;
unity is impossible.
That's why Judas laughed
and the angel surrendered.
The other drops are divided,
each drop to itself
or in groups of three
like the soldiers' guns
standing in a row
lined up three by three.
In the factories, in the unions,
in armies made of desperate soldiers,
in the houses, in the fields,
in the outskirts of the town,
they're despised by all the bosses
and they're flattered by the thieves
they are robbed by all the rich men
and they're lied to by the priests,
and a few good men among them
suffering for everyone
suffering for all the scoundrels,
who deserve it least of all.

Nothing can grow in the factory,
neither blade of grass nor grain;
not even a goat likes to graze there,
but weariness grows very well there
in that peculiar terrain.
The factory, my enemy,
is neatly bandaged up
and hides its sins and evils
behind a pile of muck.

Illness or treason
whichever it was
kept me imprisoned

in this agony
without company
away from my home
always alone.
I would like to run away
take the tram or take the train
clear across the hills and plain
of Lombardy.
I would like to run away
Oh, a hundred times away.
Or a flying trip I'll take
far above the Candia lake
and I'll see my land sublime,
mine, a hundred times all mine,
tiny like a photograph
that I carry in my heart.
There the little patch of grass
there the hedge behind the mist
there the lake shore, and they're part
of a well-remembered list.
Illness or treason
whichever it was
go from my soul
go from my home
go from my hand
go from my bones
a hundred times over, go.
Go, sorrows of prison,
sorrows of youth,
returning from France,
to Italy;
sorrows begone
from my memory,
from my factory,
all lies begone.
Death to hypocrisy
and all the company
in the infirmary;

death to a Tortora
and to the spy
who tried to poison me.
Fioravanti's agent
charlatan, dirt,
false friend of mine,
go leave the earth.
Trot away like a platoon of cavalry
trot away,
trot away down the street
give me back all the laughter and revelry
of a young boy who follows the cavalry
as it's trotting away
down the street.
Illness or treason,
whichever it was,
a hundred times over
begone.
Triumph, oh, triumph, democracy
in the garden of eternal harmony.

When I didn't abandon myself to my poetry, when I regained my mind and kept it entirely for myself, then I found that it was as sharp as a blade, eager to open something within me and find my thoughts. Carefully I would examine my entire history and my situation in that sanatorium. I have written most of this story during these moments, but my thoughts on the matter have been more numerous and more profound than the thoughts I have been able to set down on paper. I also have written many letters, but I haven't kept them. I have written letters to the social assistant, to Tortora, to the president of the company and to Gualatrone.

In the meantime my health has been improving. A silent young woman doctor looks after me. She used to call me by name from the door of her office, and then she wouldn't speak to me again. The only thing she ever said about my illness was that she didn't know whether the doctors were the cause of it or not, but she knew it was there. She managed to satisfy her sense of honesty by telling me this half lie. Honesty and truth are at the Santia station. I'll never see their like; trains don't come this far. What can you do if you want all the truth and you're not satisfied to let half truths lie? A trainful of truth is leaving, it travels from A to B, but never the truth you'll see, if you do not live in A. The voyage is never made, from the stations B to A, for the truth will always stay with those who've known it always.

I had learned that my young doctor didn't believe in God and toward Easter of the second year, one day during Holy Week, a day when I had slept soundly and felt very calm, I had the courage to ask her about it. "In God, no, I don't believe in God." She looked at me and by way of our mutual consolation she added, "But I do believe in saints. The world is full of saints, especially in here, and I can stick not only my finger but my entire hand into their wounds. I believe in the saints, even the old ones with half a cape, a loaf of bread, and leprosy, but above all I believe in the saints I see all around me. How many were there in the factory?"

I thought about Grosset but I also thought about the factory.

There is a saint in the factory,
he wears a long white beard;
he also wears a uniform.
You'll find him ready
all day long
to give the weary, cheer.
If you're working by the hour,
of this saint you'll not tire;
courage, patience
for the whole assembly line.
His hand is ready
and outstretched
to those who work
in offices.
His eyes are rays of shining light
for those who mount
the pieces right.
Underneath the smock and belt
is a man who wants to help.

He helps those in the foundry
out of their quandary.
He brings fresh air without a taint
to those who labor spraying paint.
He takes away the roar, the clang
from those who work motors by hand.
This saint his saintly hand has lent
to the men
in the department,
to the men who work
behind plate glass
in a square foot of space
while the hours never pass.
To the men who work standing up
hour after hour
in the cold that depresses,
the heat that devours.
Work on, work on
everyone
never stopping
ever on.
And the saint seems to be saying
work on, work on, everyone,
and the saint seems to be praying
do not waver, do not faint.
Are you tired? you are saints!
There are no altars here
only benches here
standing in a row.
Let them always be
lined up precisely,
lined up in a row
all alike.
What a show,
saintly men
in a row.
In the factory we say
a little prayer at end of day.

Let us leave the factory
so we can bless the day we've spent
working, sweating, wretched, bent.
We will bless it
none too soon
with a breath of air
and a look at the moon.

And I knew that the fresh air was already circulating outside
the sanatorium. The fresh air that would do me so much good the
day I breathed the first long breaths outside the gates. Air from
the valleys of Lombardy blowing gently over the woods, far from
the plains, standing still as you should on the roof tops of the hills,
fearing that you will turn into water as you pass over the lakes
of the textile towns whose names end in "ate," or the skyscrapers
of Milan. And so with the air I would fly over this bit of geog-
raphy and remember the deep breaths I would take in the evening
as I stood looking down on the lake on the way up the hill to my
home.

There is a lake
near my home.
I say
my longing-filled compass
points that way.
I miss its outline
in the vague horizon,
never harsh,
where the earth and water
form the marsh.
I miss the sound
of the querulous wind
speaking fright
in the smoky arcade
of the night.
Birds come
from between the peaks
of the hills

they perch
in the nearby woods,
still.
I see a hunter
on the dock
point his gun
and the flock
rises as one,
a white scream
in its wake
circling the courtyard
of the lake.
Their breast feathers
are the humble color of the waves
that the wind herds
into the stockade of the shore.
I too flew over the lake
like a sorcerer in their wake
searching for the place
where night is born
seeking to know why
the clear air turns
into a darkened sky
and brings with it the fear
of one more bitter night.
At that hour the town
with its broken doors
and its twinkling lights
gazed into the lake,
sank into the lake
leaving on the shore
one last living trace
of a red-roofed street
like an open ditch
of freshly turned earth
winding through the woods
in the darkness of
those first months of spring

walking narrow lanes
walking in the wake
of the white scum trace
that the round moon leaves
on the darkened lake.
But the trees remain
and their branches hover
over the bright image
of the red-roofed street.
Into the sky they rise,
the bones of the constellations
resplendent over the graves
of the generations.

IX

LAST CHAPTER. I left the sanatorium, and I arrived home the sixth of May, 1956. I spent the summer still looking after myself and waiting for all the summer storms, leaning out my window. When the heat became unbearable I would go and spend whole days on the shores of the lake. I didn't do very much, and I didn't think very much. My story was ended. The doctors and the factory could do anything they wanted with me. I can't say what my life was like or what the life around me was like during that summer because I don't remember, even though it was only last summer.

I could tell about the lake and the tadpoles, I could tell about the August moon and the crickets, but I had nothing to do with the life of these things that I saw every day and were so close to me. My mother would often talk out loud but always standing at the edge of the garden turned toward the flowers, and always when there were at least twenty meters between us or when I went out of the house and she went in or vice versa.

On the first of September I went to the Personnel Department. I didn't care too much about starting work again. I did it without any purpose, resignedly. It certainly wasn't the way I had wanted to work three years before, and I knew that I couldn't ask them for anything. As a matter of fact, I had to wait a month before they assigned me to my new job, and in the end they asked me if I would like to be a guard. They put me outside the factory to look at the shadows on the wall. A man, still young, assigned to guard a crack in the wall. I wasn't even a real guard but a sort of care-taker, something barely alive, like a dried stick planted in the ground. No one would have given me any other type of work, and by this time both my troubles and I belonged to the factory that kept ruining me and curing me.

The strongest feeling I felt during my caretaking hours was the feeling that I had become factory property. Even the factory should have understood that if I were reduced to such a state I could only be a useless weight on both of us. If they had allowed me a little more freedom, my freedom would have become its freedom, and I could have done something more worthwhile for the factory. But that's exactly what the factory doesn't want. So I kept looking at the shadows of the outbuildings. Every once in a while I would think of something as I stood and looked at the huge buildings standing in the sun. I noticed that the sun shone on the factory the same way it shone on the trees and the surrounding hills, and I thought that only the sun could understand everything. No foreman, not even all the foremen, nor the doctors, nor the people who worked in the offices could understand everything. How could they if everything that happened took place in spite of everybody or against everybody without anyone being free to do anything on his own?

I watched the yellow vans going back and forth from the warehouses. I watched and listened to the people who came and went through those side doors. After only two months I was sorry that I wasn't one of them, and when they passed I would fall into step with them and try to catch a bit of their conversation.

At home, the only thing my mother said to me was to be careful. She would tell me the same thing every morning as I passed by her room on my way downstairs. She saw me alive and fat and working once more in the factory, and she didn't think for a minute that something could be wrong with me. She was always at the same point of time, in the house, in her years, and in her comments. She drank quite a bit every evening; she drank nearly to the point of getting drunk, but this is what preserved her in that moment in time where she no longer had anything to live for, in that moment at the top of the stairs. Nothing lived around her any more, not even her room, or the gestures she made when she washed herself, or combed her hair or got dressed behind closed doors. Her conversation was only for herself, or else it was nonsensical like the noises she made when she called the chickens at feeding time. She walked around the house and kept chattering away till the last kernel of corn had disappeared. But it always seemed that she was the same. When she disappeared behind the barn her chatter never stopped; there were never any pauses in her talk that evoked the image of a new movement or gesture on her part, the hint of a small attempt at a mystery that would awaken my curiosity and in turn become a truth.

I realized that even though I had loved her, I had also hated her bitterly, and I knew that this was true because recently the hate had vanished. Perhaps I didn't hate her any more because she seemed so miserable, because she was a drunk, and that was that. Whenever she drank too much she would go and vomit in the garden. Recently she hadn't even bothered to hide the fact. She would call the chickens to come and pick at the vomit but her cries were feeble, without conviction. I'd often bring her a few bottles of *Barbera* wine and leave them for her on the kitchen table.

Those bottles kept me company on my way home, much better company than the wine inside them. They represented the best of my mother, the silent proof of her presence and of a secret affection without pretenses. I left those bottles on the table with all the tenderness I would have used if I had been placing my mother's hands on the table, if the possibility of a tender gesture between us had still existed.

During my hours of caretaking I never thought about my mother or my house. Sometimes I thought about the lake; that only happened when some half-formed thought would prevail over my other thoughts helped along by the suggestive essence of a crack, a cloud, or a scratch in the sky, or else, when I needed an immediate escape from my memories and my most recent thoughts about the behavior of doctors in general. However, I don't think about doctors and their reasons too often any more.

During my hours of caretaking I have learned to examine people more closely, the people from the factory. I have learned to notice the dirty dark-blue mechanics, the women with their black aprons, and the workers dressed in royal blue. I have learned to notice their common habit of standing up straight once they leave the factory, the way they look around and the way they walk.

I managed to place them all within the different departments in the factory, and I would remember all the different sections and daydream about the people I didn't know. From my point of view as caretaker I would imagine that every job in the factory was easy, at least physically, even though each job seemed to be tied to a

[223

series of complicated procedures, things you had to know, rules to follow, and above all friends whom you had to respect. All this made me realize that I wasn't made that way, that for me everything was more difficult, and now, impossible. I could never have understood or accepted the knowledge of the proper way to knock at certain doors, the right way to cross certain halls, whom to talk to respectfully and whom to avoid, what were the right things to say. Obviously this was the source of my troubles and I would see it leaving the factory like the dust whirling in a ray of sunlight, dodging the steps of the older workers, the ugly and malformed workers who could nevertheless still work inside the factory where I was not allowed to go.

Whenever I saw anyone leaving by the side door I would always wait for that moment when they invariably straightened up. They would lower their heads as if to avoid a blow or as if they were unloading a great weight, and I would see their sad faces twist in a rapid and ferocious grimace. I realized that this gesture was not always a gesture of freedom, it was more like a revelation of treachery, of hidden slyness, like a glutton who has trouble swallowing. I would often feel like screaming out against the workers who derided their own good luck at being inside the factory, united with their work.

One day I listened to three workers who were walking even more slowly than usual across that stolen moment of time between one door and the next. They were talking about striking. I was sitting in the sun like an Indian sentinel next to the mechanism that opened the door. I could see the doors, and in the distance I could see the tall lines of the buildings. The resentment I felt before that show of strength gave me the idea for an assault: an attack was to be launched from the factory and I had to stop them with a machine gun. What was happening was that the workers wanted to leave the factory as a protest against true Communism. This crowd not only was composed of workers but also included the heads of the departments, the guards, the directors and many of the *agents provocateurs* who had been hired by the factory. Manzino and Pinna were with them and so was Giuliana and all the people who worked in the infirmary. Gualatrone was their prisoner, and they kept him in the center of the factory tied to a ma-
224]

chine. I was standing alone in front of the doors, and my duty was to stop the instigators from leaving the factory. Their password was "strike" and they used it on purpose to augment the confusion. I was holding the machine gun. There they were, two of them standing by the door. I fired. My lips measured the volley of fire.

"Strike," a short burst of fire. One of the men grabbed his side, and the other fell to the left. Three others appeared immediately, then two, then one. They came one after another in order to fool me. "Strike . . . strike." One burst of fire after another.

Then more men approached the gates. My fire increased. "Strike . . . strike . . . go ahead and strike." "Come on, come on. Strike, strike, go ahead and strike. Strike, strike, come on."

I fired into the midst of the crowd of men who were trying to protect themselves as best they could. The space in front of the gates was always clear because the sun would devour the dead bodies as soon as they fell under the fire of my machine gun. I killed all of the people who tried to leave, and my desire was implacable, like the sun that devoured all the dead bodies. I could burn them, destroy them, as if my hands were really part of the sun. I was as big as the sun, and I reached everywhere like the sun. As they came out during the noon break I even threw bombs, and every man who darted off on his motorcycle was like a wounded particle of the explosion. I believed in what I was doing, and I had even arrived at a conclusion and formed a judgment: after an hour, when the sun changed position, casting shadows on the place, all those who had been killed would find their bodies and their lives. It was a dance between the sun and the shadows, taking place in the clearing in front of the gates. Once outside the gates it was a dance for the living and the dead, the living and the dead who worked in the factory.

When I returned to my place after lunch I was unarmed. As soon as I sat down, I saw three workers coming toward me. They were followed by a very short man with red hair. He asked all sorts of questions I couldn't answer.

"How can we strike like this?" he asked the others raising both of his little arms. The others kept on walking and disappeared into the warehouses. Before following them, the red-haired man turned toward me and gave me a piece of paper.

I toyed with that piece of paper all afternoon. I folded it a hundred different ways, and I measured the shadows on the wall by the edges of the paper. Two words appeared on one of the borders of the paper like birds in the evening sitting on the wire fence around the garden. The words aroused my curiosity, and I followed them on the paper through a labyrinth of folds and behind every corner, like a person who follows the writing along the walls of a building.

WORKERS, ASSEMBLING DEPARTMENT B–18

In our department there is an attempt being made by the Board of Directors and in particular the Scheduling Department to make our working conditions even more unbearable than they are now. This attempt is being made, section by section, in an effort to destroy and isolate any possibility of retaliation on the part of the workers. Once they succeed in our department, they will go on victorious to the other sections and in a very short time all the departments will be affected.

Here are some examples:

——The women inspectors have taken on six more operations per day for no apparent reason.

——The workers who check in line 1A have to check the output in percentages, thereby increasing the already high quota. Once this system is approved it will be extended to the other lines.

——With the establishment of line 14A, the manual laborers, the substitutes, and the repair men will have extra work to handle without increased benefits.

——The line 2A has been forced to add four machines per day to their line as a consequence of the increased output in line 1A. The same thing will happen to line 3A.

——All this demonstrates that there is a definite effort being made by the directors to render our working conditions ever more precarious with the sole aim on their part to increase the general output.

WORKERS OF ASSEMBLING DEPARTMENT B–18!

We must focus our attention on the dangerous consequences to our health caused by the terrible working schedule that every day becomes more intense.

How long can those people resist when their only prospect in life is trying to work impossible hours?

We all know that when a worker loses even the smallest part of his working power he is immediately taken off his job under the so-called "disability" clause. We must think carefully about all these things. If we continue this way, every one of us is running headlong into physical and psychical ruin and losing his human dignity by becoming merely a tool in the hands of the master.

We are denouncing this state of affairs as we have shown by the number of signatures on the petition we passed among you a month ago. We ask all the workers to rise above their personal loyalties and to unite in the fight for better working conditions before we are reduced to conditions of unbearable servitude.

—UNION LOCAL No. 16.

I still have this piece of paper, and I have copied it here to reveal the truth. I held that piece of paper, and I felt as if I had written it myself, word for word, during my many years of trial in the factory and each one of those blessed, crushed, black words were fruits of my nights and of my thoughts. I consoled myself thinking that others had written these words, that they had passed through the heads of other men and therefore there must be other men like me in the factory. I didn't want to know the outcome. I knew, and I still know that since the moment I held the manifesto in my hands many new things were in store for me. In the evening, at quitting time, I looked at the crowds who were beginning to gather in front of the doors. The only positive aspect of my job is the fact that I can witness the union of the life of the factory with the life outside the gates. Another rewarding part of the job is the resentment against the factory which allows you to judge things with a proper amount of cynicism.

As a matter of fact, the competition for prizes, the desire for promotions, the wish to ingratiate yourself with the foreman, all these things that go on continuously in every department lead you to lay aside your judgment and take on the defense of the factory's interests even though they are to your detriment and to the detriment of the other workers.

At whatever level they may be, how wrong people are if they think that they can ever become part of the factory! The minute they think such a thing the factory has taken their place, as a matter of fact it has become more important than they are, and that's what starts you off on the road of mistakes that ruins your life. It's better to be a caretaker and escape that possibility. But I have always fought against this, and I have been able to remain free even though I ache in every fiber of my being. I would care even if I were only a caretaker! I would look at the scenery more than at the factory. I would look at those square, lined places where the factory and the houses around the factory attacked the countryside. I would realize how much the countryside, born together with mankind, could lose. I would see how the garbage, the stones, the dust, the metal, and the streets robbed it of life. And men gathered in those square, lined places the way flies gather on a wound.

That evening the groups that left the factory were more compact, and they didn't explode quickly down this road and that but kept on moving in groups here and there. In the middle of the crowd I saw the short, red-haired man waving his arms. He was still there half an hour after closing time when it was my turn to quit work.

In the locker room I found out that they had declared a strike for the entire afternoon of the following day if the Directors didn't satisfy their demands by morning. As I was walking to the station the red-haired man passed riding a big red motorcycle. His hands barely reached the handle bars, but he drove with great confidence. The motor purred smoothly, rhythmically, like the hammer blows of a good blacksmith.

The next morning when I got to the factory, the guards were already there. I watched them going back and forth, two by two. I got bored watching them just as they must have gotten bored walking up and down the road without knowing or understanding anything. For that matter they might have been walking up and down any other road.

In that moment I saw a group of people coming toward the exit. These were the members of the Internal Commission who had unanimously approved the strike. They were returning after having been received but not listened to by the Board of Directors. I don't know why they wanted to leave. They were all screaming at the same time, and you couldn't understand a thing.

Other guards came running, and even the Public Security guards took several steps in their direction. I walked toward the group, and I managed to find out what was going on. The Commission wanted to urge the cooks and all the people who worked in the cafeteria to strike immediately so that the other workers, not finding anything to eat at noon would go home and assure the success of the strike. The Directors didn't want the people of the cafeteria to go on strike before all the other workers because it was contrary to the agreement made the day before that the strike would begin in the afternoon. If the cafeteria went on strike before the rest of the factory it would upset the replacements and the other employees.

The factory guards were about to be overpowered because the people of the Tool Department had joined the crowd from the Internal Commission. At that point the Public Security guards took two steps forward and in the meantime another squad arrived. They were armed and wore helmets. They stopped when they reached the door and they formed a line.

I heard someone scream from within, "Strike now, in all departments. Strike now, strike now." These words were accompanied by a burst of applause. This was like a signal to the men of the squad that had just arrived. They took a long step forward and they took out their night sticks. By this time the crowd was pushing against the doors and the walls of the factory. They stood three lines deep. I saw the night sticks, and I raised my eyes toward the sun. The place where I was standing was in the shadow of the outbuildings.

The sun was shining on the factory, and it was only in the rectangle around the door that you could see the green shadows of the guards. They were like poisonous fungus. No one could go out the door.

Then I started going back to my place, and I realized that I was heading in the direction of the cafeteria. From my position the road went downhill till it reached the door of the cafeteria. I walked quickly, crossed the entrance, and went around the inside of the building till I reached the service entrance. The kitchen windows were a few feet above the ground. I looked in, and I saw that the cooks were standing ready, around the huge pots. I leaned forward, and I said: "They sent me to tell you to strike now, right now without preparing the meal." One or two of the men turned toward me, but they didn't understand. "You must strike, strike now. No one must eat." The cooks listened and looked at me in silence lifting the great lids from the pots and moving about the kitchen. When they noticed that they had moved from their usual places, they became terribly confused and just at that moment all the pots began to boil. Leone rushed in, and he started waving his arms around straining the buttons on his tight vest.

"They told me to tell you to strike immediately, right now," I repeated more loudly, inspired by the confusion.

Then Leone rushed to my window and started moving about excitedly like a bad sergeant, or like another of those dancing pots.

"So it's you," said the faithful Leone. "It's you my fine friend. Who says we should strike?" "Me, the orders . . ." I answered immediately. "The Internal Commission. The police have blocked the doors."

"And you're their little messenger . . . Fine gratitude you're showing the president. Don't pay any attention to this lunatic. Fine gratitude you're showing the president . . ."

His senseless arguments and his anger convinced everyone that I was telling the truth. The cooks and the women started to uncover and remove the pots from the fire, and they even turned off some of the stoves. I kept on repeating that they had to strike because I wanted to encourage them and to encourage myself. Finally one of the guards led me away to the Personnel Department.

After a brief interrogation they suspended me from work for three days, and they told me that they would send me a written dismissal.

I returned home on a bus that went to Turin, a bus that left at one o'clock from the public gardens. The road was deserted and yet it seemed much narrower than usual, and it seemed as if you could see farther in front of you, as if you could see around the curves. The trees had already lost some of their leaves, and the entire countryside was lighted by a wide rose-colored light. There were flickers of light from the vineyards, especially from the sections where the leaves were thickest and the grapes had not been gathered. It was a day without birds, one of those days in the year when you don't see any shrikes or any other of the friends who sit thoughtfully with their black and white tails on the fence posts along the road. In the harvested vineyards, the ones lower down on the hillside, you could see the open spaces and the torn lace of autumn, and that trace of rust that colors the last apples of the season. In a few days my letter of dismissal would arrive and so would the pointed flocks of starlings, the gluttonous thrushes and those other scavengers with beaks as sharp as an ax. They'll make a great deal of noise and they will foul the leaves in the vineyards with their droppings.

I got off at the crossroads after a very fast trip, and I started walking home. As usual, I watched the lake grow, little by little, as I climbed the hill. At a certain point in the road it lay directly beneath me breathing softly between its banks. I saw all the roofs of the village, red and orderly as if they didn't harbor the evils of humanity. In the clear afternoon the lake lay devoid of shadows or tints, without reaching out to the countryside and the trees. It lay enclosed between the shores. It didn't shine, and its reflection didn't spread along the edges.

I had reached the place where I was level with the garden of my house. The climb was over, and there were only twenty feet of flat ground to cover before I reached my door. Exactly at this point I have realized that no one can help me now.

MY TROUBLES BEGAN

The text has been composed on the Linotype in Baskerville, an adaptation of the type face designed and cut between 1750 and 1754 by John Baskerville of Birmingham, England. The display type is Onyx, American Type Founders version of an extra-condensed bold modern face.

The book is printed by letterpress on Warren's No. 66 Antique paper.

Composed, printed, and bound by H. Wolff Book Manufacturing Company, Inc., New York.

DESIGNED BY CHARLES FARRELL